Best Of Me

A SAVANNAH'S BEST BOOK

MAYA ALDEN

BEST OF ME

MAYA ALDEN

CHAPTER 1
Aurora

"**B**aby, I'm so sorry. I promise to make it up to you this weekend," Gabriel said again and added, "I love you, Aurora, so very much."

It was a pity *I love you.* Another apology. I heard them a lot lately.

"I know, and it's okay. I understand."

I heard his daughter call out to him, and he hurriedly hung up. This was the third date in one month that Gabriel had had to cancel at the last minute because Sophia, his thirteen-year-old daughter, had a crisis.

"Wow, look at you. Gabe is going to swallow his tongue," my colleague and friend Luna said as she walked into my office.

Since my last meeting ran late, I'd brought a change of clothes to the office. The cream raw silk dress I knew worked well with my café latte complexion. As a family that was mixed-race in more ways than one—we had

African, South American, Irish, French, and even Middle Eastern mixed in. People always wondered where I came from. I told them I was born and raised right here in Savannah.

My father was half African and half French, born and raised in Martinique before he'd moved to the United States. My mother was half Brazilian, a quarter Irish, and a quarter Lebanese. My parents were not together and hadn't been since I was eight, which was why I appreciated how much Gabriel loved his daughter and put her first. My father had not. He'd made a new family and forgotten his first. My mother had dragged me around until finally, at the age of thirteen, I'd had to find a way out to survive and stayed with my aunt in Savannah. The only reason she took me in was because she needed help.

When she passed, it had hammered home to me that I was alone. Even though she wasn't a loving and caring adult in my life, she'd at least been in my life.

I'd grown up without attention, so when I finally got it from Gabriel, I'd been swept away by his charm, his elegance, and his kindness. He had a big heart. He laughed openly and loud. He was also a true Southern Gentleman, except in bed, where he was by far the best lover I'd ever had.

"He canceled," I sighed, sitting down. "So, he won't be swallowing his tongue."

"Not his daughter again," Luna complained. "You know that little brat is trying to break you guys up."

"No, she's not. She's thirteen, and Gabriel has set his life up, so even though he and Iris share custody because they

2

live next to one another, Sophia has both her parents always."

"And you don't mind that his ex-wife is at his place all the time? Or he's over at hers?"

"They're friends, Luna. I wish more divorces were this friendly; it would be better for the children."

Gabriel Rhodes had built two homes after he and his wife, Iris, divorced. They were next to one another and connected through the gardens and pool area. He'd told me privacy wasn't an issue, but it was. Iris had walked in on us making out on the kitchen counter once because she was running low on cream. I'd been mortified.

Iris had made a fuss about Sophia seeing us having sex. Since then, we kept our sexual activities in his bedroom after we locked the door. Which was why I asked him to come over to my place the weeks he didn't officially have his daughter. My house was a condo and not the opulent home of an old-money Rhodes fortune heir—but at least no exes or impressionable daughters were lurking around.

Speaking of daughters and despite my efforts to make it work with Sophia, the fact was that she didn't like me. As soon as Gabriel's back was turned, Sophia turned mean. I'd asked Gabriel if there any chance of reconciliation between him and his ex, and he'd assured me it was dead and buried. But I didn't think his daughter or ex-wife had gotten that memo. I couldn't tell him that his setup with his ex was a significant problem for me because his devotion to his daughter was one of the things I loved and admired about him.

"I love you, Aurora, but you're kidding yourself, honey." Luna looked at me with concern mixed in with pity, the emotion I hated most. "This isn't working for you."

I was twenty-nine years old, and I wanted to get married and have children. When I met Gabriel, I thought it would be something short-term. But a year had gone by, and we were still together. He had become my best friend, and I knew I was his.

"I love him," I said bleakly.

"Love isn't supposed to hurt you like this." Luna rubbed my shoulder and leaned to kiss my cheek. "You have to talk to him, tell him how you feel."

"I'll lose him, Luna."

"If you can lose him so easily, do you really have him?"

I closed my eyes. "Is it pathetic that I want whatever I can get with him?"

"No, sweetheart. But relationships are give and take. No matter what decision you make, I'm with you all the way."

I started working at Savannah Lace Architects & Designers three years ago. Luna had been my colleague first and now boss. We'd become close friends. We were opposites. While I was an introvert, she was an extrovert. I wore a lot of sheath dresses with high heels, while she wore a lot of jeans with boots. She stood out in a crowd, while I blended into the wallpaper. She dated a lot. I had been in two long-term relationships in my life. I wanted to be her when I grew up. She was an attractive woman, definitely, but what was arresting about her was her confidence. She was a fantastic architect as well and a friend who cared about me. She didn't

4

judge, which I loved, but she was also honest about how she felt. I hadn't had a lot of friends growing up since we moved so much, and by the time I settled in Savannah as a teenager, I'd become used to my company. No one would call me mousy, but they would say I was quiet. They'd say I was a peacemaker but not a pushover. I was a softie with a spine of steel. Except, apparently, when it came to the man I'd fallen in love with. My spine seemed to have melted.

I decided to put in a couple of hours of work on a new hotel project on Tybee Island and distract myself from the romantic dinner I'd been looking forward to.

My phone buzzed, and I smiled when I saw it was Gabriel.

Gabriel: *Baby, I miss you. I'm so sorry about tonight.*

It was our first anniversary, and he'd booked a romantic dinner at Circa 1875, an exclusive restaurant. We were going to go to my place after. I'd even taken the following morning off so we could sleep in and have a lazy breakfast.

Me: *It's okay, honey. Take care of Sophia.*

Gabriel: *You want to come over here tonight?*

He was trying, I knew. But the last time Sophia had had some crisis, and I'd gone to his place, I'd spent the night alone in his bed while Gabriel had been at his ex's house. He'd fallen asleep on Iris's couch, he had explained to me full of apologies when he came back early in the morning and *then* immediately packed to leave for a Rhodes Hotel opening in New York.

The walk of shame was a hundred times worse when you had slept all alone.

I didn't mind that our work schedules kept us apart. As part of my job as an architect, I traveled quite a bit, and he, as the President & CEO of the Rhodes Hotel chain, was on the road as well. But he made it a point to be home every other week when he had his daughter officially with him.

He'd introduced me to Sophia six months ago, and it hadn't gone well. She loved her dad, and it was apparent she wanted her parents back together. I'd tried to bring it up with Gabriel that he and his ex-wife living so close together and being in each other's homes so much was confusing for a child. He'd told me not to be jealous, and that I was the only woman in his life.

I couldn't begrudge him for loving his daughter and for prioritizing her. He should. But I wanted to be important to someone. I wanted to be a priority. I'd never had that. My aunt was old when I moved in, and more than her taking care of me, I'd been taking care of her. My father had checked out, and I didn't even get token Christmas messages as I used to some years back. I had no clue where my mother was.

When I first met Gabriel, I was involved in a project to refurbish the conference area at the Rhodes Hotel in Savannah.

The attraction had been instant. He asked me out, and I said yes *first* and *then* checked with my then-boss, Nina, if it was okay to date a client. I was more reckless than I had ever been.

Nina was blasé about it. *"Gabe is a professional. If some-*

thing goes wrong between the two of you, it's not going to become a work issue."

The sexual part of our relationship was intense, and just thinking about him made my nipples pebble, and I became wet. God, he was sexy. At five foot seven, I wasn't short, but he still towered over me even when I wore heels. He wore suits as well as he wore jeans; and worked out with a personal trainer four days a week. His ex-wife also had a slim body that looked like it went through a gym several hours a *day*. If I managed a few Pilates classes a month, I was lucky.

But all my insecurities went out of the window when he was with me because he looked at me with such hunger that I had no doubt that he found me attractive. Gabriel Rhodes was a handsome and very wealthy man. He had no reason to pick me when there were probably women lining up everywhere for him.

Me: *It's late, and I'm going to put in some work on the Tybee Island project. Rain check?*

His response was immediate, and I wondered if he was relieved. Maybe he didn't really want me at his place. It was always weird because of Sophia. I wasn't sure why Gabriel had introduced me to his daughter. He'd told me it was so that it would make it easier for us to spend time at his place when he had her. It hadn't worked out that way.

Gabriel: *Are you free tomorrow evening?*

Me: *I think so.*

It took a couple of minutes, and Gabriel wrote back: *Damn. I can't do tomorrow, baby. Sophia has something at school. How about Friday?*

I hated how I felt—annoyed about him being a good father. I wish he'd balance his personal life and parental duties just a little.

Me: *I can't on Friday. I'm going to New Orleans for the Carter Hotel opening on Saturday.*

Gabriel: *I'm away next week. It's Fall break.*

He was taking Sophia to Paris. He hadn't asked me to join them, and I understood it was a father-daughter trip. He was so excited about taking her to one of his favorite cities in the world that it was hard not to feel happy for him.

Me: *We'll see each other when you come back.*

Gabriel: *Can you cancel New Orleans? You weren't the chief architect on that project.*

I felt something snap inside me. He couldn't change Sophia's school plans, but he wanted me to change mine.

I stared at his last message and ran a hand through my hair. I'd had it blow-dried and left it loose because Gabriel liked that. I opened my drawer and found a hair band. I twisted my hair into a messy bun, keeping it off my face while I worked.

I decided not to respond to the message. I didn't know what to say. I went into the kitchen; found a salad that had been left there from the company-catered lunch. I took it my office and ate while I looked through the Tybee Island hotel blueprints.

My phone rang, and I saw it was Gabriel. I was tempted to not pick it up, but that would be petty, and I was a grown up.

"Hey," I said coolly. "All okay?"

"You mad at me?"

I wanted to say yes. How can you ask me to change my plans, something I am excited about? I'd spent days and nights working on the New Orleans hotel project even though Nina had been the project lead, and I wanted to see how it had turned out.

"No," I lied.

"You sure?"

"Yeah."

"Baby, I miss you."

Then spend time with me, damn it.

"Me too." I felt tears prick my eyes as the knowledge that this relationship was not going to work established itself in my mind. I loved him so much; and yet I felt that ending our relationship swiftly—like ripping off a bandage—would be better instead of the death our affair *by a thousand cuts* or a *thousand missed dates.*

"I miss you too."

"You still at work?"

"Yeah."

"I'm watching some chick flick with Sophia. I stepped out to talk to you."

"She okay?"

"Yeah, just girl drama. Did you have a lot of that?"

"No." Because no one would put up with it.

"You sound angry with me. Quiet."

"Just tired. I still have an hour of work to do before I head home."

"Come over." There was a hint of desperation in his voice, like he knew we were slipping away from each other.

"Gabriel, it's not a good idea. Remember last time?"

"I know, but...fuck, Aurora, I won't see you for over ten days."

"I know. I'm sorry. I can't cancel New Orleans. It's an important project and—"

"I should never have sent that stupid message. Of course, you can't. I was being selfish."

And I fell for him even more. How could I not?

"Ah...do you want to come to New Orleans?"

I heard his long-suffering sigh. "I wish. My parents are doing the Rhodes Family annual charity luncheon lunch thing this Saturday; we'll be there all day."

By we, I knew he meant Iris, Sophia, and him. His ex-wife attended all the family events, which was why I hadn't been invited to any of them. He'd been up front about it, saying he'd like to introduce me to his parents one-on-one and not at some big party or event. And because Iris would be there, he didn't want it to be awkward.

But each time it happened, it made me feel dejected, and this time something cracked inside me. I felt like I was his mistress. Not good enough to take to see his parents, not good enough to be invited to Paris. Not good enough to be part of a family. Just plain not good enough.

"Well, I'm sure it'll be fun."

He paused. "You're wondering why I didn't invite you?"

"No. In any case, I'm not here, anyway." I didn't want to talk about this because it hurt to hear him prefer to spend time with his ex-wife over me, even if that wasn't exactly what he was doing. He was keeping his divorce friendly for his daughter's sake.

"Baby, I hate doing this over the phone. Can't you come over?"

"Gabriel—"

"I promise it won't be like last time. I'll be in bed with you. Please?"

Damn it! My spine was liquid around him. I felt pathetic, but I knew I'd go see him, take whatever scraps he threw my way. Oh god, but these kinds of thoughts and resentment would kill us and destroy me. Gabriel was a good man. He was making the best of his life and I'd walked into it willingly. He wasn't throwing me *scraps*. He was prioritizing being a good father. That's all this was.

"Okay. I'll be there." I gave in.

"Thanks, darling. And—" I heard Sophia call out to him then. "I'll see you soon. Go straight to my place. I'm at Iris's, but I'll come over as soon as you get here."

CHAPTER 2
Gabriel

Managing my relationship with Aurora and my daughter was killing me. I knew I was hurting Aurora by canceling as much as I did, and she said she understood, but even I knew that I was stretching it.

For the first time in my life, I'd fallen in love with a woman, and Christ, being with Aurora, made me happy. After minutes in her company, everything in my head quieted. She was gentle, kind, and so fucking beautiful that it hurt to look at her. She had an innate grace about her; she was almost ethereal.

All the mixed heritage in her background had come together in an intensely striking face that you couldn't look away from. Our sex life was off the charts. I'd fucked plenty before I married Iris and after our divorce three years ago—but it had never been the way it was with Aurora. I was hungry for her all the time, my body addicted to being inside her. She was a generous lover and never, ever turned me down. Compared to the shit show of rejection my marriage had been, Aurora was a breath of fresh air. There was no stress with her.

But even I knew I'd gone too far when I asked her to cancel her trip to New Orleans, and then I'd put my foot in my mouth by telling her about my mother's charity luncheon. We'd been dating for a year. She'd met my brother once. I'd introduced her to Sophia so we could see each other even when I had my daughter, but it was apparent they didn't like each other. According to Iris, Aurora was nearly thirty and had no children; and maybe she wasn't very maternal. I knew Sophia tried with Aurora, but the elegant quietness that I loved about her probably turned off a teenager. Aurora had met Iris, of course, but I hadn't taken her to see my parents because the instant I did that, I was announcing how serious this relationship was—hell, it already was with my introducing her to my daughter. I couldn't imagine not being with Aurora. I had contemplated asking her to move in with me, but knowing how Sophia felt about Aurora, I didn't know if it would work.

So, I did what I was good at. Left the long-term to figure itself out and managed the short-term. Right now, I wanted her in my life, and who knew how things would turn out later? And, why worry about that now?

"Daddy." Sophia snuggled into me. We were sitting in the living room at her mother's house. Because our homes were next to each other, we had an almost joint household.

It worked for us, especially because Sophia never felt she had to choose between her parents or follow the court mandate of when she could be with me or Iris.

"Yes, Sweetpea."

"Can you stay the night here?" she asked, her blue eyes glistening. She'd had some issue with a friend at school that involved a boy. Teenage years were tough.

"Aurora is coming, so I'll go over to my place." I stroked her hair.

She frowned. "Please, daddy."

I sighed. "I'll be right next door." Even if I stayed, I slept in the guestroom. It was no different from being at my place.

Sophia didn't like Aurora. *And* I knew that Aurora tried to avoid Sophia. I was between a rock and a hard place. But my priorities were clear. Sophia came first. If she didn't accept the woman in my life, there would be no woman in my life.

Sophia sulked, but nodded and laid her head on my shoulder.

"Why don't you like Aurora?" I asked.

She shrugged. "She's...I don't know...quiet and cold. Mama said that because Aurora is old and has no kids, she doesn't...you know...."

I actually didn't know. But then I'd never seen Aurora with kids, only Sophia, and she was thirteen going on thirty. I sometimes had trouble with her, so it was possible that Aurora had similar issues. *Or* she wasn't the maternal type. Though I couldn't accept that, knowing how considerate and sweet she was.

"And I've tried, Daddy. You know I have." She looked so solemn that I kissed her forehead.

"I know, Sweetpea."

"Are you going to marry her?" she asked, and her eyes were so troubled that I felt a wave of regret inside me. I had to break up with Aurora. Fucking hell.

"No. We've just been seeing each other for a year." And most of the time, between my job, my life, and her job, we didn't spend all that much time together. The sex was amazing, and I loved talking to her and did every night, whether we were in the same bed or not—she'd become a lover and friend. Losing her would hurt, but the panic in Sophia's voice was a wake-up call. I couldn't be with a woman my daughter didn't like.

"Good."

That one word slammed into me like a freight train. This problem was rearing its ugly head now. Between Sophia and Aurora, there was no contest—I'd burn down the world for my daughter.

Iris came in fifteen minutes later. "It's a school night, Sophia. Time for bed."

"Okay." Sophia made a face and looked at me gravely. "You won't stay here, Daddy?"

"Not tonight."

I'd pleaded with Aurora to come over. I couldn't expect her to sleep alone like last time, and I didn't want to sleep without her. I hadn't seen her for a week, and I wouldn't see her for another ten days. I missed her. Not just the sex, though I did miss that a lot; it was everything. It was her quiet support and her gentle smile. She never judged, never demanded. After spending a decade with a wife who'd always taken and not given much in return, it was great to be in a relationship with someone who gave openly and was grateful for whatever I did.

When Iris was annoyed with me, and she used to be that a hell of a lot, I used to buy her jewelry. It always worked. With Aurora...it had been a year, and I'd never felt she was ever truly *angry* with me. No matter how many times I canceled at the last minute or was not able to live up to a commitment, she just smiled and said she understood. She didn't do it like some women did who said it was alright and then proceeded to make your life miserable. She genuinely meant what she said.

Aurora didn't call or text me incessantly. In fact, I initiated most of our conversations, and I liked that. I didn't feel like I was obligated to be with her or talk to her all the time. When I did, it was because I wanted to, not because I was pleasing *her*. It was the least demanding relationship I'd ever been in, and I enjoyed it.

Did I feel guilty from time to time that I canceled more dates than I was able to actually attend? And imposed on her time whenever I was free and demanded she make time for me? Sure. But she didn't make a big deal out of it, so even though I sometimes felt I was taking advantage of her, I didn't feel I had to change.

Maybe I could keep seeing Aurora and just not have her come over. That way, she didn't have to interact with Sophia. I'd been with other women but had never introduced them to my daughter. Aurora was the first, and it wasn't going well. Maybe I should keep this relationship purely casual.

Even as I thought it, I knew that was bullshit. I loved Aurora. I knew it in my bones. Ending my relationship with her would break my heart, but better my heart than my daughter's.

I kissed Sophia goodnight and was walking to my place when Iris stopped me. "Gabe, you know Sophia wants her family back together."

I closed my eyes. I knew that, but there was no chance of that. Iris and I were not happy. When we were married, we fought all the time. The yelling and screaming, the banging of the doors. I just couldn't do that shit anymore.

"Iris, we broke up for a reason."

"I know, but we're different people now...better people. I love you. I know you love me."

She was a beautiful woman. Had always been. But ten years with her had dulled it in my eyes. She wasn't beautiful when she was calling me a loser for forgetting a commitment, an asshole for missing a flight and coming home late, or a jerk for wanting to make love with my wife the few times she deigned to put out for me.

"Iris, I'll always love you because you gave me Sophia. But we're not happening."

Her eyes shimmered with tears. I used to hate it when she cried. Now, I didn't give a shit. She'd used up my supply of sympathy. Aurora never cried—she dealt with things differently. She was gentle, and I'd never even heard her cuss.

"Fucking hell, Gabe. We're a family. Even now, you eat dinner with us more nights than not."

"I do that for Sophia."

She stepped to me and put a hand on my chest. "Do you feel nothing for me? Remember how we used to spend days in bed?"

Before we got married, we had—but then she got pregnant, and we rushed into a marriage that had not been a pleasant one. I'd hung on to it for Sophia, but after a fight where Iris began to throw things at me, I knew it was done. I wasn't much of a fighter. I shut down and preferred to keep my mouth shut rather than say something nasty. Iris didn't have such a problem.

I removed Iris's hand from my body. "We're not good for each other."

My phone beeped then, and Aurora's name flashed with a text message.

"It's because of her, isn't it?"

I looked at Iris, confused. "Aurora?"

"Yes."

"You think you and I are not together because of my girlfriend? Christ, Iris, we've been divorced for three years, and a year before that, we were separated. I've been with other women in the meantime. You and I are the problem. Aurora's got nothing to do with it."

Aurora was at my place. I smiled, texting her back that I was on my way.

"Is it young pussy, Gabe?" Iris snarled when I had my hand on the knob of the front door.

Here it comes. This is why we weren't suitable for one another. If I didn't give in, Iris would get cruel and sling insults. I'd tuned her out a long time ago.

I ignored her comment. Iris was my age, and Aurora was just seven years younger than me, so it wasn't a huge age gap.

I walked out, feeling a dark cloud hang over me. I regretted marrying Iris, but never Sophia. She was mostly a good kid, though her mother's influence was becoming more and more apparent. She'd wanted some designer clothing, and I'd flat out said no, but then Iris had gone ahead and gotten her some three-thousand-dollar purse or some shit. It wasn't the money. I had plenty, and Iris was well taken care of.

That was the other thing about Aurora. She never took anything from me. The only gifts she accepted were flowers. Once, I bought her jewelry because I missed a date— she had taken one look at the diamond earrings and gone pale.

"You don't like them?" I asked. They were expensive as hell. Iris would have grabbed them.

"Gabe, look at what I wear?" She'd pointed to her small pearl earrings. "And this is so expensive. I'd be scared to lose them. Please. No jewelry. Just buy me flowers and chocolates. Actually, you don't have to buy me anything. We're both professionals with busy lives and these things will happen. Now, can I get my kiss hello?"

While Iris bulldozed, Aurora was sweet. Fuck, but she was. So goddamn loving and lovely.

As soon as I walked into the living room, the smell of

lavender pervaded my senses. Aurora was here, and the dark cloud that I'd felt at Iris's lifted.

She was in the living room, looking at the pool in the back. I'd had it designed so the pool was common to Iris's and my place. Sophia loved it, especially in the summer when Savannah was hot as Hades.

I wrapped my arms around Aurora, pulled her back to my chest, and breathed her in. I couldn't let her go, I thought. I'd have to make this work. She brought me such peace and calm. Just holding her took the tension away.

I nuzzled her neck. "Thanks for coming, baby."

She put a hand around my neck and turned her face to kiss me. She was willing and inviting. In the first years of our marriage, Iris used sex as a weapon until I just stopped giving a shit about it. The more I wanted sex, the more she withheld. Finally, I stopped wanting, and if she made advances, we'd fuck, but there was no passion. By the end of our marriage, we were in what was called a sexless marriage. My right hand got a lot of action. After the divorce, I had all the sex I could find, and I could find it easily. I kept my philandering for when I traveled because Savannah was a small town at the end of the day. If Gabriel Rhodes was fucking a woman, it would make the gossip pages, and I didn't want Sophia to be impacted by it.

Aurora was the first woman I'd dated and not just had sex with. She wasn't the kind of woman you had a one-night stand with.

"I missed you," I murmured, trailing my lips over her silky cheek.

"I missed you too."

"I'm sorry about dinner tonight."

"It's alright. Have you eaten?"

"Yeah. I had dinner with Sophia and Iris." I felt her stiffen at that, but it was such a small instant that I wasn't sure if it was even there. Did she resent my relationship with my ex? I'd told her how we'd set up our households. She'd confided in me that her father had all but abandoned her after the divorce. She respected how I was doing everything in my power to continue to give Sophia my time and make her my priority.

"How about you?"

"I did. I'm sorry I can't cancel New Orleans."

I turned her to face me and was stricken by her beauty. My god, but she was stunning. Big brown eyes, long lashes, angular cheekbones, and the softest lips.

"I should never have asked. I was being a selfish asshole."

"I know it's hard to make time for each other when we have so many other commitments," she soothed. But she wasn't the one who canceled on me, ever; it was always me. I had a daughter, and she seemed to have only work.

"Let's go to bed, baby."

Again, I felt something go through her.

"Hey, are you okay?" I asked.

She nodded. "Of course."

"The housekeeper dry-cleaned your clothes from last time, so you have a change of clothes here," I offered.

Over the past six months, our belongings had begun to migrate between our homes. She left a few items at my house, while I accumulated considerably more at hers: a couple of suits, a drawer filled with underwear and socks, dress shoes, running gear, toiletries—essentially, I had a lot more of my stuff in her condo than she had at my place.

"You know you can leave more of your things here, so you don't have to go home on your way to work." We walked up the stairs, my hand on the small of her back.

"That's okay."

"Aurora, why?"

She smiled awkwardly. "It's just that the last time I left some things, Sophia wasn't pleased. I don't want to create any issues between you two."

"What do you mean Sophia wasn't happy about it?" I demanded once we were in my bedroom. I began to unbutton my shirt, as she leaned against the closed bedroom door.

"She told me that she didn't like seeing my things at your place and—"

"What? Sophia?" *No fucking way.* "You probably misunderstood, Aurora."

She smiled. "Maybe."

"So, stop worrying and just get comfortable here. Okay?"

She nodded and then looked at her watch. "Ah...Gabriel, would it be alright if I left *after*? I have an early morning meeting."

I removed my shirt. "After?"

She looked so lost suddenly that I walked up to her. "Hey, what the fuck is going on?"

"I just...I thought after we had sex, I could leave. I can't stay the night."

"So, this is a booty call?" I felt anger surge through me.

She licked her lips. "I...well...isn't that why you—"

"Is that what our relationship is? I'm asking you to feel at home in my house, and you're treating me like some dude you met on Tinder to get your rocks off?" I put my hands on her arms and curbed the desire to shake her. *How dare she?*

"I'm sorry." She lowered her eyes.

I deflated and hugged her. "I love you, Aurora."

She curled into me, pulling me close. "I love you too. So, so much."

I felt her tears on my chest. "What's going on, baby? Talk to me."

She shook her head. "Nothing. Just that I love you. And I'm sorry. Is it okay if I take a quick shower."

I nodded and watched her go into the master bathroom. I followed her, and while she showered, I brushed my teeth. By the time I got into bed, she was done and slid in next to me.

I loved this part of my night when Aurora was there, and the smell of lavender filled my room. Even after she left, my sheets smelled like her until the housekeeper changed them.

Damn it! Why couldn't Aurora get along with my daughter? Maybe I could talk to her and ask her to make an effort. I didn't want to lose her.

"You know you're the first woman I introduced Sophia to since the divorce," I began when she was nestled against me, her warm body making me hard. But I needed to explain why I hadn't invited her to the Rhodes Annual Charity Luncheon and, *more importantly*, discuss why she needed to mend her relationship with Sophia.

"I do know that, Gabriel."

"Sophia is important to me, as are you."

She kissed my chest and stroked my stomach.

"I want you to meet my parents, but not at an event like this. They invite way too many people, and it's an obligation for my brother and me."

CHAPTER 3

Aurora

I wanted to ask him then why Iris was going to be there with him.

"Iris's parents and mine are friends. They're always invited and so is she," he explained, even though I hadn't asked. "*And* she's Sophia's mother."

How do you win that contest with an ex?

I felt enormously guilty for demanding more than he was prepared to give. Relationships had always been complicated for me. Throughout my life, I had tried to accommodate others—my mother, my aunt, and even my father, as I attempted to maintain a relationship with him, only to be rejected. I was not needy or clingy, but I worried that I might have been acting that way with Gabriel. If that were the case, then our relationship would undoubtedly have ended soon. I loved him like I had never loved anyone else, and I wanted to give it my all to see if we could build a future together.

It didn't seem likely, even I, the perennial optimist, had to admit.

Sophia didn't like me—it wasn't personal; I think she wouldn't like any woman her father was dating. She wanted her parents back together, it was obvious.

I'd left my perfume and a few makeup items in Gabriel's bathroom a few months ago. The next time I was there, they were gone. I was looking through his drawers when Sophia came into her father's bathroom, arms crossed, and said, "I threw your stuff away."

"Why?" I was shocked.

"I don't want you leaving your things in our house." She swiveled around and left me staring at her back open-mouthed.

Luna had been furious with me for not telling Gabriel what Sophia had done, but I didn't want to come between him and his daughter any more than I already had.

"Gabriel, I'm sorry if I made you feel bad about not inviting me to your parents' party...luncheon...whatever," I told him sincerely.

He stroked my arm and pulled me in for a kiss. "You are too sweet to make me feel bad about anything. I love you, Aurora. I've never loved anyone but Sophia and then you."

I snuggled into him, wanting to feel comforted by his words, but I couldn't.

Then you? First Sophia and *then afterward* me. But that was fair, wasn't it? He *should* love his daughter more than he loved me.

"I need you to try with Sophia. It's tearing me apart that

you both don't get along. I need you both to be friends. Can you please make that happen?"

I felt a chill go through me. How was I supposed to do that? I didn't have any responsibility or authority when it came to his child, and she was rude and insolent with me. Oh, she put up a good act when Gabriel was around, but the minute he wasn't there, she was a whole different kid.

"Please, Aurora."

"Of course."

"When we're back from Paris, why don't you and she go do something together?" he suggested.

I stifled a sigh. Didn't he get it? I'd done everything I could. His daughter would never ever get along with any woman he dated.

This was hopeless.

"Baby?" he pulled me onto him, so I was lying on top of him.

We were eye to eye, and I could feel his erection against me. My breathing stuttered as it always did. His eyes were midnight blue, and his face, carved by angels, made my heart stop.

"I need you to make it work with Sophia," he growled, his hips moving against me.

Was that a threat? I wondered. Yes, it was. If I couldn't make it work with his daughter, he'd end us. I didn't blame him. How could I when I'd wanted the same thing from my father when I'd been Sophia?

"I will, honey. I promise," I vowed. I'd do whatever it would take. I loved this man, and he loved me.

"Good."

His hands on my hips ground me to him as he kissed me. I slid down his body to take him into my mouth. I couldn't wait.

"Fuck yeah," he muttered and fisted my hair to lift my head. "Look at me, baby. Look at me when you suck me off."

I did as he said and continued to take him deep. It was just us here. The two of us. No daughters, ex-wives, no one. Just Gabriel and me.

He moved his hand to control my movements. I loved how he took charge. I loved it when he let me take charge.

"How do I taste, baby?" he asked as he pulled me up.

"Intoxicating."

He pushed me down on him and, at the same time, lifted his hips to hit the back of my throat. I whimpered, and tears filled my eyes.

"Fuck. Fuck." He kept pushing until I could barely breathe. He'd told me if I needed to stop him, all I had to do was tap his thigh, but I never did. I loved it when he lost control with me.

He came, and it was sudden, and he was so far back in my throat that I could barely taste him. He groaned as I pulled away, breathing hard.

"You have the perfect mouth."

I rested my forehead against his taut stomach, catching my breath and feeling my arousal intensely.

"On your knees, baby," he ordered, and I scrambled to do as he asked.

"You're so wet." He stroked my pussy, I moaned. "You're swollen and soft. You want to come?"

"Yes," I cried when he slid a finger inside me.

"What if I make you wait? What if I edge you?"

He'd done that once, brought me to the brink three times before letting me come. He'd had to hold me after because I was shaking for a good five minutes, sobbing.

"Not tonight." I was desperate for him.

He licked me then, and I saw stars. The orgasm slammed into me with such force that my hands slipped, and my face met a pillow.

I heard his low laugh. "Baby, you're so fucking sexy. You come so hard for me."

He palmed my ass cheeks and licked the length of my pussy, feasting on my release. He slapped my butt hard, and I moaned louder.

I'd slept with two men my whole life, and my previous boyfriend had never done that. When Gabriel had, for the first time, a part of me had been scandalized, and the other thrilled. I loved being dominated; I knew that, and that had been a major problem with my previous boyfriend, who had wanted me to take charge.

Gabriel slapped my ass again and squeezed a cheek. And then he sucked my clitoris as I writhed. He spanked me harder, alternating between nibbling at my clit and stinging my ass cheeks.

When I was about to come again, he pulled away, and I felt him, hard, ready against me. He turned me onto my back. He liked to watch me when he was inside me. My eyes could barely open, I was so out of it, so consumed by what was happening to my body.

"Look at me," he commanded as he teased my pussy with the tip of his erection. He moved a hand to my breasts, squeezing my nipple *hard*.

"Ah," I groaned in pain. He snapped his hips and entered me; his mouth fell on my breasts. He suckled me hard, teeth and tongue and lips. He knew I liked the bite; it made my pussy wetter and tighter. I didn't even know that about myself until I met Gabriel; that pain and pleasure blended for me.

He raised his head and lifted my thighs over his shoulders. I was stretched, and he was going deep. His eyes never left mine as he hammered into me.

"Say you love me."

There was a shift in his eyes, something almost cruel and selfish. "I love you," I whispered, all self-preservation out of the window.

"Good, because you're mine," he grunted.

I was his, but I was afraid that he wouldn't take care of me. I hadn't realized that was what I was afraid of until right now, as I was on the brink of another orgasm.

"Say, you're mine. Say, my fucking name." He bit my bottom lip.

His movements became jerkier and stronger; he was losing control. I knew he was about to come. And I gave him my complete surrender.

"I'm yours, Gabriel."

But I knew even as I exploded into a million pieces along with him that even though I was his, he was not mine.

CHAPTER 4
Gabriel

"I hear you're dating," my mother asked me when we had some privacy during the Rhodes Annual Charity Luncheon.

The opulent family estate in the Isle of Hope on Skidway River was designed for casual coastal living. I didn't live too far in The Landings, which made it convenient for Sophia to drop by as she was close to my parents.

Betsy Rhodes was not your traditional southern woman; in fact, she was from Boston and had met my father when he was studying at Harvard. She came from old money like my father did but was not *southern* with a big S.

"Heard from?" I queried as I topped her glass with champagne.

We were sitting by the river where my parents had built a small pagoda. It was private, and right now, with the gardens and estate full of people, it was nice to have some time alone with my mother.

"Sophia. She doesn't like your lady friend."

"Did she say why?"

Betsy chuckled and sipped her champagne. "She doesn't have to. I know why."

"Why?" I asked, puzzled.

"Because she isn't Iris."

There was absolutely no love lost between my ex-wife and my mother. They were opposites. My mother spoke her mind and was mostly down to earth despite growing up and marrying wealthy. She managed the Rhodes Charitable Foundation, where Iris had dabbled when we first got married until she realized it was real work, not just parties and socializing.

"She knows Iris and I are never getting back together."

"Knowing and hoping are two different things," Mama pointed out.

"Is it really that simple?" I wondered.

"For Sophia? Yes. Iris is manipulating that kid."

I sighed. "Mama, no, she isn't."

My mother scowled for a moment and then breathed in, closing her eyes. When she looked at me again, she was calm. "Look, you and Rafe are independent and live your life on your own terms. When Rafe said he wanted to pursue academia and not the family business, we let him. When you said you wanted to marry Iris because you knocked her up, we celebrated."

"What's your point?"

"I don't like to interfere in my children's lives, so when I do, I expect you to pay attention." There was a bite in her voice. "You have created living conditions that are not conducive for you to have a relationship with a woman."

"Christ, Mama, can we give the whole you live too close to your ex business a rest?"

She never approved of my living arrangement with Iris, but I was convinced that Sophia thrived from having both her parents so close and accessible.

"How does it work when Iris is dating someone?" she asked.

I shrugged. I had absolutely no idea if my ex was seeing someone, and frankly, I didn't care. Sophia hadn't mentioned anything either, so I assumed Iris was being as discreet as I had been. When she met someone serious, she would introduce him to Sophia, and I would support that.

"Tell me about this woman you're seeing?"

The thing with Mama was that she never held a grudge. She'd say her piece, and if we didn't listen, she didn't hold it against us.

I smiled as soon as I thought about Aurora. "Her name is Aurora Turner. She works for Nina Davenport."

My mother nodded appreciatively. She'd never liked it that Iris was a full-time socialite. "What does she do at Savannah Lace?"

"She's an architect. I met her when she was working on a Rhodes Hotel project."

"Is she from Savannah?"

"Born and partially raised."

"What do her parents do?"

I stilled. I didn't actually know. "Her father is in Memphis and her mother is god knows where. Neither is in the picture. She was born here, moved around with her mother, and then returned at Sophia's age to live with her aunt in Savannah."

I knew her childhood had been difficult, though I didn't know all the details. She had shared that her father started a new family and abandoned her, which is why she respected my efforts to stay close to Sophia.

"Do we know the aunt?"

I chuckled. "No, Mama. We don't. In any case, she's not alive."

"Poor girl, she has *no* family."

"I guess she doesn't." I knew that, but I hadn't actually given it much thought. She was not the kind who advertised how she felt. She never talked about her family much. I had the basic details and nothing more. Why hadn't I asked? She knew everything about my family. She knew because she'd asked, she'd been curious. What does it mean that I hadn't been?

My mother grinned. "So, she's not some stuck-up Savannah socialite?"

I laughed. "As far from that as you can imagine. She's a career woman. In fact, this weekend, she's in New Orleans for a hotel opening. She was an architect on that project."

"Is that why you didn't bring her today?"

"I want you and Dad to meet her in a quieter setting... when I'm ready for y'all to meet."

My mother raised an eyebrow. "But you introduced her to Sophia?"

"Yeah, and I think I might have made a mistake. They're not getting along. I told Aurora that after we come back from Paris, she needs to make it work with Sophia. I love her, Mama," I confessed, "but if she can't find a way to be friendly with Sophia, we're over."

My mother finished her champagne and rose. "Gabriel, break it off with Aurora because there is no way that she and your daughter will ever get along. And not because of anything Aurora says or does; it's going to be because Sophia is too much under her mother's influence to allow that to happen."

"Mama, you're getting this all wrong. Aurora is nearly thirty and doesn't have children. She's not used to being with kids. I just need her to spend more time with Sophia, and...it's just that Sophia thinks Aurora is cold."

"Do you find Aurora cold?"

Aurora was warm and loving. Kind and generous. "She doesn't know how to be around kids. She just needs to learn," I maintained.

"Is Aurora in love with you?"

"Yeah."

"Poor girl," my mother said. "Well, let's get back before your father sends a search party. By now, he must be sick and tired of everyone, and if I don't go back, he may kick everyone out."

My father, Atticus Rhodes, was an introvert, a lot like

my brother Raphael. Rafe was three years my junior and a tenured professor of quantitative economics at Emory University. The son of a bitch was a geek and one of my closest friends.

He'd met Aurora once, and he'd liked her.

However, he'd remarked, "She's too soft for what Iris will put her through."

"What will Iris do?" I asked, baffled.

Rafe just shook his head. "You've got blinders on, brother. If you don't take them off, you're gonna die a bitter old man with Iris on your arm."

"What the fuck does my relationship with Aurora have to do with Iris?"

"You're still living with your ex-wife, Gabe."

"We have separate homes."

"You keep telling yourself that."

The thing was, no one in my family liked Iris. Sure, she came from the same social circles as us, but that didn't seem enough for my family as it did for Iris's. Her parents had been beyond thrilled that I'd gotten their daughter pregnant —because the wedding would be one for the ages. It had been a bit over the top, and my mother had let Iris's mother run the show.

"It's a catfight I don't want to win," she told me.

My mother was far too busy to plan a society wedding, and it wasn't her thing. This Annual Luncheon was a way to raise money for the causes she supported, and pretty much everything my mother did was to drive the agenda of the

Rhodes Charitable Foundation. My father had turned over the reins of the company to me nine years ago because he'd wanted to work with my mother.

"At some point, son, you realize it's not about the money but what good you do with it," he said. "So, go make some more so your mother and I can spend it on doing some good for the world."

Iris didn't fit in at all with my family, and she'd known that. Every time my parents visited, or we had to spend time with them, she'd made a drama out of it. Now, I couldn't stop her from attending every party and event that my mother threw.

"Just because we're not married doesn't mean I'm not your daughter-in-law," she protested when Mama had asked why she wanted to continue to attend Rhodes family gatherings.

"Actually, Iris, that's exactly what it means," my mother replied, and because I glared at her, she added, "But you'll always be the mother of my granddaughter, and that makes you a Rhodes for life."

I wondered how Aurora would fit in with my family and painfully realized that she'd fit in just fine. My father, who was a hotel man, would talk to her about architecture until the cows came home, and my mother would enjoy her intelligence.

That was what Rafe had said the one time he met her. "She's smart. Went to Georgia Tech." I hadn't known then, but Rafe had informed me it had one of the most prestigious architecture programs in the world. Aurora had never shown off about it; she wasn't the type who would.

I found Rafe in the library, alone.

"You snuck out?" I asked and sprawled on an armchair across from him.

"I did the meet and greet," he sighed. "How come Aurora isn't here with you?"

"I wanted her to meet the parents in a quieter setting," I repeated what I'd told my mother, what I'd told Aurora.

"Bullshit," Rafe snorted, "You didn't want to have a fight with Iris and Sophia."

I cocked an eyebrow. "What the fuck?"

"Yeah, that's why she's not here."

"No. And she's in New Orleans this weekend for work." But he'd touched upon something true. A part of the reason I hadn't wanted Aurora here was the shitshow Iris would bring down on me. It just wasn't worth it. And wouldn't it be easier for her to meet my parents at a restaurant where it was just us? If she resolved her issues with Sophia.

"I'm surprised you guys are still together," Rafe provoked.

"Why?"

"Because your kid and your ex-wife control your life. I mean, it pisses us off when every time there's a family thing that doesn't include Iris, you and Sophia don't make it."

"What nonsense."

It was partly true. Sophia didn't want to go if her mother wasn't going to be there as well. Not that she was hanging around Iris at such gatherings, they did their own thing, she just wanted her Mama around.

I was about to get up to leave when he added, "How many dates do you cancel with Aurora versus the ones you go to?"

I leaned back. "I have a thirteen-year-old. She's at a vulnerable age."

"*That* many canceled dates?" Rafe mocked.

We looked like brothers, except he worked out more than I did, and it showed.

"You're a serial monogamist; I don't think you should give anyone relationship advice," I muttered.

"If you love her, you need to fix your life."

"My life is great." Now, I did stand up. "What's up with all of you? Mama was saying the same thing."

"Then maybe you should pay attention, Gabe."

"My daughter is my highest priority."

"I love Sophia, Gabe, but she's turning into Iris." I felt my temper flare inside. How dare he? Rafe raised his hand when I was about to speak. "Don't say anything you'll regret."

Before I could answer, there was a knock on the library door, and my father looked in. "Your mother is looking for both of you."

Rafe marched out, and I grabbed my father's arm. "Do you also have a problem with how I'm living my life?"

My father frowned. "What part?"

"That Iris lives close by, and we share parenting responsibilities?"

My father, who was a good reminder for me as to how I'd look in another thirty years, waited a long moment and then said coolly, "It's none of my business, son. You do you."

And that was that. It was Atticus Rhodes' motto, "live and let live."

My kid was my priority, and that was that as well, I told myself, but there was a niggling seed of doubt inside me that maybe my family wasn't judging me but trying to help me.

CHAPTER 5

Aurora

There were four messages from Gabriel when I got back to my room around midnight from what had been a fantastic party in the ballroom of the hotel that I'd helped design. I'd not looked at my phone on purpose. When I was busy, and he was not, Gabriel tended to demand my attention.

I never initiated contact, whether by message or call, unless it was for something practical, like informing him I was running late. Initially, his delayed responses left me feeling rejected, so I stopped trying. Our vastly different lives didn't require daily communication.

Did it make the relationship one-sided? Yes. Did it make me a simpering moron? Yes, to that as well.

The messages from Gabriel spanned four hours. The first one came around seven thirty in the evening: *How's the hotel? Are you having fun?*

The next message was forty-five minutes later: *I was*

wondering if you're free next weekend? Maybe you and I can do something after I come back from Paris.

The third message came an hour ago: *Aurora? Baby? You there?*

And the fourth message that came fifteen minutes ago: *Call me whenever you get in.*

I contemplated that last message as I stood on the balcony of my suite and looked out at the beautiful city of New Orleans. I went back inside the room and opened the bottle of champagne the hotel had left for me. I poured myself a glass and then texted Gabriel: *Are you still awake?*

The phone rang within seconds. I'd barely had time to put my earbuds on.

"Where the fuck have you been?" he demanded.

"Well, hello to you too." I took a sip of champagne. I knew he was irritated. He got this way if he didn't hear from me right away. I hadn't avoided my phone to rile him up; I'd done it so I could enjoy an evening without thinking about him, without him being with me emotionally.

"It's late."

I laughed softly. "It's midnight. The party was still roaring when I left."

"Put me on video," he demanded.

I accepted the video call, and he was in bed, naked even though he was covered waist down by his duvet. We'd had phone sex—sometimes, it was all we could manage because of our various commitments and because Gabriel canceled more dates than he kept. If possible, he'd show up late at my place for what Luna called a booty call even after he canceled

—after his daughter was asleep and would leave before she woke up like he was sneaking out to see me. I didn't like it, but he'd tell me a variation of, "She's having a meltdown, blah blah blah."

"Drinking champagne?" he murmured as I raised my glass to him.

I set the phone down to lean against the vase on the table on the balcony and sat down.

"Holy shit. You wore that?"

I looked down. I wore a navy blue sheath dress with a long slit. But it covered me from neck to ankles, leaving my arms and back bare. I'd paired the dress with blue sandals and put on my only expensive jewelry, a pair of dropped gold earrings that I'd bought from Cartier when I'd gotten my first bonus. Since then, I spent all my money on my condo on River Street, which had a priceless view of the Savannah River. It was a historic property with exposed brick, hardwood floors, and iron detailing. It had an open design with a spacious kitchen, dining, and living space. I loved how it was within walking distance of everything. It stretched my budget, but as someone who'd never owned anything, I'd desperately wanted *my* place. Of course, compared to Gabriel's mansion, it was tiny, with just two bedrooms and two baths. But it was perfect for me.

"You look beautiful," Gabriel continued. "Fuck, but you do."

I smiled. "How was your day with your family?"

His eyes flickered with irritation. "It was a charity luncheon that my mother hosts, so it was more than family."

His tone said he didn't want to discuss it any further. I could feel the chasm between us growing, and I was certain he could as well.

"Did a lot of men hit on you tonight?" he asked.

He was a possessive man, and I'd told him more than once that he didn't need to be where I was concerned.

"Luna is with me," I laughed and drank some more champagne. "No one looks at me when she's around."

"Luna is okay, but you're stunning, Aurora. You know that."

"I'm glad you think so."

But did he? Or was he with me because I was such a doormat, letting him get away with treating me like...well, a doormat?

Compared to his ex-wife, I was the epitome of plainness. My schedule didn't allow for luxuries like manicures or hair appointments. Engulfed in sixty-hour work weeks, my scarce free time was dedicated to Gabriel, whenever he was free.

As junior architect, which I'd been for four years now, I contributed to projects without leading them. Climbing the career ladder in my field meant embracing long hours and accepting the grind. Long exhausting hours were part of the package.

"Show me what you're wearing under that dress," Gabriel whispered, his eyes bright with arousal.

I smiled and took the phone inside the suite. I placed the phone on the dresser and moved further away.

"God, you're beautiful."

I unzipped my dress and slowly peeled it off of me. He

shifted I knew to touch himself, take himself in his hand. I loved to watch him come. We masturbated to each other sometimes, even when we were together.

Underneath the dress, I wore a pair of lace panties. I hadn't worn a bra because the dress came with built-in support.

"Turn around," he whispered in my ear.

I did as he asked.

"Oh, baby, I wish I could put my hands on your ass. Did you like how I spanked you last night?"

"Yes."

Heat pooled between my legs, and I felt the urgency for release. I turned to face him.

"Your ass turned such a beautiful shade of red. Christ, I wish you were here with me." His frustration came through to me loud and clear.

"Me too." I bent and removed my panties and heard him gasp.

"Are you wet, Aurora? Show me."

I put my hand to my pussy when he cursed, "Fuck, baby spread your legs."

I knew what he wanted. I moved my legs apart, and he groaned when I touched myself. "Put a finger inside you."

I did as he asked.

"Show me."

I did.

"Taste yourself."

I did.

"Fuck, yeah. Did you bring your vibrator, baby?"

"Yes."

"Get into bed and show me how you can come hard with me."

No one had ever made me feel this abandoned when it came to sex. I couldn't believe the things he made me do.

I set the phone propped up so he could see me with the small clitoral vibrator I had stored in my bedside table.

"Yes. Just like that." He was pulling hard, jacking himself off.

Watching him was erotic because no one looked as beautiful as Gabriel when he came. I turned on the vibrator, and my eyes closed.

"No," he snarled. "Look at me, damn it. I can't touch you, so give me that. Come with me, baby. I love you so much. I miss you so much."

I opened my eyes and felt tears run down my cheeks. I was so turned on and overwhelmed with emotion. It happened sometimes when we made love, and he licked my tears away.

"Oh, baby." I watched as he came in his hands, his eyes still on mine. "Come on, sweetheart, come for—"

"Daddy?" I heard Sophia and a thumping on his bedroom door.

"Fuck," Gabriel growled. "Sweetpea, give me a minute. I'm so sorry, I—"

I hung up before he could say anything else. I felt humiliated. Had his daughter been listening to us? The experience that was, so us and made me feel so sexually empowered now seemed tawdry.

I wiped my vibrator clean with a tissue and went into the bathroom to take a shower. There would be no orgasm for me tonight.

I leaned my head against the wall of the shower as the water cascaded down on me. This relationship was consuming me, driving me crazy. My insecurities were being stoked, not being assuaged.

I remembered what Nina Davenport always said about relationships, "Personal or business, it's a pooling of resources. A relationship should make you more than you are, not less."

This relationship with Gabriel was making me less. It was making me feel insecure. It brought back all my feelings of abandonment. I couldn't do this anymore.

I put my phone on silent and cried half the night before falling into fitful sleep.

CHAPTER 6
Gabriel

P aris was a nightmare. My sweet child had turned into a monstrous teenager, and I had no idea what to do with her. It appeared that Iris let her buy whatever she wanted, and Sophia went a little nuts with my credit card.

Rafe and I grew up with money, but we were never allowed to spend it freely. There was no fucking way I would have considered buying a pair of two thousand dollar shoes at the age of thirteen. So, when Sophia asked for Chanel boots, I told her that wasn't going to happen. She sulked and whined. It was a scene that repeated itself several times in Paris.

She liked playing tourist—going to the Louvre, the Eiffel Tower, the Arc de Triomphe, and the Notre Dame—but what she really wanted to do was to buy things so she could go back to school and show them off.

I called Iris and asked her what the hell was going on,

and she said, "All the kids are doing that. Don't be stingy, Gabe."

This had nothing to do with being tightfisted and everything about being responsible. I wanted my kid to be more excited about seeing the fucking Mona Lisa than walking into Prada. Maybe Mama was right, and Sophia was being influenced by Iris, who lived and died by designer brands.

The time difference meant that I never got Aurora for more than a few minutes on the phone. I missed her. I ached for her. The phone-sex we had the night before I came to Paris left me raw. I knew it had hurt her feelings because I'd had to cut it short. Pump and dump, man.

I'd tried to call Aurora after Sophia went back to sleep but she didn't pick up. I tried again before we left for Paris and got her voicemail. I texted her, and she replied with a: *Have a wonderful time in Paris with Sophia.*

I refused to believe she'd end us because I had to prematurely end our phone-sex session. It made no sense. Well, I was going to make time to see her once we were back in Savannah, and in all honesty, as much as I loved the kid, I needed a break from Sophia.

We got home early on Friday morning, and I went straight to work. When I called Aurora, I got her voicemail. It was starting to piss me off.

After my morning meetings, I called Aurora's office and asked the front desk to connect me to her.

"Aurora Turner, how can I help you?" I heard her crisp voice.

"Well, for one, you can talk to me," I stated.

There was a long pause. "Hey. I'm sorry. It's been crazy busy."

"Or you're avoiding me," I tried to joke, but I could feel the fear of losing her in the pit of my stomach.

"No. Not at all. Are you back?"

"Yes. Can I see you tonight?" I paused and then added, "Please."

"Yes, of course. Can you come over to my place? I can cook dinner."

"Yeah?" It was all okay, I thought, relieved. She wouldn't suggest cooking for me if she was breaking us up. In any case, I wasn't going to let her. She loved me, and I'd take advantage of that to keep her with me.

The past week, I'd missed her; hungered for her. There had been an ache inside me, not just for sex but for her. When I talked to her and listened to her laugh, her calm voice settled and centered me. No one had ever done that for me.

This was the first time since we started seeing each other that I'd had trouble getting a hold of her. Usually, she'd be there, available for me.

As I thought that, I felt something move inside me. Available for me? And what about when she wanted to reach out to me? Was I there for her?

But she never reached out to me. Why didn't she? How come she never called, never texted? She responded, but she didn't initiate. I didn't mind it so much. Aurora and I didn't fight or argue. It was always pleasant and easy. And I wanted to keep it like that. I wanted a smooth relationship with no bumps.

I said as much to Beau Bodine, one of my closest friends who ran a tech company that was headquartered in Savannah. We'd grown up together, and I thought of him as a brother. We often met for either drinks, dinner, or a meal—though it had become increasingly difficult with Sophia becoming needy and me trying to juggle having a girlfriend and a teenage daughter.

"Looks like you have it made. A woman who revolves around your schedule, I wish I had that. Every woman I date wants to take up space and time to where I'm keeping it to *only* sex," Beau remarked when I told him how things were going with Aurora and how lucky I was to have an uncomplicated relationship with her.

"Aurora doesn't revolve around my schedule." I protested.

"That's what it sounds like." He browsed the menu even though we came to eat at The Olde Pink House often and knew it by heart.

We went with our usuals: fish tacos for him and crab cakes for me. We got a glass of white wine each. It was a Friday afternoon, and we'd knock off work early. And I was a little jet-lagged to boot.

"My parents think a relationship with Aurora can't last because of how close I live to Iris."

He shrugged. "But you're not looking for a relationship, are you? You're looking for someone to have sex with on the regular, and it looks like that's what you have with Aurora, and it's good quality sex, yeah?"

"I'm in love with this woman," I snapped. I couldn't believe he was being so callous.

Beau chuckled. "Come on, Gabe, you don't introduce her to your parents, you cancel more dates than you keep. I mean, you missed your one-year anniversary because Sophia had a meltdown. It's clear where your priorities lie."

"What's wrong with prioritizing my child?"

"But that's not what you're doing, Gabe."

"Explain to me then what it is I'm doing?" I barked. He was irritating the shit out of me as my parents were. I was a damn good father, and it was important for me to remain that way.

"You're asking Aurora to prioritize your daughter."

"Isn't that what happens in such relationships?"

"I have no clue. I've never dated a woman with a kid... and wouldn't want to. Since Trevor is now engaged, I'm hoping he'll keep my Mama happy with grandkids."

Trevor was Beau's younger brother, and his new fiancée was a carbon copy of Iris. Good luck to him. But that's what men in my social circle did. We married a woman who'd look good on our arm and be the best hostess, fuck us once a week, have a couple kids, and then Trevor would find a side piece, and everyone would be happy.

Iris had suggested why I couldn't just have an affair like everyone else instead of getting a divorce when I'd told her we were done; that I was done.

But I wasn't a cheater and I'd told Iris that; insulted that she thought so little of me.

We moved to less lofty topics centered on the health of

our businesses and the upcoming social calendar so we could coordinate the few events we could attend together to be able to stand them.

"You going back to work after lunch?" Beau asked when we walked out of the restaurant.

"I think I'm going to stop by Tiffany and then go to Savannah Lace. Maybe I can convince Aurora to leave work early," I decided on the spot.

"Tiffany?" Beau arched an eyebrow.

"Yeah. I should buy her something."

Beau scratched his jaw. "Don't take this wrong way, man, but I've got to tell you. This relationship ain't lastin'."

"Why?" I demanded.

"Cause no woman is gonna put with your family drama in the long term," Beau explained.

"I don't have family—"

"You live with your ex-wife, brother. And you just told me that you had to end a fucking phone-sex session because of Sophia."

I sighed. "That's not drama."

"It is. And from what you've told me about Aurora, which isn't a lot, and I don't get women, but I can tell you she isn't the type who's gonna be swayed by a tennis bracelet. I don't think she's like Iris."

"And how the hell would you know?"

"Cause I know people. Come on, when was the last time you bought something for this woman that had her light up?" Beau handed his ticket and some cash to the valet. I did the same.

I thought about it. "I bought her chocolates from the airport in San Francisco."

"Yeah?"

"She told me it was because she knew I thought about her when I was traveling."

He smirked.

"I should've picked up something for her in Paris."

Beau put a hand on my shoulder. "Honest to god, do you want to make it with this woman?"

"What does that mean?"

"Do you want to marry her and have kids with her?"

"Whoa! I barely know her."

"You've known her for a year," Beau said solemnly. "Stop stringing this woman along. If you can't commit to her, then let her go. I mean, if buying her something in one of those light blue boxes is gonna make you feel better, go for it, but I don't think she'd give a shit."

"And what the fuck do you know." The valet thankfully got my car first so I could leave because Beau was annoying the hell out of me. I felt like when it came to Aurora, literally, everyone I'd spoke about her to was certain it wouldn't last, and not because of her, but because I was choosing my daughter over my love life. Well, if that was the case, then so be it.

And the hell with Beau. I went to Tiffany and bought Aurora a tennis bracelet, which I was certain she'd like.

I'd just parked my car and was on my way to Aurora's office in downtown Savannah when my phone rang. It was Iris. I groaned but answered.

"Gabe, where are you?"

"Out."

"You've got to come home. Sophia is in pieces."

"About what?" I ran a hand through my hair in frustration.

"It's some boy...she's crying and..."

"Iris, can you handle it. I'm in the middle of something."

"Of what?"

"Just something." I walked to the main door of the Savannah Lace building.

"You're seeing her, aren't you? *She's* more important than your daughter?" Iris demanded.

I took a deep breath. "I'm not seeing her," I lied to keep the peace, "I just have work. How about I get there in an hour or so?" That would give me enough time to drop Aurora's present off, go see my kid, and then come back for dinner.

"Whatever." Iris hung up.

Christ! My life was a mess. *Was it supposed to be this hard?*

"Mr. Rhodes," Nova King, Nina's executive assistant who saw me in the lobby greeted me. "Does Nina have an appointment with you?"

"No. I just came to see Aurora. Is she in?"

Nova looked at her watch. "She's in a meeting. Why don't you wait in her office, and I'll let her know you're here?"

"Thanks, Nova."

I walked into Aurora's office and sat down in one of her

client chairs. I pulled my phone out and saw it was blowing up with messages from Sophia.

Daddy, are you coming home?

Mama is being mean.

This is so hard.

I can't believe Ashley is seeing Jason. I was gone for one week.

I put my phone face down on the table, feeling utterly weary.

"Gabriel," I heard Aurora's voice from behind me, and part of my fatigue evaporated, just like fucking that.

I rose and smiled. Her beautiful face always made me happy.

"Hey, gorgeous." I pulled her into me and hugged her close and just held her. "Christ, it feels good to hold you. It's been so fucking long."

I kissed her, wanting to immerse myself in her. When I lifted my head, we were both breathless. She put a hand on the chest and stepped away.

"This is my place of work." Her eyes twinkled with amusement.

"I bought you a present." I pulled out the blue Tiffany box from my suit jacket pocket and held it out to her.

She looked at it like it was on fire.

"Gabriel," she whispered.

I opened the box. "Do you like it?"

She closed her eyes for a long moment, and I wished I'd picked up chocolates like Beau had suggested.

57

"It's beautiful." She closed the box. "But I can't take that."

"Why?"

"*Please.*"

"Why the hell can't I buy you anything, Aurora?" I demanded harshly. "Is this your way of keeping me at a distance?"

She looked at me in shock and walked to the door of her office to close it. "Please keep your voice down," she mumbled.

"Well?" I didn't keep my voice down. I was fucking furious. I'd missed her and wanted her while she was still playing games with me.

"It's not that, Gabriel. I hardly wear any jewelry." She held up her hands. She only wore earrings, small, delicate ones. "And it's so expensive I'd be afraid to wear it."

"If you lose it, I'll buy you another."

She shook her head. "I've told you before. I don't want these types of things from you."

"What do you want then?" I growled.

"You...time with you. I want your attention. That's all," she replied softly, her eyes shimmering with emotion.

Fucking hell, this woman twisted me around. I set the box on her desk and pulled her to me. "I'm here. I'm with you. I think about you all the fucking time. I'm so in love with you, Aurora."

"Really?"

"Yes."

My phone pinged with a message, and she stiffened. I

ignored the phone and kissed her softly. "I'm here with you. Even when I'm not."

Her eyes lit up at that. This was her love language— being there with her for her, as it was mine. That's how she showed me she loved me by making time and room for me, and I had to do the same.

"So, what time should I come over for dinner?" I asked. "And what are you cooking?"

"How about seven and duck?" she grinned broadly and warmed my heart. I loved how she made duck breast, and I knew she'd especially gone shopping to please me. She didn't usually have duck in her freezer.

"Excellent. And for dessert, I can eat you," I murmured and enjoyed watching her eyes turn glossy with arousal. "I've missed being inside you."

She lay her head on my chest and hugged me tight like she'd never let me go, and everything felt right in my world.

There was a quick knock on her office door, and it opened before Aurora could respond. Luna Steele walked in. Luna came from the same society as I did but she was no socialite. One of the most sought-after architects in Georgia, she was a few years older than Aurora. She was her mentor, boss, and friend.

"Hi, Gabe."

Even though Aurora struggled, I held her to me. I knew this was a workplace, but fuck it, I hadn't had my hands on my girl for ten days.

"Luna."

"Aurora, the client is here."

She looked at me, and I stepped away from her. "Go, have your meeting, and I'll see you later."

She picked up her laptop and hurried out. Luna stayed with a challenge in her eyes.

"Yes?"

"You're hurting her," she simply said.

My jaw tightened. "Luna, I don't think your friend would appreciate us discussing her."

"She won't."

"My relationship with Aurora has nothing to do with you."

"I'm her friend, one of the very few she has, maybe the only."

"I don't know what you want me to do." I picked up the Tiffany box and put it in my pocket.

"If you love her, stop hurting her."

Luna didn't back down.

"I do love her, and I'm not hurting her."

"She's too much of a sweetheart to say anything, and she's shit scared of losing you. But when you always put her second to your kid—"

"Stop right there," I snarled. "You don't get to talk about my daughter. You crossed a line."

Luna nodded. "I know. But it had to be said. You take care of yourself, Gabe."

She walked away, leaving me feeling like an asshole. Why was it that everyone in my life was blaming me for loving my daughter? I was a thirty-six-year-old man who knew myself and knew how I wanted to live my life, and as long as Aurora didn't have a problem with it, Luna and the rest of the world could go fuck themselves.

"Come on, Sweetpea, I told you I have dinner plans." I was exhausted being with Sophia. Her moods were all over the place, and she was clingy and needy. According to Iris, it was because I was not paying attention to her. I called bullshit on that. I'd just spent a week with Sophia in fucking Paris, carrying shopping bags for her.

Her eyes filled with tears. "Please, Daddy."

I ran a hand through my hair. "Why don't you come with me?" I suggested.

"To her place?" Her eyes went wide.

"Gabe, I don't think that's such a good idea," Iris piped in.

We were on Iris's porch, watching the sun go down. I had a half hour to get to Aurora's place, which was a twenty-minute drive.

"Aurora is making dinner," I ignored Iris, "it's your favorite, duck breast with orange sauce."

At least here, she couldn't say Iris did it better because my ex couldn't cook for shit. We had a cook that we now shared.

She looked at Iris, who was shaking her head.

"Sophia?" I asked. "Look, I'm going to go one way or another. It's your choice." Enough was enough. I wanted to be with Aurora, and this would be a great way for her and my daughter to engage on Aurora's turf.

"Give me ten minutes to get ready," Sophia said with a big smile.

"Great. I'll be at my place. Just come by, and don't take too long."

I called Aurora as I walked through Iris's garden to mine.

"Gabriel," she answered, sounding so sad that I realized she thought I was calling to cancel.

"Hey, baby. I can already taste the duck. Would it be okay if I brought Sophia along?" I was asking, but really, I was telling. "It would be good for you both to spend some time together."

She didn't hesitate, and my heart filled with something warm and pleasant. "Absolutely. Does she like duck? Should I make something else?"

"She loves duck with orange sauce. It'll be a big hit."

"Ah...does she like chocolate? I'm making souffles."

My mouth watered. Aurora was a damn fine cook. "Baby, she's going love it all."

CHAPTER 7
Aurora

"He's bringing Sophia along," I told Luna on the phone, panicked. "I don't know how it's going to turn out."

"You shouldn't be afraid of a thirteen-year-old."

"This is not your garden-variety thirteen-year-old." And I should know. I spent enough time with Nina's daughter, Bianca, who was thirteen as well, to know Sophia was going through something.

Bianca wanted to be an architect, and we spent every other Sunday afternoon together with the goal of seeing one historic building in Savannah at a time and learning about it. After we had lunch. I always enjoyed my time with her. Bianca was a lovely kid, curious and smart.

Sophia, I had a feeling, was a good kid who was stuck trying to save her parents' relationship and was acting out because of that pressure. Gabriel would never see it, but his ex-wife was doing everything she could to get him back and no matter how often he told me that was never happening, I feared that it would. The lure of being a happy family would be hard for a man like Gabriel, who was so dedicated to his daughter, to resist. If that happened, I promised myself I'd let him go with a smile. I wasn't a home wrecker. I wanted him to be happy.

I set a third place on the table and turned up the lights now that it wasn't going to be a romantic dinner for two. It was a beautiful April day in Savannah, and I opened the balcony doors to let the air in. The candles on the dining table flickered.

I looked around my home. It was warm and cozy. I'd always had an affinity for Native American art and style, so my home had a lot of colorful pueblo-design throw rugs and a bright red couch. The art was eclectic from impressionism to modern. Everything in my home was something I'd purchased and had meaning for me.

The dining table had been an impulse buy at an antique fair. It had been in abysmal shape until Stella—who in addition to being an amazing landscape architect was also a remarkable furniture restorer—gave it some TLC. I paired the beautiful redwood with modern leather chairs. It was a small table with seating for six people, maximum.

I had also changed the bed sheets, but I needn't have bothered because Gabriel would not be staying the night. And somehow, that pleased me, that he wanted to spend time with me without sex being involved. He was bringing his daughter to my place. He was making a commitment. I'd do everything I could to make it work with Sophia, I vowed. Everything and anything.

But an hour into dinner, it was becoming increasingly difficult to keep my promise to myself. Sophia was chipper because her father was there, but her remarks were getting increasingly hostile, even if she was delivering them with a smile.

"It's really a small condo...but you live alone, so I guess it works for you," she said, looking around at my place.

"Isn't it noisy to be on such a busy street?" she asked. "Daddy likes it quiet; that's why we live where we live, right, Daddy?"

"I love your dress. Did you buy it at Zara? In Paris, we went shopping everywhere. My favorite was Chanel."

She was thirteen, and she was behaving like a...well, *spoiled* thirteen-year-old who was competing with me. I didn't want to compete with this kid.

Gabriel looked so pleased with himself that it was painfully obvious he had the biggest blinders on when it came to Sophia. He simply couldn't see what she was doing. Poor girl, I thought to myself, having to learn such underhanded behavior at such an early age. My heart went out to her and to Gabriel.

His phone rang, and he sighed. "It's my father, I have to take this."

We'd just finished our soufflés, and they'd turned out really well, which I was relieved about. As soon as Gabriel stepped out onto the balcony, Sophia went from Jekyll to Hyde, but with a twist this time.

"Why are you doing this?" she asked.

I was taken aback. "Doing what, Sophia?"

"Breaking up my family."

I felt a sledgehammer go through me. "Honey, I'm not doing that."

"Look, I can see you don't have a lot of money, and my dad does. Is that what you want?"

I sighed. "No, Sophia, I love your father. I'd love him whether he had any money or not."

She sniffled. "You're just a gold digger, and we all know that."

She was a beautiful girl, like her mother. Blonde, blue-eyed, devastatingly good-looking features. The words gold digger coming out of her mouth sounded obscene.

"Sophia. Your father would like us to get along and—"

"I don't like you."

I licked my lips and smiled gently, "Tell me why? What can I change for you to like me?"

"Leave my father," she declared.

"Honey, your father and my relationship doesn't have anything to do with how he feels about you. You do know that, right?"

"Either you leave him, or I'll make sure he leaves you."

I frowned at that. "What?"

Gabriel walked in then, and as if on command, Sophia burst into tears. "Hey, Sweetpea." Gabriel crouched in front of his daughter. "What happened?"

"I told Aurora that I'd like for us to be friends, and she said that kids and grownups can't be friends."

I stared at her, horrified. I'd never expected her to outright lie.

Gabriel looked at me in confusion. "Aurora?"

"I..." I didn't know what to say.

"What's going on?" he demanded, pulling his daughter up from the chair and holding her.

"I didn't say that, honey," I tried patiently.

"What exactly did you say?" Gabriel asked harshly stroked his daughter's back as she sobbed.

Sophia pulled back. "I'm trying, Daddy, but she isn't...I don't know why you have to keep dating someone like her."

Gabriel shook his head. "Aurora?"

I took a deep breath. There was no winning this, was there? I felt tremendously sad for Gabriel and me, but especially for Sophia. How terrible for a child to lie and cheat to bring her family back together? Maybe that would be the best course here.

"You should get her home," I mumbled. "We can talk later."

Gabriel looked at me, confused. "What the fuck is going on?"

I just shrugged. "She's really upset, Gabriel."

"I can see that. What I want to know is what you did to make her so upset?"

I'd been foolish to think this could work. His arrangement with his ex and his daughter made it impossible for

Gabriel to have a relationship with another woman—I had always known that, hadn't I?

Sophia pulled away. "As soon as you're not around, she's so mean to me, Daddy. Do you know that?"

Gabriel looked at his daughter, disbelief running through him. I could feel his conflict. He couldn't imagine his Sweetpea lying to him, and he couldn't believe I could be mean. I knew who'd win this tug of war.

"She tells me that I take up too much of your time. Do I?"

"No, honey. You're my baby girl." Gabriel stared at me with anger. "Come on, Aurora, that's not something you tell a kid."

I felt the weight of the world on my shoulders. I could throw a hissy fit if I knew how to, but I didn't. I could tell him that his daughter was lying, but that'd hurt him, and he'd never believe me, anyway. This was what was called a no-win situation.

"I never said...," I said weakly. "I'd never say that."

"You did. You just did when you said that your relationship with my father has nothing to do with me. It has everything to do with me. He's my father."

"I only meant that it doesn't change how your father feels about you, Sophia." I didn't even know why I was trying. She'd just lie some more. The poor kid was brainwashed by her mother that I was the evil stepmom who was upending their family life, regardless of the fact that Gabriel and Iris had never been happy together.

Gabriel pulled out his car keys and gave them to Sophia. "You know where the car is parked?"

"Yes, Daddy."

"Sweetpea, go and wait for me. I'll be there in five minutes."

Sophia walked away, sobbing, and gave me a triumphant look. I only smiled back sadly. *Yeah, kid, you won, but at what cost to your conscience.*

I turned to face Gabriel, who was enraged. I could feel the anger emanating from him, directed towards me.

"You know I was warned that a woman who's nearly thirty and hasn't been in a relationship and has no kids is maternally unsuited to be with me. I didn't listen because I was so fucking hot for you. I should have."

Despite the anger, his voice was calm. I knew how Gabriel handled his temper. He said his piece and walked away. He didn't discuss, didn't want to hear the other side of the story—he just said what he had to and moved on.

"I'm so sorry, Gabriel." I had no idea what I was apologizing for. Probably everything. That he had a child who was off the rails. That he was still mired in his marriage after he'd worked so hard to get away from it. For breaking my heart over a love that never had a chance, not the way he managed his personal life.

"Fucking hell, Aurora. I wanted you to make it work with her. Do I mean so little to you? What's wrong with you?"

"I never meant to hurt her," I said lamely. "I never said those—"

"Well, there's no point dancing around it, is there? We both know it's not working. You're too cold to be with someone who has a child."

Cold? My heart almost stopped beating and the punch to my gut made me feel hollow.

This was it. *We were ending.*

Everything inside me was shutting down. I loved this man. I'd do anything for him. But I couldn't convince his daughter to give me a chance.

He ran a hand through his hair. "I've got to go. You have a good life. Ah...I have stuff at your place, and some of your things are at mine."

I nodded.

"Just drop by with my things and take yours...do it during the day. I'll make sure your code works for the next few days."

"Thanks."

I wanted to hug him one last time. Kiss him one last time.

He looked at me. "Are you so jealous of my daughter that you couldn't even try?"

"No. I'm not jealous of—"

"Now I can see why your father and mother walked away from you. All this calm and quiet is an act, isn't it? I can't believe you're so selfish. The minute I'm not there, you're attacking my daughter?"

I closed my eyes. He knew me well. Knew what buttons to push. How to hurt the most. But, see, when you'd been abandoned by pretty much everyone who was supposed to love you all your life—you learn to steel your heart. So, I did.

"You're not even upset we're ending, are you?" He looked devastated.

I smiled weakly. "Take care of yourself, Gabriel."

I left him standing in the living room and went into my bedroom. I heard the front door slam shut, and then, after I was sure he was gone, I let heartbreak take me.

CHAPTER 8
Gabriel

I t had been a week since Aurora and I ended, and my life was a mess.

I still loved her desperately.

I missed her. I couldn't sleep.

I was aware that I'd let my temper get the better of me and had said things to Aurora that I couldn't take back.

Sophia was cagey about what exactly Aurora had said to upset her so much, and I suspected that she'd overreacted. But then, so had I.

It didn't go unnoticed that Iris was happier than she'd ever been, and Sophia was not having as many meltdowns. Was she doing that just to keep me from seeing Aurora? I couldn't believe my kid would be that manipulative.

Beau had absolutely no sympathy for me. "I told you."

We met for a drink at Rocks on The Roof on the riverfront. My evenings were freer than they had ever been. Sophia was behaving like a normal teenager who went out with friends, and since I didn't have a girlfriend, I could actually see my friends.

"Told me what? Come on, man, Aurora handled Sophia poorly."

Beau shook his head as he took another sip of his Lagavulin Scotch. I didn't know how he drank that smokey, peaty crap but to each his own.

Since Aurora left, I had been nursing Macallan 12, and I was beginning to wonder if I was turning into an alcoholic to dull the pain of losing her.

"Or Sophia made sure of it."

"She's thirteen."

"Whatever you say."

"Beau?"

He sighed. "You live with your ex-wife, who wants you guys to get back together. Imagine the pressure on your kid?"

"I'm living like this so Sophia can have both her parents close by. So, she doesn't have to choose between us."

However, it was getting tiresome to eat dinner as a family of three when I didn't want to spend my time with Iris. But it made Sophia so happy that I didn't protest.

"Maybe you should go on a trip like you used to get your rocks off," Beau suggested. "How about New York? I have a meeting there next week. Come along."

The idea had potential, but in all honesty, I couldn't imagine being with any other woman. I wanted Aurora. I wanted her breathy moans. I wanted her mouth on my cock. I wanted her pussy. Fuck! I needed to stop thinking about sex with her because even after the stunt she pulled with my daughter, I wanted her. Just the thought of her made me hard.

"I'll be your wingman," he continued.

Beau was a handsome motherfucker and the wrong kind of wingman to have. A woman caught one glance at his handsome face and well-toned body and chose him over me. I knew this because it had happened. It wasn't just about looks; Beau was charming and a proper Southern gentleman. I didn't have that skill set. I was rough around the edges, as Iris liked to say, and not as sophisticated as was expected by the Savannah society set. Well, fuck 'em. When you were a Rhodes in Savannah, you didn't have to conform, and thanks to my mother, who was a bit of a rebel herself, neither Rafe nor I had.

"I don't know. I'll think about it," I demurred.

"Too heartbroken to fuck around?" Beau asked.

I sighed. Two women who came into the bar eyed us. Beau raised his glass to them.

"Come on, man, I'm not in the mood," I groaned.

"Hey, I love a menage," Beau said.

"You're such an asshole."

"Maybe, but I'm getting laid while you're...moping."

"I'm not moping." I was a grown man, and grown men didn't fucking mope. "Those two look young enough to be your daughters."

Since Beau was in his late thirties like me, and these girls looked like they were in their early twenties, it was a stretch.

"I always wrap it up, so I don't have to worry about that

shit," he proclaimed and grinned. "It's been a dry week for me, so I'm going to mosey on."

I watched him walk up to the bar and chat the women up. He didn't have to worry about sleeping with women in Savannah. Beauregard Bodine, a notorious playboy, vowed never to settle down and enjoyed the company of women— as long as they weren't expecting a ring on their finger.

I paid the tab and walked out of the bar, feeling the urge to reach out to Aurora. I had a free evening and when we were together, I'd be with her...unless Sophia made sure I couldn't.

Fuck! I was starting to doubt my daughter. Sophia used to be an adorable, easy-going kid, though the teenager she'd become was alien to me.

I got a text message, and my heart lifted when I saw Aurora's name. The lasted for a nanosecond when I read her message that simply read: *Gabriel. Would it be okay for me to pick up my things and leave yours tomorrow? I can come by your place around 1 p.m.*

I felt anger at her message. Here, I was nursing a broken heart, and she was worried about her stuff.

It was unfair; she wasn't materialistic, no matter that Iris called her a gold digger. The proof was that tennis bracelet that she refused to take, the one that Sophia had found when she'd hugged me. She'd grabbed it and shown it to Iris. They decided that it was too big for Sophia, and Iris had put it on.

"It's beautiful. Did you get it for me?"

"Ah, it was—"

"Daddy, that's so sweet of you."

Sophia hugged me tightly.

I kept the peace and foolishly didn't protest. I also didn't admit that I had bought the bracelet to make amends with Aurora, but she turned it down, saying what she really wanted was my time and attention, not a bauble.

I replied to Aurora, annoyed: *Sure.*

My phone beeped again with a: *Thank You.*

Just to make sure that Sophia wouldn't be home at that time, I texted her to let her know that Aurora would be picking up her things tomorrow. Sophia replied with a thumbs-up emoji. Since Aurora and I had ended, Sophia had been in a better mood.

I walked down the riverfront aimlessly, feeling adrift.

I should go home and catch up on work. Or I could call Rafe and see if we could meet for a game of pool. But neither had much appeal. I wanted to be alone and stew in my misery.

CHAPTER 9
Aurora

Luna agreed to come with me to Gabriel's place.

"I don't know why he's making you schlepp his stuff around. He could've asked one of his many minions," Luna complained as she drove her SUV toward The Landings, where Gabriel lived.

"I don't know. Maybe he wants me to collect my things myself. It's not much, just a few clothes that his housekeeper dry-cleaned and a pair of shoes, I think. I didn't leave much there."

"You mean after Sophia threw your stuff away?"

I winced. "That poor kid is all kinds of messed up. She needs help."

"She needs a kick in the ass."

I shook my head. The way I had grown up as an outsider had instilled in me a lot of patience—and I didn't judge. It was not my place. People had their own reasons, and I tried to be as understanding as I could. But I also had let Gabriel get away with saying things I wouldn't normally allow. Sophia was one thing; she was a child, but Gabriel? I still couldn't believe he'd said that I was selfish, which was why my parents had abandoned me. His words replayed in my head on a loop, and with each repetition, they inflicted a fresh wound.

Never again would I let anyone talk to me like that, no matter how much I loved them. I deserved better.

"You should've told him his kid was lying, Aurora."

"And how would that help? If she was lying, it means the underlying problems are something they need to deal with as a family. And I don't think Gabriel would have believed me."

"That son of a bitch is in denial." Luna changed lanes to the exit toward Gabriel's house.

"He's struggling with raising a teenager," I defended him, "but...regardless, he didn't have to be cruel to me."

Luna patted my hand. When I'd told her what Gabriel had said, she'd been ready to punch his lights out.

"I can't believe you let him get away with that. You know, at work, you're the Ice Maiden. Everyone knows they treat you with disrespect; you'll freeze their balls off."

"Love makes us do weird things. But, yeah, never again. He devastated me, Luna." The pain was still pretty intense, and everything inside me hurt.

"I know, honey. He's an asshole."

"Then why do I still love him?" I sulked.

"It'll pass," she said, concern lacing her voice.

I took a deep breath after Luna parked in front of Gabriel's place. I looked at the identical house next door and realized that our relationship didn't have a chance. He was too involved with his ex-wife.

"Christ, his ex-wife lives so close?" Luna looked at my line of sight.

I nodded.

"Are the houses connected?"

"Through the garden. They walk in and out of each other's homes all the time."

"It's like he's still married, isn't it?"

I shrugged. "None of our beeswax. Let's go get my stuff."

I'd packed Gabriel's things as neatly as I could. His suits were in a suit bag. His toiletries and shoes were in a box. Luna carried the suit bag, and I the box.

I used my code and thumbprint to get into the house. We walked into the living room, and I set the box down and looked around. "Do you think he packed my stuff, or do I have to go look for it in his room?"

Luna rubbed my back.

I didn't want to go into his bedroom that smelled like him, where we'd made love. This was so hard.

"You want me to—"

"No. I'm fine." I took the suit bag from her. "I'll hang it. You bring the box?"

I walked upstairs quickly, wanting to get done with this. As soon as I stepped in, Sophia confronted me. My clothes were at her feet crumpled. What was up with this kid?

"Take your stuff and get lost," she cried out.

She snatched the suit bag from me and threw it on the bed.

I closed my eyes and bent down to pick up my clothes. There were not that many, and I could hug them to me. I didn't know where my shoes were, but it wasn't worth it to look for them.

"I told you, if you didn't leave my father, I'd make him leave you," she said triumphantly.

"Sophia, is this how you want to be? Lying to your own father?"

She snorted. "I'm doing it so we can be a family. You won't understand. My father told me how your own parents didn't want you."

Direct hit! I almost stumbled when she said those words.

I smiled wanly. "Take care of your father."

"I don't need you to tell me that," she bit back.

I turned around and walked out. Luna had heard the whole thing because she'd left the box at Gabriel's bedroom door. She put a hand on my arm and all but dragged me out of there. I felt tears prick my eyes when his ex-wife walked into Gabriel's living room.

"Oh...Ariel, is it? My husband mentioned you'd be here to take your things. Hope you didn't take anything that isn't yours."

Husband?

"Wow, Iris, that's low even for you," Luna said, and Iris noticed her for the first time. They came from the same social circles and knew each other.

"Luna," Iris said politely.

"Christ, no wonder your kid is so fucked up," Luna said.

I wasn't listening. Iris was wearing the bracelet that

Gabriel had bought for me, the one I'd asked him to take back. He'd given it to her. Well, it looked like Sophia had succeeded. Her parents were getting back together.

"Don't talk about my daughter," Iris snapped.

"Fuck you, bitch." Luna pulled me out of Gabriel's house. Threw my clothes in the backseat and, within seconds, got us the hell out of dodge.

I leaned my forehead against the SUV's window and began to cry,.

Luna kept patting my back, making soothing sounds as I wept.

"Hey, you're better off without him. His family is batshit crazy."

I chuckled tearfully. "They're pretty mean, aren't they?"

"You should meet Atticus and Betsy Rhodes, his parents. They're fabulous people. Betsy works so hard for her charities. It's not just throwing parties; she's hands-on, and so is Atticus. I don't know how Gabriel ended up with someone like Iris," Luna explained. "She's nothing like the Rhodes. His brother is a darling."

"I met Raphael." I wiped my tears. "He seemed nice."

"He's a sweetheart. And the thing is, so is Gabriel. But I don't know what to say about his recent behavior. Having seen for myself how Sophia and Iris spoke to you, I'm relieved the relationship is over. You deserve so much better."

She was right, I thought, and grabbed her hand and held it. "I'll never ever let love do this to me again. "

"Oh, honey. True love, healthy love doesn't do this."

"I thought what we had was true." *But maybe not always healthy.*

"Okay. It's a Friday, so let's go to your place, order pizza, open a bottle of wine, and get drunk while we watch *Real Housewives of Atlanta.*"

"Sounds good. But could we watch something else? Like...*Narcos* or *Griselda*?"

"Oh, yeah, I love that dark mafia romance shit."

CHAPTER 10

Gabriel

I t had been eight weeks and five days since we broke up when I saw Aurora again. But who was counting?

Things had gotten somewhat better at home. I was relieved that Sophia had stopped being clingy and needy. That had now transferred to Iris, who called me at least once a day to ask what we should have for dinner like we were a couple. When we were married, she hadn't given a shit.

"We should go together," Iris insisted about the Annual Savannah Hearts for Healing Ball, an event designed to support children's hospitals.

I checked my cufflinks and began to look for my phone. Iris was sitting on my bed in a brand-new red chiffon gown that looked damn good on her, and her neck, wrists, and ears were lit up with diamonds. She was wearing the tennis bracelet that I'd bought for Aurora. I wish she'd stop wearing it, but it was too late. If I didn't want an argument with her before, now it would only get worse.

"I don't see why."

"You don't have a date, and neither do I."

"I'm going with Beau."

She scoffed. "Please."

"Iris, we're not presenting ourselves as a couple to the Savannah society." *And especially to our daughter*, who'd begun to ask at least once a week if Iris and I were getting back together. I kept telling her it wasn't going to happen. I had reached the end of my patience with both of them.

"Please, Gabe."

That pout, ten years ago, had been a turn-on. Now, on a woman in her late thirties, it was embarrassing as hell.

"Don't beg," I clipped and added, "And, Iris, you can't just walk into my bedroom."

"Why not?"

"Because this is a private space. I could have been changing."

She hadn't even knocked, just walked in like she was still my wife. We'd never lived in this home as a couple; she had absolutely no excuse.

"I've seen you naked, Gabe; in fact, we have a child together."

"Iris, I'm trying to keep the peace here, but you cannot just walk into my home and my bedroom."

"Our daughter lives here, Gabe. You wanted this set up so we *could* walk into each other's homes."

I could almost hear Mama say, I told you so in my head.

"My bedroom is off limits," I used my this-is-the-end-of-discussion tone.

She huffed.

"Mama," I heard Sophia call out, "You look really nice."

"Well, your father doesn't think so. He just banned me from coming over."

"What?"

I stepped out of my bedroom. "No, just from coming into my bedroom, Iris."

"Whatever, Gabe. I don't know why we can't go together to the ball since we live together."

"We don't live together, Iris. We're divorced," I said patiently.

"Yes, I know, but only because you forced it down my throat, you son of a bitch. It's not what I wanted."

I closed my bedroom behind me, hating that I was still fighting with my ex, that she was still here, still doing what she'd done for ten years of marriage.

"What? You won't talk now, Gabe?" she jeered as she stood at the top of the stairs, her fists on her hips, her stance one of fighting.

I turned to Sophia. "Miss Kayla is downstairs all night. I shouldn't be back much later than ten or so."

I had to make an appearance, and my plan was to get back as soon as humanly possible.

"Can you at least do me the decency to talk to me?" Iris screeched when I continued to ignore her.

"Give me some sugar, Sweetpea." I ignored Iris and leaned in to give Sophia a kiss. Her eyes were wide, her lips trembling. I hated seeing her like that—upset and frightened. I hated that Iris was screaming in our house again.

"Gabe, I'm talking to you," Iris yelled.

"Please stop fighting," Sophia interjected, a plea in her voice. "*Please.*"

"Well, then ask your father to be a little nicer to your mother," Iris demanded and then flounced away.

Sophia looked at me with watery eyes, and I pulled her into an embrace. "Sweetpea, we're not fighting. Your mother is just upset, and she'll be fine."

Sophia pulled away angrily. "But it's your fault that she's like that. You ended your marriage, and now...I have to..."

"You have to what?"

"Nothing." She wiped her tears with the back of her hand. "Why can't you both just get back together?"

"Because I don't love your mother the way I should a wife, Sweetpea. I told you that several times."

"Why can't you love her?" she asked.

"Because that's not how love works," I smiled sadly. If I could control the damn emotion, I wouldn't still be breaking my heart over Aurora. If there was a switch I could pull, I would, so I could stop hurting.

"Can't you try?"

"Sophia, what's going on?" I asked.

She shook her head. "Nothing. Just...are you dating someone again?"

I was taken aback by the question. "No."

"Then why can't you just be with Mama?"

I put my hands on her shoulder. "For the last time, Sophia, your mother and I are divorced. There's no going back. I don't want to be married to her. I love you, Sweetpea, but our marriage was not a good one, and we're not right for each other."

"But you and Aurora, were you right for one another?" she snarled, and I saw Iris in her face.

"Aurora and I broke up, you know that," I whispered.

"Did you love her? Like you can't love my mother?"

I stepped away from Sophia. What the fuck was going on with my kid?

"I did love Aurora very much," I replied gently. I still do. "But that's the past now."

She nodded sadly. "I'm sorry, Daddy. It's just...Mama is so depressed about the divorce and..."

"Baby, our marriage is not your responsibility. You still have two parents who love you very much."

She nodded again. I kissed her forehead.

"Daddy, Mama loves you," she whispered.

I wish I could explain to her that her mother didn't love me anymore than I loved her, but Sophia was thirteen.

"You sleep tight. I'll check up on you before I go to bed."

By the time Beau and I arrived at the Perry Lane Hotel for the ball, I was already in a bad mood, which only worsened when I saw Aurora there with a date.

"Stop staring," Beau urged as we stood at the bar after the speeches and before the dinner bell rang.

"I'm not staring. Who the fuck is that guy?"

"It's Pierce."

"Callum Pierce?"

"Yeah," Beau was amused. "She's an architect on one of his real estate projects in Atlanta."

"How do you know that?"

"I had a meeting with Nina Davenport last week and saw him there, she told me."

I took a sip of my drink. "You building something?"

He nodded. "Yeah, we need to expand the headquarters, and I wanted to speak to her about that."

Callum Pierce was a real estate developer. Not old money but new. He was in his early thirties, so younger than me. He was nice enough looking and—.

"Wasn't he married to...that Hawthorne girl?"

"Divorced. Two kids. Shared custody," Beau filled in.

I drank some more.

From there, the night quickly went downhill. In hindsight, I drank more than I should have and found myself watching Aurora. She was in a simple yet elegant structured black gown that hugged her curves as if it were a lover. Her hair was pulled back into a loose bun, with tendrils softly framing her face. She laughed...a lot, and Pierce frequently placed his hand on her shoulder...a lot. I was fucking furious.

Dinner didn't improve my mood, and finally, Beau asked if I could stop drinking. "Coffee, please," he instructed a server.

"What?" I snapped. "I can handle my liquor."

"Sure, you can," he mocked.

"Are they dating? She moved on quick enough, didn't she?"

"I don't know if they're—"

I got up, and Beau did the same. "What the fuck do you think you're doing?"

"I know Pierce. Let's go say hello to him."

"Darling." Like my life wasn't fucked up enough, my ex-wife slipped her arm into the crook of my elbow. "How's your evening? I just spoke to your mother, and she's so excited about our summer party."

"Your parents' summer party, Iris. It's not ours." I gently removed her hand from touching me. "Don't fuckin' make a scene here."

"You're the one doing that," she hissed and then looked at Aurora as I had been and raised an eyebrow, "Looks like your tart has found a new rich guy to gouge."

"Jesus, Iris, what the fuck is wrong with you?" I snapped.

"Beau, how are you?" she turned to my friend, who raised both his hands, palms up.

"I'm not your friend, Iris. Keep me out of it," he mumbled.

"Iris, darling," someone called out, and mercifully, she left.

The server handed me a cup of coffee that I downed, and then I downed another.

"I can't believe she moved on, Beau." I could barely sleep without her, and she was laughing with some guy.

"Come on, Gabe, you dumped her."

"I think Sophia may have overreacted."

"And so did you."

"Yeah."

"What do you want to do?"

"Get drunk."

"About Aurora."

"Get drunk."

Beau nodded. "Enough drinking, let's—"

"Beau." Nina Davenport greeted and then hugged both of us.

"Your mother is precious, Gabe. This is such amazing work she's doing. Savannah Lace is so happy to contribute."

I nodded. "Thanks, Nina. I know Mama appreciates your support."

Nina patted Beau on the shoulder. "Beau, we're working on some great plans for you."

"Thanks, Nina. Who do you think will work on our project?"

"Most likely Luna."

"She's top-notch," Beau said, watching me as if I were a grenade with a loose pin.

"Come say hello." Nina led us to the Savannah Lace table, and Beau stifled a groan, giving me a 'don't make a scene' look.

After all the hellos and how do you dos, Nova, Nina's executive assistant asked us politely if we'd like to join them at their table.

I sat down and stared at Aurora, who smiled softly at me. "Hello, Gabriel."

Her voice went straight to my dick. "Aurora."

"You know each other?" Pierce asked.

"Yes," I said, "We dated."

Aurora looked shocked for an instant and then recovered, wearing one of those masks I'd never seen her wear with me. She'd let her feelings through, but in the beginning, when we first met, she schooled her emotions. She looked exactly like this, hiding.

"Oh." Pierce patted Aurora's hand. "I hope this isn't awkward, darlin', a current date and an ex at the same table."

Fucking hell. They were dating.

"Of course not," Aurora said with a quiet smile, "we're all grownups."

"I hear you're working on Pierce's Atlanta project." I ignored Beau's kick under the table.

"Yes." She smiled fully now. "I'm so excited about it. Callum has a great vision for building sustainable and affordable apartments."

Callum? Fuck. I stopped a server and asked for a Macallan 12.

Luna who was sitting next to Aurora glared at me. "Gabe, I just saw your wife."

"Ex-wife," I muttered.

Music was playing, and couples were dancing. The conversation around the ballroom was pleasant and cheerful. The tension at the table I was at could be cut with a knife.

"How long have you both been dating?" I asked, pointing to the space between Aurora and her date. It was borderline rude, but I was past giving a shit.

"This is our first date," Pierce chirped, "I hope the first of many."

Aurora looked down at her hands, and I felt like an ass for making her uncomfortable. But I couldn't stand it. I couldn't fucking stand seeing her with another man. She was mine. Didn't she know that? *For fuck's sake.*

The server brought me my drink, the one I shouldn't have drunk, but I did.

"I hear you're divorced with kids," I said recklessly.

"Yeah." Pierce wore a broad proud smile, "My son is six, and my daughter is four."

"Well, be careful with this one," I lifted my glass to indicate I was talking about Aurora, "she didn't grow up with parents, so she's not particularly maternal." As soon as the words were out and the gasp that went around the table, I knew I'd fucked up. Aurora's mask fell, and the hurt in her eyes, *fuck me*, tore me apart.

Beau pulled me up from my chair. "I'm so sorry, everyone, but we have to leave. Come on, Gabe."

I closed my eyes. "Aurora, I'm—"

"Please, leave," Luna cut me off.

"I got him," Beau assured her and dragged me away.

We left the ballroom and exited the hotel. Beau asked for my car to be brought around. I had my Cadillac with a driver, and we had picked up Beau from his place on our way here.

He waited until we were in the car and had the privacy screen up when he handed me my ass. He didn't have to. That look in Aurora's eyes told me how badly I'd fucked up, how much I'd hurt her.

"That was cruel, Gabe."

I dropped my face in my hands. "I know."

"I can't believe you said that."

"I know."

"How bad do you feel about it?"

I looked at him and let him see.

"Not badly enough, not compared to how she looked."

"How did she look?" I asked.

"Like you peeled her living skin off her flesh."

He was disgusted with me, no more than I was.

"Are you staying the night with me, or do you want to go home?" he asked.

"I have to go home. Sophia," I explained.

"You still love Aurora?"

I nodded.

Beau scoffed. "You better get over her because you just railroaded any fucking chance you ever had with this woman."

"Tell me something I don't know."

"I love you, Gabe, I always have but what you did today? You do something like that again, we won't be friends any longer."

93

CHAPTER 11

Aurora

I was humiliated. I sat still, hoping I wasn't crying—because I couldn't feel my body—and that would only add insult to injury. I couldn't believe what had just happened.

Pierce put his hand on my shoulder. "Hey, you okay?"

I looked at him, still in shock. "Yes, of course," I said as if on automatic pilot.

"I'm sorry. It's my fault. I never should've insinuated to him that we were on a date," he apologized. "But he was being such an arrogant ass that I wanted to rile him up."

"Well, you riled him up good," Luna scoffed. "Aurora, snap out of it, honey. He ain't worth it. What this shows is you dodged a bullet."

"I am sorry, Aurora," Pierce persisted.

"Please don't be," I said easily. The mask was back on. Fuck, Gabriel Rhodes. "We are out on a date. It may be casual, but he doesn't get to be an asshole about it."

Nova whistled. "Did our Aurora just cuss?"

"Bless her heart, she did," Luna chimed.

I chuckled.

Nina Davenport sat down and looked at me pointedly. "Do you want Savannah Lace to drop Rhodes Hotels as a client?"

I was flabbergasted at the question. "What?"

"No one talks to my people like Gabe just did. I'd be happy to kick them to the curb."

Nina was, first and foremost, a businesswoman. She didn't let emotion rule her, and the fact that she was supporting me made me feel validated in ways she couldn't imagine.

"Nah," I said breezily, "If we get the Miami Beach hotel project, it'll be a few million in the bank. Maybe you can negotiate a better contract, squeeze him for more of his money."

Nina grinned. "Yeah. Let's make that motherfucker pay."

"Ah, I'm in your good books, right?" Pierce asked. "Cause I don't want to be on the wrong side of y'all."

I laughed even though my chest felt tight.

Gabriel had been jealous. He was always possessive, but I didn't think he'd be so now. He was the one who ended us, and yet, he was seething with envy when he saw me with Callum. A part of me loved that. A *very* small part. Mostly, I was humiliated.

I had no defense for the "she's not maternal" statement. My parents *had* abandoned me. I had grown up alone. My aunt had only taken me in because she needed a caretaker herself, and since she had no children, it fell upon me. She wasn't mean, but she wasn't loving either.

I managed to convince everyone that Gabriel hadn't affected me—well, everyone except Luna, who cornered me on my way to the ladies' room.

"You okay?"

I nodded. "Of course."

"Stop with the *of course*, will you?" she snapped.

I leaned against a wall by the sink of the opulent restroom. "I'm hurt. I'm humiliated. I'm embarrassed."

She was about to say something when the door opened, and two women walked in. One of them, because the universe hated me, was Iris Rhodes.

She came to stand in front of the mirror and opened her bag, ignoring Luna and me.

"Will you be coming for the Mason engagement party next Saturday?" Iris's friend asked her.

"Oh, we can't. Gabe is taking us to the Rhodes vacation place in South Beach. You know they're building a hotel there." Iris put on her lipstick.

"Are you and he getting back together?" Iris's friend asked in surprise.

Luna tilted her head, indicating we should leave. I pulled away from the wall.

"Looks like," Iris said with a big smile and looked at me through the mirror. She lifted her wrist. "See this? He got it for me."

"Tiffany?"

"It's a little bauble, sure, but you know, it was his way of saying let's get back together."

Well, at least Sophia will be happy, I thought. Maybe not Gabriel, though. I felt sad at the thought. I still loved him even if right now I couldn't stand him. He'd never been happy with Iris, he'd told me. They'd gotten married because she was pregnant, and he'd stayed married for as long as he could stand it for Sophia. But when Iris became violent, throwing things at him, a glass vase crashed at his feet, and he'd had to go to the ER to sew up his foot; he'd decided enough was enough.

"She did that on purpose," Luna quipped me as we walked back to our table.

I was so tired. The heartache. The headache. All of it was too much. "I'm going to go home," I announce.

"Yeah?"

I nodded. "I'll call an Uber."

She kissed my cheek. "I love you."

"I know."

I went out to the lobby, called for an Uber, and waited outside by a magnolia tree, enjoying the scent of the blossoms.

When Gabriel had first shown attention, I'd decided to reject his advances. Wealthy men like him wanted a woman for just one thing, and I wasn't one-night stand material. But he'd taken his time with me. He didn't rush me. I honestly believed that he cared for me. After he introduced me to his brother and daughter, I'd convinced myself this was the real deal. He said he loved me, and I trusted him. But the man who'd so callously used my lack of love and support as a child against me just now —that man didn't love me. Sure, he was jealous, but he'd said what he had to inflict pain. It was mean and cruel. And so unnecessary, especially since he was getting back with his wife.

Maybe it wasn't jealousy, I decided, perhaps it was just some alpha male bullshit.

He'd ask me to say I was his when we made love. Maybe it was some kind of twisted sense of ownership.

But all in all, it was my fault, wasn't it? Someone with my background and pedigree couldn't compete with the old-money, affluent, white Savannah society.

My Uber arrived, and I got in.

My phone beeped with a message. It was from Gabriel. I didn't read it. I just went to my contacts and blocked him. I didn't want to hear from him. I didn't want to see him again. It hurt too much. He hurt me too much.

That night, as I struggled to fall asleep, I decided that love wasn't worth it, and I'd steer clear of it. My parents had taught me a lesson about love, and though I'd forgotten it for a moment, I would not do so again. I wouldn't fall for its allure. The pain and chaos it brought seemed far too high a price to pay for fleeting moments of happiness. Instead, I resolved to focus on myself, my ambitions, and my well-being, building a life unencumbered by such emotional turmoil.

CHAPTER 12
Gabriel

S he blocked my number. It was what I deserved. I'd apologized by text messages until I realized they weren't getting through, and it became even more apparent when I tried to call her.

I had drunk just enough to be an asshole—and I had been. Christ, the hurt in her eyes when I'd talked about how she wasn't maternal, how her parents had abandoned her, still made me want to throw up. How could I have done that to the woman I loved?

I went through the weekend like a zombie, ignoring Iris while we played fucked up family at some social gathering at my ex-in-laws' place. Sophia had wanted me there, and I'd gone instead of picking a fight.

My mood sucked when I got to work on Monday, and everyone, including my executive assistant, was on alert.

I could guess the whispers.

"He broke up with that architect."

"Damn it. He'd been in such a good mood while he was with her."

"Well, Angry Rhodes is back."

Apparently, Aurora had made me tolerable, and now I was back to being Angry Rhodes.

There was a knock on my door after my morning meeting, where I'd chewed up a few people.

"What?" I barked.

Luna Steele walked in. "Your EA is petrified of you, but I told her it was fine; you'd want to see me."

I closed my eyes. If I couldn't reach Aurora, maybe Luna could help me get through to her, though the way she was looking at me, she wanted to knee me in the balls.

"Have a seat." I gestured toward one of the client chairs.

She pulled out her phone from her jeans and sat. "I'm sending you something. It's a video. I want you to watch it. I was never going to show this to you. But after what happened at the ball, I think you need to see this and lay off Aurora."

I leaned back on my chair and picked up my phone. "Okay."

The video was of Sophia in my bedroom.

"Take your stuff and get lost," Sophia said. *She took something from...Aurora and threw it on my bed. A suit bag. My clothes, I deduced, the ones I left at her place.*

The video showed Aurora bending down to pick up what I recognized as her clothes that had been dry-cleaned by my housekeeper but were now crumpled on the hardwood floor. A chill ran through me as I understood what I was watching.

It broke my heart when I heard my Sweetpea say, "I told you, if you didn't leave my father, I'd make him leave you."

Aurora looked so sad when she said, "Sophia, is this how you want to be? Lying to your own father?"

"I'm doing it so we can be a family. You won't understand. My father told me how your own parents didn't want you," Sophia yelled, and my heart broke.

I'd done this. I'd given Sophia the ammunition. I'd allowed this to happen.

But the knife went deeper when Aurora smiled and said, "Take care of your father."

"I don't need you to tell me that," Sophia replied belligerently.

The video was shaky after that and only showed the floor, my floor. I heard Iris's voice. "Oh...Ariel, is it? Gabriel mentioned you'd be here to take your things. Hope you didn't take anything that isn't yours."

"Wow, Iris, that's low even for you." That was Luna's voice.

"Luna," Iris said.

"Christ, no wonder your kid is so fucked up," Luna said.

"Don't talk about my daughter," Iris said.

"Fuck you, bitch," Luna replied.

The video ended.

"First things first," Luna began, "Aurora doesn't know I made this video, and I don't want her to know. She'll kill me if she finds out I came between you and your daughter. But you needed to see this because you need to know that the fact your kid and Aurora didn't get along has nothing to do with Aurora."

My hands shook as I put the phone down.

"This is how Sophia has been treating Aurora. The reason Aurora didn't leave things in your house was because the first time she left some makeup, Sophia got rid of them."

Aurora had told me that Sophia hadn't liked her leaving things, and I had dismissed her, saying she must've misunderstood. Despite that, Aurora had not tattled on my daughter.

"Your wife insulted her whenever she was there, and you weren't, which is why she started to ask you to come over to her place," Luna wasn't done.

I was having trouble breathing. I couldn't believe that my sweet child had done what she had, said the things she'd said, and probably lied about how Aurora treated her. I should've known. Aurora was kind and sweet. It didn't match up with how Sophia looked at her, and yet I didn't see it because I hadn't wanted to admit that my kid was, as Luna put it fucked up, that I'd fucked her up.

"Aurora feels hurt, humiliated, and ashamed after what you said at the ball. Looks like your daughter comes by her meanness and cruelty, honestly; she gets it from you."

I closed my eyes then and grabbed my desk because Luna's words hit me hard. She wasn't wrong. I could be a downright asshole.

I opened my eyes after a long moment. "Thank you for letting me know." The words came out hoarse.

"Now, please stay away from my friend. She deserves better."

I nodded, and for the first time in decades, tears filled my eyes, surprising me. I'd hurt the woman I loved, and I'd damaged the child I loved to where she'd lied to me, treated another person with such cruelty, just like I had.

"Why didn't Aurora ever say anything?"

"Would you have believed her?" Luna challenged me. "Without a video like I just showed you?"

I shook my head. "I wouldn't have."

"You know what Aurora said when I asked why she didn't tell you? She feels sorry for Sophia for carrying the pressure of keeping her parents' marriage together, and yeah, she knew as well that you wouldn't believe her." Luna got up.

"I fucked up."

"Yeah. You lost an amazing woman. It just sucks that you hurt her so much that it's going to be a long while before she trusts a man again, if ever. But I'm hoping she does because no one deserves to be loved, to have a family more than Aurora." Luna's eyes were also shimmering with tears. "The way you talked about her parents? Have you any idea how hard it must've been for a kid to have her father abandon her and her mother drag her around to fend for herself?"

I dropped my head in shame.

"Do you think it was easy for her to have to protect herself as a child when her mother put her in dangerous situations?"

I looked up at her now in horror. Aurora had never said.

"Oh yeah, her mother would just go to some commune where they were high all the time, and little Aurora would have to hide from some sick fucks who liked young girls."

I ran a hand over my face, frustrated with myself.

"Her only choice was to come to Savannah, and you know how her aunt agreed to it? Do you know, Gabe?" Luna demanded.

"No." I just knew that she'd lived with her.

"Because she had COPD and needed someone to take care of her. So, thirteen-year-old Aurora went to school, took care of her aunt, cooked, and cleaned, and worked a part-time job to pay for rent. She had to pay *rent* at that age."

I didn't know any of this because Aurora never told me, because I'd never bothered to ask. I knew about her work, and she knew about mine; but mostly, the truth was when we met, we fucked. We talked every night, but I realized now it was always about me and my work. She would mention her projects, and I knew she worked hard, but I hadn't grasped the significance of her job and career until Rafe mentioned that Georgia Tech, where she studied, had the one of the best architecture programs in the country.

"She took care of her aunt until she died when Aurora was in her last year of high school. She got a scholarship and went to Georgia Tech. This has been her life, and you ridiculed her for her childhood, blamed her for your kid's behavior." Luna tucked her hand in her jeans. "I hope now you understand how much you hurt Aurora."

"I do. And I'm sorry. I'm so fucking sorry, Luna. I texted her and tried to call her this weekend, but—"

"She's blocked you. Nina Davenport is this close to dropping Rhodes Hotels as a client because your behavior has been reprehensible."

"I didn't know about her childhood," I said defensively.

"Oh please, you didn't need to. Couldn't you guess?"

Shame was a heavy burden, and my shoulders slouched. "I lost my temper, Luna. I love Aurora and—"

"Oh, shut up," she snorted, "if that's how you treat people you love, I can see why they call you a barracuda in business, Gabe; you probably eviscerate people you hate."

There was absolutely nothing I could say in my defense. I'd fucked up royally, and now I had to figure out how to fix my kid and, if I could, find a way to get my love back. I didn't know how to do either.

Luna pulled out something from her pocket and threw it on my table.

"When I was growing up, I got into a lot of trouble. A therapist helped me. She's a tough cookie but great. I recommend you and your daughter get some counseling," Luna advised. "You have a nice day."

With that, she left.

I picked up the card and reviewed the details of a family therapist.

CHAPTER 13
Aurora

I t took me nearly a week to confront Sophia after Luna showed me the video.

"Hey, Sweetpea." I sat down on the couch next to my daughter in the living room, where she was watching Netflix while she dug into a bowl of popcorn.

I'd thought about how to talk with Sophia and had called the therapist that Luna had recommended to figure out how best to handle this conversation.

Dr. Monica Ryan had been frank with me after I explained what had happened. She was worried about Sophia and insisted that my approach needed to be one of understanding and that we'd probably need counseling as father and daughter to rebuild what was fractured.

"Hey."

"Can we turn this off?"

She looked at me with confused eyes and picked up the remote to turn off the television. "Is everything okay?"

I smiled wanly at her. "I don't think so."

"You look serious."

I nodded. This was going to be harder than watching the video that had gutted me. However, at thirteen, Sophia couldn't be blamed for my sheer stupidity in allowing her to treat my girlfriend disrespectfully.

"So, remember the evening we had dinner at Aurora's condo?"

I saw panic flare in her eyes.

"What did she tell you about me? Are you still seeing her? I thought you broke up?" There was dread in her voice, and I hated hearing it.

"She didn't tell me anything. And, no, I'm not seeing her," I said sadly. "You told me she said some mean things to you."

Her eyes became defiant. "She did."

"I don't think so, Sweetpea."

"You think I'm lying?" she challenged me.

"Yes."

Her lips quivered. "You just believe her because you're having sex with her."

Christ on a crutch! Kill me now.

"I told you to not be home the day Aurora came to pick up her things."

She shrugged. "Whatever."

"But you were at home. Her friend, Luna, made a video of what you said to Aurora and showed it to me." The therapist had said I'd have to establish that I knew the truth early on in the conversation so we could get past

107

the defiance and lies to the root cause of Sophia's behavior.

Now, she was in full-on anxiety mode. "Her friend made it up. You know, these days, you can make stuff up with AI and—"

"Hey, it's time to come clean," I coaxed. "You said some terrible things to Aurora."

"She deserved it."

"No, sweetheart. She didn't."

Aurora hadn't deserve it from me, not from Sophia, and not from Iris. All she'd done was love me and every member of my family had been cruel to her.

Her eyes filled with tears. "Why are we talking about this? You broke up. It's over."

I took her hands in mine and held them. "Why was it so important for you that we broke up?"

She licked her lips. "Because then you and Mama would get back together."

I nodded. "But I've told you that's not going to happen."

"Mama doesn't think so," she retorted. "Mama said that...you just...that...Daddy, it's fine. You bought Mama the bracelet, and we're going to Miami Beach tomorrow as a family."

"I bought that bracelet for Aurora. She refused to take it because she said it was too expensive," I told her honestly. "When you found it and your mother decided to take it, I just didn't say anything. I should have, but I didn't. And that was wrong of me."

Her eyes flickered with fear and shame.

"I just want you and Mama to be together."

"Why?"

"Because that's the way it's supposed to be. Mama keeps saying that. And she's so angry about the divorce. I just don't want her to be mad anymore."

Fucking hell! I pulled her into my arms for a hug. The poor kid.

Dr. Ryan had told me that the way Iris and I were living was confusing Sophia. We had officially divorced, but as my family and Beau had all been hammering at me and I'd refused to listen, it did seem a lot like we were still living together. For Sophia, overhearing Iris's hopeful talks of reconciliation translated into a burden—she felt pressured to mend the situation in a bid to bring joy to her mother.

"Daddy, why can't you just get married to mama again?" She burrowed into me.

I pulled her away a little so I could see her face. "Forget about your mother for a minute, Sweetpea. What did you think of Aurora?"

Her face fell. "What do you mean?"

"How did she treat you?"

"She was alright."

"When you were rude to her or mean to her, how did she treat you?"

Her eyes filled with tears. "She wasn't mean back."

"Did you feel bad about how you talked to her?"

She shrugged. "I just wanted her gone. Mama said that if she wasn't there, then you'd both be together."

"What else did your Mama say?"

She looked so forlorn that my heart was crushed. Dr Ryan suspected that my ex had been putting pressure on Sophia to get Aurora out of the picture.

"That...if I was not nice to Aurora, she'd leave."

"And that's why you were mean to her?"

"Yeah. And Mama said Aurora just wants you for your money," she added and then sadly, slowly, added, "But she didn't even take the bracelet."

"No, she didn't," I agreed.

Because Aurora had never cared about my money. She'd wanted me. She wanted time with me. She loved me. Truly loved me to put up with my family drama, my kid who was rude to her, my ex-wife who pretended we were still together. *Christ*, I don't know how she put with my shit for an entire year.

"Daddy, I don't know what to do," she admitted. "I...just don't."

I kissed her forehead. "I know, Sweetpea. But here is the truth. What you said to Aurora was not cool. In fact, it was cruel."

"You mean the thing about her parents not wanting her?"

She knew I thought what she'd done was wrong. At least, that was something.

"Yeah."

"It's because of me your relationship ended, isn't it?" Tears were now freely flowing down her face. I wiped them with the palms of my hand.

"No. I was cruel to her as well and...I messed up. Don't

get me wrong, what you did was not okay, but I'm the one who ended that relationship." I didn't need her to carry the guilt for something that was definitely my fault.

"Every time I'm alone with Mama, she only wants to discuss how I should convince you to get back together with her," she confessed.

"And you want that?"

She blinked. "I guess so."

"Why?"

"So, Mama won't be so upset."

"Forget about Mama for a moment. Do you want us to get back together? How do you think things will change for you?" I stroked her blonde hair and wanted to kick myself if I could. My parents, my brother, and my friends had been warning me about this, and I'd ignored them because I was an arrogant fuck.

She shrugged. "I don't think anything would change."

"And how do you think things would change for you if I were to have a girlfriend?"

She eyed me thoughtfully. "You'd spend less time with me."

"I was with Aurora for a year, did I spend less time with you?"

She thought about it some more and shook her head. "No. The week I'm with you, you're always home."

"The past few months, you kept asking me to be with you during your week with your Mama as well. What was going on?" I asked.

She sighed. "I feel bad telling you this."

"You can tell me anything and never feel bad about it. I'm your father, and I'm going to love you no matter what."

She looked at me with unblinking eyes. "You promise?"

"Yes."

"Mama knew when you were going out with Aurora, and she'd ask me to insist you come back home. And I like being with you so..."

How the fuck did Iris know my calendar? It took me a minute, but I guessed how she did and decided to deal with it when I got to work next week.

"And when you wanted me to sleep over at your Mama's place?"

She licked her lips. "I..." She just shrugged then and shook her head. "I love Mama."

"I know, Sweetpea. And you should. She's your mother."

"But she's so unhappy since the divorce. And you're *so happy*...it just seems unfair to her."

My heart clenched. I had been happy since the divorce. It was wonderful to be free of everyday endless conflict.

"You're not responsible for your mother's or my happiness, Sophia. No one can make the other person happy—that's something we have to do for ourselves."

"But other people can make us sad."

"Yes." I hugged her close and rested my chin on her head.

"I made Aurora sad," she whispered.

"How does that make you feel?"

I felt her tears before I heard them. "Really shitty, Daddy. But Mama was so happy when you broke up. I was so relieved."

I pulled away to wipe her tears. "This has been a shit-show," I said with a small smile.

She sniffled. "No shit."

I laughed and didn't ask her to clean up her language this time. "Would you like to talk to someone about how you feel? About what's happening?"

"You mean like a psychologist?"

"Yeah."

"Lilah does." She was a friend of Sophia's whose parents had recently split up.

"And?"

"She likes it. She especially likes it when her parents are with her, and she can tell them...openly what's going on."

I nodded, hearing her loud and clear. "How about we meet with a therapist that was recommended to me? If you don't like her, we can find someone else. And then come up with a plan on how we make sure your Mama and I are there with you. Sound good?"

"Daddy, since you broke up with Aurora, you haven't been happy," she told me. "It's...like how you were before... when you and Mama were together."

I wasn't happy; there was no sugarcoating that. I was devastated and hating myself for hurting the one woman who'd given me more than she'd taken.

"Aurora and I were together for a year; it's going to take a minute for me to stop feeling bad about it ending," I admitted. That was the other thing Dr. Ryan had told me was important, and that was transparency. This hiding stuff and pretending things were okay when they were not wasn't helping Sophia and increasing her level of anxiety and confusion.

"You loved her," she whispered, and it broke my heart to see her in so much pain. But it was also a good thing, I knew. If she felt guilty, it meant that she understood that what she'd done was wrong.

"I did. I do. But these things happen."

"I broke you guys up."

"No, Sweetpea, I did that all by myself," I assured her. "You're not responsible for my relationship with Aurora, just as you weren't for your mother's and my marriage."

She nodded slowly.

"Got it?"

"Yeah, Daddy. I do."

I kissed her on her forehead. "Alright, I'm going to leave you here for a minute while I talk to your mother."

"You're going to talk to her about this, aren't you?"

"Yeah. I am."

CHAPTER 14
Gabriel

I found Iris on the phone on her porch.

"No, darling, we're off to Miami Beach tomorrow," she was telling someone.

I hadn't knocked on her door before coming in, I realized. Yeah, so this shit needed to change. I was going to start ringing the fucking doorbell and would ask her to do the same. This walking in and out of each other's homes, having dinner several times a week as a family—all of this was not helping Sophia; it was fucking her up.

Iris waved at me, asking me to step out on the porch. I looked at the garden we shared and the pool in between and wondered how I'd now separate these two homes. Maybe the better option would be to buy a new place and sell this off. Iris could figure out what she wanted to do and where she wanted to live. I needed to stop taking care of her and her life. I didn't mind. I had enough money, but I was probably even giving Iris mixed signals by allowing her to live off of me.

When we divorced, she took a lumpsum based on our prenuptial agreement—but I'd continued to pay for the car, the house, the cook, groceries...everything.

"Alright, I'll see you next week." She hung up, and I heard her come up behind me and wrap her arms around me. "Hey, baby."

Fuck me! Since Aurora and I broke up, she'd upped the touching and hugging, telling me that she wanted me.

I unwrapped her arms from around me and set her aside. "We need to talk."

She beamed. "Okay." She sat down on a sofa and settled herself like she was modeling for a magazine.

I sat down across from her, leaning forward, my elbows on my thighs.

"Sophia has been lying to me," I began.

"Oh?" She sounded nonchalant, but I caught the slight anxiety in her eyes.

"She's been working quite hard to break up my relationship with Aurora. She's been mistreating Aurora whenever I wasn't around, as have you. And she's been lying to me about how Aurora talked to her as well."

"Don't blame Sophia for your affair with that slut."

I felt my temper rise, but I needed to stay calm and not let the rage take over as it had with Aurora. That helped no one.

"According to Sophia, you've been pushing her to talk to me about you and me getting back together."

"So?"

"So, Iris, Sophia shouldn't carry that burden. She's thirteen. She's a fucking kid, and you've been asking her to fix our marriage."

Iris waved a hand. "I just told her that she should let you know how much she likes us to be a family. I see nothing wrong with that."

"You also told her to make sure she's not nice to Aurora."

"I did not say that. Sophia just didn't like your slut."

She was baiting me by using the word slut.

"Aurora is a beautiful, intelligent and kind woman who I had the good fortune of being in a relationship with. The fact that it is over is my fault and my loss," I hissed. "Here is what we're going to do. I'm going to sell these houses."

"What?"

"I don't want us to live so close together."

"Gabe, please, don't do that. I...I can't not see Sophia for an entire week. This works for us."

"No, Iris, it doesn't. Sophia keeps thinking that there's a chance you and I can get back together. And that's never happening. Do you understand that? I'll fucking die alone before being married to you again." Full transparency, even if it meant hurting Iris and right now the way I was feeling, I *wanted* to hurt her.

"Gabe." She rose and came up to me, crouched in front of me. "We love each other. We have a daughter together." She put her hands on my thighs.

"I don't love you. We married because you were pregnant. I have never loved you. Do you know how I know this?

117

Because I did fall in love, Iris, with Aurora and found out what it means to love and be loved." I pushed her away gently. She tried to leap back onto me and lost her balance, fell on her ass. I didn't help her up.

"My lawyer will be in touch with yours."

"About what?" She stood up, now furious.

"About amending the custody agreement, making it a little clearer. When I have Sophia, you cannot come into my home and vice versa unless there's an emergency. I'm removing your access to my house and mine to yours. You want to come in; you have to knock like everyone else. And I'm putting the houses on the market, so you better find a place to live." I put my hands in my pockets.

She got up, and I waited for the show. Her blue eyes widened with anger. "You're paying for my new house then."

"No. I gave you a lumpsum as you'd wanted when we divorced. I was generous to buy this house and let you stay here, but the house is in my name, not yours."

She walked up to me and slapped me.

I took a step away from her. "I will let my lawyer know about this."

"What?"

"The physical violence, Iris. I will document this slap. I will document every fucking thing, so be very careful as to how you want to play this because I have more money, more influence, and better lawyers."

"What are you threatening me with?" she flared.

"I will make sure you don't ever see Sophia unsupervised if you don't fucking straighten yourself up."

"How dare you?" She flew at me, and this time, I held her hand, not to hurt but to restrain her.

"You don't get to hit me."

She struggled. "Damn it, Gabe."

"No. And the agreement will also insist that you attend one counseling session a week with Sophia and me." I released, and she stepped away from me.

"And talk about our personal business with a stranger? Absolutely not."

"Yes, you will. Trust me, Iris, you don't want to cross me and find out what a contentious divorce means." I kept my voice level.

"Oh, please, you can go—"

"Be very careful," I continued. "One word from Betsy Rhodes and your social life will end. And you know she'd enjoy that."

In the Savannah society food chain, the Rhodes were much higher up than Iris's family.

"Your mother doesn't have that kind of power."

I smiled. "Test it out at your own peril. Oh, and you're not welcome to any more Rhodes family events and parties."

"What? Why?"

"Because you've been poisoning my child, Iris, confusing the fuck out of her. Driving her to be a jerk. This is damage control. You, I don't give a shit about. It's always been Sophia that I've cared for and done everything for."

"I'm coming to Miami Beach tomorrow. Don't you dare cancel that. Sophia is counting on it."

"And that will be the last time."

"You're an asshole, Gabe."

"Dixie will contact your lawyer and set up a time to meet."

Dixie Chassay was one of the best divorce lawyers in all of Georgia and had made sure that my divorce agreement with Iris was air-fucking-tight just as she'd made sure my prenuptial agreement had been. She'd make sure the amendments would be the same.

"Fuck you, Gabe."

"No, Iris, not in this lifetime."

I was whistling a tune as I walked out of there, realizing that for the first time I truly felt like I was rid of her.

CHAPTER 15

Aurora

I t was a Sunday, two weeks after the ball, when my doorbell rang. I had blueprints spread on my dining table and my laptop as I worked on Callum Pierce's project.

I looked through the peephole and felt a chill. I'd just managed to calm myself down and stop obsessing over Gabriel Rhodes, and there he was at my doorstep.

I opened the door and ignored the feeling of discomfort that I was wearing ratty jeans and a loose T-shirt that kept falling off my shoulder. When you grew up the way I did, appearances became important—so you wouldn't be quickly identified as poor and destitute. But like hell, I was going to change and put my face on for Gabriel. He'd have to take me in my home wear with my hair tied in a messy bun and my face makeup-free.

At least I was wearing a bra, one I'd put on to go buy myself a quick sandwich for lunch and hadn't taken it off yet.

"Hi." He smiled.

I nodded nervously.

"May I come in?"

I took a deep breath, unsure of what I should do.

"Just for a few minutes, Aurora."

"Of course." I opened the door to let him in. I walked to the dining table and poured myself some more red wine. I'd opened a bottle of Merlot the night before.

"Would you like a glass?" I asked politely.

"No, thank you."

"Water?"

"No, thank you."

I waved a hand at my living area and walked to sit down on my couch. I tucked my feet under me, feeling vulnerable.

He sat down on an armchair, facing me. He was in jeans and a T-shirt, and neither were ratty. He wore some snazzy shoes that I knew were Gucci because I'd seen them before. He looked devastatingly handsome, and I regretted that we weren't together anymore. I couldn't run a hand through his disheveled hair or kiss his jaw.

It wasn't cool at all that he still looked so good to me. The universe was a right-on bitch.

"What can I do for you?" I asked after taking two fortifying sips of wine. Because I was worried, my hands would begin to shake, I set the wine glasses down on the coffee table and set them firmly on my thighs.

"Thank you for letting me talk to you. After how I behaved, you have every right to not speak with me again."

He seemed to stop after that and wait for me to say

122

something. I just stayed silent and looked at him, schooling myself to be expressionless. I wouldn't give him the satisfaction of knowing how much he'd hurt me. I had my pride.

"First, I want to...I'm so fucking sorry, Aurora."

His voice was hoarse, filled with regret and emotion. I steeled myself against it. Men like him only cared about themselves and how they felt. This was about his guilt for shaming me in public. It was apparent from the way his friend Beau dragged him out of the hotel ballroom that he'd not been happy with Gabriel's behavior.

"Okay," I said coolly.

He nodded and then rubbed his face with his hands. He did that when he was frustrated.

"I know Sophia lied about you." He surprised me. I'd not expected that at all. "I know she's been treating you horribly. She's been trying to break us up."

Wow! I nodded dumbly because I could hardly believe that he knew the truth and that he accepted it.

"I'm so sorry for everything."

I waited to check if he was done, and when I was confident he didn't have more to say, I straightened. "Okay. Anything else?"

I saw a harshness enter his eyes. I'd seen it before when he wasn't getting his way, and he'd assess the best way to proceed.

"Can you forgive me?"

"Of course."

It was his turn to be surprised. "You forgive me?"

"Yes," I said easily. "I don't like carrying anger." This was true. I had forgiven him, I just had to find a way to forgive myself for falling for him, for making this mistake. It was not his fault that he'd taken advantage of me; it was mine.

"I wish you'd yell at me and call me names."

I smiled. "That may make you feel better, but how will it help me?"

He chuckled. "Yeah. It would make me feel better. Make me feel less guilty."

"It's not all always about you."

"I know." He looked at me, his blue eyes filled with remorse. "I hurt you."

"Yes."

"It tears me apart that I hurt you."

"Again, it's not all about you...Gabe." I couldn't call him Gabriel. Everyone called him Gabe. Gabriel was something between us, almost an endearment. He didn't deserve it anymore, and I didn't have the right either.

"Gabe?"

I shrugged. "Look, it's all fine. I'm sure things will work out for you. I hear you and your wife are reconciling."

He frowned. "You heard? From whom?"

I licked my lips. "Your wife."

"Ex-wife."

I didn't reply. My hands were not shaking, so I picked up my wine and drank a little. This man wasn't going to rattle me again. I wouldn't let him.

"Iris told you she and I were getting back together?"

"Yes. At the ball. I mean, she was talking to a friend, but

she was really telling me. It was in the ladies' room," I explained.

"We're not getting back together, Aurora."

I didn't want to call him a liar to his face, but I also wasn't going to let him get away with it. "She showed me the bracelet you gave her."

"Fuck, I didn't give it to her. Sophia found it, and...Iris liked it."

I nodded. "Well, if that's all, I have some work to get through and—"

"I love you."

CHAPTER 16

Aurora

His words echoed in my head, mixing with the other words he'd said.

He called me cold, unwanted, not maternal. And now he was saying he loved me? This was too much. He couldn't say these things to me because the control that I was hanging on to by a thread would slip.

"No, you don't."

"Don't tell me how I feel, baby." There was iron in his voice.

"If you loved me, you'd know that I'd never do what Sophia accused me of. If you loved me, you'd not have humiliated me in public by bringing up how I was cast aside by my parents."

He leaned over and picked up my glass of wine. He downed it and slammed the glass down. "Fucking hell," he muttered and stood up as if he couldn't sit. He paced a little and then stopped to look at me. "I didn't want to believe I'd fucked up my kid, okay? It was easier to believe you fucked up."

I sighed. "Like I said, it seems to me that everything is all about you. So, I don't know why you're here. We're done. It's okay. I'm not asking you for anything, not even an apology. You owe me nothing."

He stalked up to me and crouched so we were face to face. "You don't feel anything for me?"

"Can't you see that how I feel about you doesn't matter anymore?" My voice was steady. He didn't get the authentic Aurora anymore. He got the woman I'd made myself to be, to protect myself from the world. The one everyone at work called Ice Maiden.

"Why? You forgive me. You love me. I love you."

"I loved my father and my mother, even my aunt, and where did that leave me?" I smirked. "I love you, Gabriel, but you cast me aside as well. You used the pain of my childhood to hurt and humiliate me. That isn't love. I'll *never* trust you again. I don't know if I'll ever trust anyone again."

He looked stricken at that.

"Oh, baby."

My mask slipped. Kindness was my Kryptonite.

Tears filled my eyes and I let them fall. It didn't matter if he saw them. I loved Gabriel and he knew that. What he didn't seem to understand was that he didn't love me like I needed him to.

"A relationship is supposed to strengthen us. It's not supposed to—"

"You did that for me." He took my hands in his. I let

him. If this was the last time we were together like this, then I'd be pathetic for a moment longer and touch him, feel him. "You made all the noise go away. I had to just look at you and I felt calm. I talked to you about issues at work, and it helped me think more clearly. I held you at night and slept better than I ever did before."

The heart could break again and again, I realized then. So, I twisted the knife in my gut deeper. "I was always afraid of losing you. You were so adamant about me making no demands on you that I never made any. I never even called you or texted you because when I had in the beginning, you ignored me."

"No, baby," he protested. "It wasn't like that."

"Yes, it was. Be honest. Didn't you like being in a relationship where there were no demands on you? Where I moved my life around to accommodate yours? Where I never made a big deal out of you canceling dates and dinners? I'd have cooked a three-course meal, and you'd call at the last minute and say your daughter needs you, and I never made you feel bad about it."

He rose from his crouch to sit next to me. He continued to hold my hands. "I'm sorry for that."

"You made my fear of abandonment come back because, for the first time since my parents and aunt, there was someone in my life that I was afraid of losing...again." I pulled my hands away from him, feeling tremendously tired. "You made me feel less by never ever prioritizing me."

"I was trying to be a good father, Aurora."

"I know, and I appreciate that. I mean, you know how

things were with my father, and I love that about you. But I've never been anyone's priority, never been important to anyone—and I want that. I think I deserve it. Don't you think so?"

He looked wrecked by what I said, and I couldn't stand his pain any longer. I got up and walked to the dining table with my now-empty glass of wine. I refilled it and stayed by the dining table, wanting distance from him, not wanting to smell his cologne.

"I felt like all you wanted from me at times was sex," I confessed. "Before you went to Paris, you told me *I* had to make it work with your daughter, as if it were *my* fault things weren't working. It felt like a threat—that if I didn't make it work, you'd leave me, and that's exactly what you did. But you never understood that I could never make it work with Sophia."

"I know that now," he barked.

"I'm glad. I hope that things will improve and that next time you're in a relationship, Sophia will handle it—"

"I don't want to be in a relationship with anyone but you," he declared and came up to me, entering my personal space.

"I don't trust you. I never will again. You broke my trust and my heart. The things you said to me were meant to wound, and you succeeded. I can't be with someone who hurts me intentionally when they get angry, or things don't go their way."

I stepped around him and walked back to the couch.

He stood by the table. "I have a temper and...fuck, Aurora, this cannot be the end of us."

"We ended when you said I was too cold to be with someone who has a child," I murmured. "I forgive you. I just can't forget what you did. Look, our social circles are not the same at all, so it's not like we'll be bumping into each other."

He came to me then in a rush. "Baby, we were good together." He pulled me up to him, the glass of wine in my hand jerked and spilled on him and me. He ignored it.

"You're not good for me," I told him. " You hurt me not just at the end, but throughout our time together—when you ignored me, when you thought jewelry could make up for it. You hurt me when you only came to me at your convenience, never stopping to consider if I might need you. You never gave me permission to take from you."

"You can take from me; everything I have is yours," he pleaded. "Give us another chance."

I pulled away and set my wine glass down on the table.

"Aurora. I know you love me."

"I do love you. But we're never going to be together," I told him calmly. "I have too much self-respect to be with a man who's still married."

"I'm divorced."

"No, you're not. That's just on paper. You live together. You have dinner with your wife more often than you do with your girlfriend. What were your plans for last weekend, Gabe?"

I felt anger run through me. Did he think he could continue to play me? That I was such a fool?

"What?"

"Weren't you at the Rhodes family home in Miami Beach last weekend?"

He nodded. "Yeah, that was the plan but.... How do you—"

"Your wife told me how she was coming along with you and Sophia. You're still married."

"No, that's not it, Aurora. My parents wanted us there, and Sophia asked her mother to come along," he protested, running a hand through his hair.

"Your wife is trying to get back with you, and your daughter is moving heaven and earth to bring her parents together. You go to family events and gatherings as a family. There's no room for another woman." My voice was raised, and I hated that. I was losing control of my emotions, which didn't surprise me. I could manage Ice Maiden at work but not with Gabriel, not the man who held my heart and then threw it away.

"Aurora, I'm just doing what's best for Sophia."

I flung my hands up in the air. "Then do that. Don't drag me into your family drama," I cried out. "*Now* we're done. I have work to do."

He looked stunned. I'd never raised my voice at him before; I was usually cool and controlled. But this man was driving me up the wall and completely shattering my composure.

He came up to me and put his hands on my shoulders. "Why didn't you tell me how you felt?"

"I shouldn't have had to," I retorted, annoyed, "You're a

grown man; why the hell couldn't you see what you were doing? And really, if I'd told you, would you have listened?"

He had the decency to shake his head.

"I'm so tired, Gabriel," I sighed. "Please go. We don't have to see each other again. I just...I just want to stop hurting now."

He rested his forehead against mine. "Baby, I'm so sorry. You're the last person I want to hurt."

"Then leave me alone."

He kissed my mouth softly, and tears began to roll down my cheeks. This was too much. All of it. The loving and the not having. The loving and the not being loved back.

"I do love you, Aurora. I fucked up. But that doesn't change that fact. You're not cold. Hell, you're the warmest, sweetest, and kindest person I've ever known. You love so openly. You give so much." He stroked my cheek with the back of his hand. "It was your parents' loss that they didn't get to know you. And it's my loss that I did and lost you. I'm worse than them because I knew what I had, and I let it go."

He kissed me again. "I love you. I'll always love you. If you need me, ever, will you reach out to me?"

I stood still as a statue.

He let out a self-deprecating laugh. "I never allowed you to feel you could when we were in a relationship, so it's big of me to suggest it now, right?"

He was too close, and all I wanted to do was rest my head against his chest and let him hold me. It was so unfair that the man I loved wasn't someone I trusted any longer.

"You deserve all the happiness in the world. And I know

I didn't make you feel like you were important to me, but baby, you were on my mind all the time. I smiled when I went to bed because I'd have you with me, either in person or on the phone. I woke up feeling giddy when I knew I'd see you." He wiped the tears I didn't even realize were flowing down my cheeks. "I loved making love with you because it was love and not just fucking. And when you said you loved me, everything inside me turned to gold."

He touched his lips to my forehead one last time and whispered, "Take care of yourself." And then, he was gone and once again broke my heart.

CHAPTER 17
Gabriel

A couple of months after we started going to counseling, it became clear that our setup at home, as I'd been told by my family, was fucked up. It wouldn't be, the therapist said, if Iris was okay with staying divorced, but the fact that she was seeking reconciliation to the point that she worked with Sophia to sabotage my relationship with Aurora meant that we had to move.

Sophia was doing much better. In fact, she'd stop having meltdowns and was behaving like the kid I remembered. Counseling helped. She could, in the weekly meetings, tell Iris when she screwed up, and Iris, who was required by our divorce amendment to show up for the sessions, or we'd be in front of a judge, hated every minute of it.

"This is humiliating," she told me while we waited outside Dr. Ryan's office, where she was meeting with Sophia. She spent an hour with our daughter and then we spent an hour as a family. It worked well, and Sophia talked to us about the things that bothered her.

"What is humiliating, Iris?" I asked wearily.

"Listening to my daughter accuse me of being a bad mother," she bit out. "And you're the good father."

"Iris, you need to stop pressuring her to fix our marriage. The one that has been over now for four fucking years." I dragged a hand through my hair, detesting every minute I had to be in Iris's company. I wish I'd seen a counselor while we were getting divorced, so we could've created healthy boundaries earlier on. This was my fault, and I was getting my ass kicked because of it.

What didn't help with my state of mind was that I couldn't get over Aurora. I'd tried. In the past month, Beau and I had gone to Miami Beach when I had a meeting, and there was plenty of pussy available, just not any I was interested in. I was like a lovesick fool, wanting the woman whom I'd treated unfairly and disrespectfully. She'd loved me, I knew that and felt it, but I'd been a selfish fuck, and she didn't trust me any longer. But as she said, I hadn't trusted her either when I believed she was capable of doing what Sophia had said she'd done. It didn't help that I decided to get drunk and be an asshole at the ball.

"I don't understand why wanting my family back together is such a bad thing," Iris continued.

"Because I don't love you, and I don't want to be married to you, and nothing you do, or Sophia does, is going to change that." I'd said a variation of this to Iris numerous times.

She crossed her arms. "Well, I'm not giving up."

"Fine, then we'll take this to a judge, and you can have supervised visits with your daughter. Iris, we have her for another few years; let's not make them miserable for her, yeah?"

"Fuck you, Gabe."

I sighed. It seemed like all our conversations ended with her cursing at me.

This week, the therapist wanted Sophia to talk about how guilty she felt for lying to me about Aurora. I'd told her there was nothing to forgive. I didn't blame her, but her guilt was eating her up.

"I didn't ask you to call her a gold digger, Sophia," Iris snapped.

"No, Mama, but *you* called her that," Sophia said sadly, "I feel really bad, Daddy."

"Sweetpea, let this go, will you? It's alright. You're not to blame for my relationship ending with Aurora or with your mother," I soothed.

"What would make you feel better, Sophia?" Dr. Ryan asked. She was in her fifties and was a no-nonsense psychologist as Luna had told me. She didn't let Iris do her dance or let me get away with my shit, either. She called it as she saw it, and I respected her for that. And the fact that Sophia was being helped as much as she was meant I was indebted to Dr. Ryan.

"Can I apologize to Aurora?" she whispered.

"Absolutely not," Iris snapped, getting off her chair. "You will not talk to that slut."

"Iris, sit down," Dr. Ryan said sharply. "And don't use that kind of language in front of your daughter. When you talk about a woman like that, you demean her, and that's not acceptable."

"Oh, please, she is a slut."

Sophia had tears in her eyes. "I don't have to talk to Aurora, I guess."

Fuck me! Iris had been manipulating this poor child, and I'd been too much of a righteous ass to see it.

"If you want to, we can set that up," I said, looking at the therapist for confirmation, which she gave me with a nod.

"No way." Iris sat back down, breathing hard. "Sophia has done nothing wrong and—"

"Iris, stop talking right now," Dr. Ryan interrupted. She never lost her temper and always stayed calm, which rattled the hell out of my ex-wife. "Sophia did do something wrong. You saying it is not, is confusing to her. Like we have discussed previously, you have to start being transparent with Sophia."

"I am," Iris smiled. "And that girl Gabe was seeing is a gold-digging slut."

Dr. Ryan sighed. "Gabe, I'm happy to write a report that Iris's influence is detrimental to Sophia's mental health and well-being if you wish to take her to a judge."

"You bitch," Iris growled.

Iris was losing her ever-loving mind, I thought.

"Iris," I whispered, "Sophia is now old enough to stand in front of a judge and tell them where she wants to stay."

Sophia licked her lips and looked at Iris. "Mama, I love you, but it's becoming too hard."

"Sophia, I'm your mother."

"I know." She began to weep, and I pulled her into my arms.

"This is you, turning my kid against me," Iris accused both Dr. Ryan and me; and left the office.

I held Sophia and looked at Dr. Ryan, who smiled at me. After my daughter calmed down, Dr. Ryan asked if Sophia would be okay if she spoke to me alone. "I just need to make sure he's okay as I do you."

I liked that about Dr. Ryan; she was always honest about what she was trying to do. It made Sophia trust her, which was vital in such a relationship.

When we were alone, Dr. Ryan grinned at me. "Well, how are you feeling, Gabe?"

"Like shit. Like this is my fault. I should've never set our lives up as I did. I thought I was doing the best for Sophia, and now I find out that I fucked up big time," I admitted.

"You're a dedicated father, Gabe. And you have an authentic relationship with Sophia. Your ex-wife's lack of self-awareness is not your fault," she said. "We've now met eight times in the past two months, and I can tell you that things are not getting better with Iris. She appears to be devolving. I hate to say this, but you need to move your home sooner than later."

I'd been searching for a place to buy without any luck in finding something suitable. Perhaps I should settle for a temporary house now and figure out a more permanent solution later.

"Okay."

"Is Iris still coming into your home unannounced?"

I shook my head. "She can't. The door is coded, and she doesn't have access. But she does come every day to see Sophia, but only when I'm home."

"And during her week?"

"I talk to Sophia every night to check in with her. She puts on a good act of being happy, but I know she's feeling like shit."

"My goal is to do what's best for the child, and usually that means having both parents involved. However, if this situation with Sophia continues, you may have to consider petitioning for sole custody," Dr. Ryan warned.

"I know."

"But you don't want to."

"Sophia is going to carry even more guilt, for hurting her mother. I just wish Iris would get her head out of her ass."

"I do this a lot, Gabe, and I can assure you that Iris is not going to change," Dr. Ryan confirmed what I already knew. "Will you be able to set up some time and space for Sophia to talk to Aurora?"

"What do you recommend?"

She took a deep breath. "I don't know Aurora, so I don't know how this meeting will go. It may damage Sophia further."

"Aurora is a sweetheart," I said, "She'll not hurt Sophia."

"Do you know your eyes light up whenever you say her name?" she asked.

I frowned. "Do they?"

"Yes. This relationship was important to you."

"Yes," I choke out because losing Aurora was almost physically painful. Worse, knowing that I'd hurt her, wounded her, was torture. I understood Sophia's guilt because I carried the same and then some.

"Any chance of reconciliation?"

I let out a short bark of laughter. "I don't think so. I lost her trust."

Dr. Ryan nodded. "I'm going to let you decide if you want Sophia to meet with Aurora. And whether you want to be there during this meeting or not."

"That is if Aurora agrees to meet with Sophia."

"From how you talk about Aurora, she seems like the kind of person who wouldn't want a thirteen-year-old to carry needless guilt."

CHAPTER 18

Aurora

"**B**aby, come for me." Gabriel was behind me, his erection nestled between my ass cheeks. His hand on my clitoris, his lips against the sensitive hollow beneath my ear.

"Gabriel," I whimpered, my hips pushing against him, wanting him inside me.

"I'll fill you up, baby, right after you come for me. Your cunt squeezes me so well when you come, you know that. You pulse around me, get wetter."

I woke up and found myself dry-humping a pillow.

I wanted to pull out my vibrator and finish off, but when I did that after I dreamed of Gabriel, I missed him even more.

Months had passed since we broke up and yet, I felt the tears come as they seemed to do whenever I thought about Gabriel.

How could it still hurt so much? How long would it go on?

It was harder on the weekends because we used to spend Friday nights and Saturdays together on the weeks Gabriel didn't have Sophia. On Sundays, he went back home as he, his ex-wife, and Sophia had lunch with his parents and brother. I felt like an outsider, a mistress.

But this Sunday, I had something to look forward to.

I had a date with Nina's daughter Bianca every other Sunday when we toured a Savannah building and had lunch. I loved spending time with her. She was curious about architecture and a fun kid.

The sun was already high and relentless by the time Bianca, and I stepped out of the Mercer Williams House Museum, our latest exploration in Savannah's architectural treasure trove. It was the end of June, and the city was wrapped in the warmth of summer, the air thick with humidity and history.

"I loved the ornate details of the cornices in the building," Bianca marveled, her eyes wide with the vivid imagination of a thirteen-year-old who was just beginning to understand the layers of stories behind the façades of such historic buildings.

I smiled at her enthusiasm. "Yes, and think about the Italianate style of the house, how different it is from the other buildings we've seen. Savannah has such a rich architectural diversity, doesn't it?"

Bianca nodded eagerly as we made our way down Bull Street towards Mrs. Wilkes' Dining Room, a place as famous for its traditional Southern cuisine as it was for the line of people that often snaked around its exterior. "The tall windows and the ironwork on the balconies," she mused, "it's like something out of a book."

"That's exactly right," I agreed. "And those features are not just aesthetic. They're functional and designed for ventilation and light in a time before air conditioning. It's fascinating how necessity shapes design."

Bianca was quick to catch on, her mind already spinning with ideas. "Well, architects do have to think about the climate and how people live when they design a building."

"Absolutely," I said as we took our seats at a table inside the bustling restaurant, grateful for the escape from the heat.

The smell of fried chicken, collard greens, and cornbread filled the air, a perfect complement to our day of historical exploration.

I ordered shrimp and grits while Bianca went for fried chicken, as she always did with cornbread, collard greens, and fried okra.

As we waited for our food, I pulled out a sketchbook and pencil from my bag and slid them across the table to Bianca. "Why don't you try sketching a contemporary version of Mercer Williams House? Think about the elements we talked about—the windows, the ironwork. Imagine how you would incorporate those features into a modern building."

Bianca's eyes lit up as she accepted the challenge, her pencil hesitantly touching the paper before gaining confidence. Watching her, I felt a profound sense of responsibility and pride. Here was a young mind eager to absorb the lessons of the past to create a future.

"Our cities, our buildings, tell the story of who we are," I said, hoping to instill in her a sense of the importance of her budding passion. "And one day, Bianca, you'll contribute to that story with your own designs."

Lunch arrived, and as we ate, our conversation meandered from the technical aspects of architecture to the dreams and ambitions that buildings like the Mercer Williams House inspired in both of us.

We were waiting for Bianca's dessert, a mud pie, when she brightened. "Mr. Rhodes."

"Hi, Bianca, how are you doing, sweetheart."

I felt him, smelled him as he leaned down to give Bianca a quick hug.

My heart was in my mouth. What on earth was Gabriel doing here? This was not the kind of restaurant he frequented. This was too low-brow for his high society tastes.

"Aurora," I heard him say, and I lifted my chin to look at him. *Why, oh why, did I have to see him right after dreaming about him?*

"Gabriel." I resisted the urge to clear my throat and reveal how nervous he made me.

He looked at the open sketchpad. "What do we have here?"

"I'm trying to fuse the historic inspiration from Mercer House, which we just toured, with more contemporary buildings," Bianca said proudly.

"Sir, will you be sitting at this table?" a server asked.

"Ah, I'm waiting for someone. You have a reservation under Rhodes."

Holy shit, he was here on a date. I'd have to see him with another woman. That was going to hurt big time.

"You can wait with us," Bianca offered.

Gabriel looked at me when I nodded—what the hell else could I do—he sat down next to me and across from Bianca. I was seeing him for the first time since he'd come to my condo to apologize, and all I wanted to do was lean into him.

Love had to die sometime, didn't it?

"We do this on Sundays," Bianca chirped, "Aurora is mentoring me. I'm going to be an architect just like her and work at Savannah Lace."

"Aurora is a great architect. You're learning from the best," Gabriel said softly, and I could feel him looking at me. I blindly stared at Bianca. It was safer.

"Every Sunday?" he asked.

"Well, every other," Bianca continued. "We tour a building that's open to the public, and then we have lunch and talk about it. I want to understand architecture and how we can learn from the past to make more sustainable buildings for the future. Am I right, Aurora?"

I had to smile. "Yes, you are, honey."

"Aurora even came to school to talk to my class about architecture," Bianca said. "Everyone was impressed."

Gabriel shifted, and his jeans brushed against my naked calf. It was hot, and I was in a white summer dress that hit two inches above my knee. My arms were bare, and the dress was held by a bow on each shoulder.

I moved so we wouldn't touch. He didn't shift his chair as I expected him to do because I was against the wall and couldn't go much farther.

"I think you'll make a fine architect," Gabriel said, "Maybe you can design a Rhodes Hotel someday."

Her eyes brightened. "Oh, wouldn't that be amazing? Mama said that Savannah Lace was going to design your Miami Beach hotel."

Nola Jolly, an architect who'd joined Savannah Lace a few months ago, would probably be the lead on the Miami Beach Hotel project. Nina had asked me if I minded being part of the team, and I'd told her I was okay with it if she needed me. Ultimately, thankfully, she'd not assigned me to the project. Mostly, I was relieved, but there was a small part of me that wondered how it would be to see Gabriel regularly again, even if it was for work.

Bianca's mud pie arrived, and so did Gabriel's lunch date. As I'd dreaded, it was a woman. Blonde and beautiful. Slender and oh so Southern. She waved at Gabriel, and he rose.

"It was nice seeing you, Bianca, and you as well, Aurora," he murmured softly.

"Have a great rest of the day, Mr. Rhodes."

I just nodded at him because words would not come out of my mouth. He was on a date. He'd moved on. Of course, he had. Why wouldn't he? He was good-looking and charming, and this woman looked like she came from the same social circle as him if her jewelry and outfit were anything to go by. That dress was a Chloe, I knew, and all the bling was not paste. Maybe his daughter would accept this woman better as she was of the same socioeconomic status as him. No one would accuse her of being a gold digger.

I dragged my focus away from Gabriel after I saw him hug the woman because I couldn't stand seeing him touch her. This was a lot worse than I thought it would be.

For the first time, I wanted to rush Bianca so we could get the hell out.

But that wouldn't be fair to her, so I just pretended Gabriel was not close by and that my heart wasn't beating like I'd run a hundred-meter sprint, and my panties weren't wet because just a whiff of him had aroused me.

CHAPTER 19
Gabriel

"Who's that woman?" asked Rose, my cousin.

"Which woman?"

"You know which woman, the one you were sitting with, the one who's trying so very hard not to look at us," Rose grinned.

"She's Aurora."

Rose raised an eyebrow. "*The* Aurora?"

I nodded.

"She's beautiful...stunning. Who's the young girl with her? She looks familiar."

"That's Nina Davenport's daughter. Aurora works at Savannah Lace. She's an architect," I explained, glad that my back was to Aurora, otherwise I'd be hard-pressed to not stare at her. That fucking dress she was wearing. I could barely stand it. She smelled like lavender, as she always did, and I wanted nothing more than to tug at those bows on her shoulder and see her gorgeous tits under the dress.

"Hmm...she's not happy about you having lunch with me," Rose declared mischievously. She got up, leaned, and kissed my cheek.

"What the fuck?" I pulled back.

Rose sat down, rubbing her hands together. "Oh yeah, she hated that."

"Rose?"

"What? Rafe told me that you and she broke up. Speaking of which, how's Sophia doing?"

"Better."

"And Iris?" Her lips curled with displeasure.

"According to our therapist, she's devolving now that she has to come to terms with the fact that we are indeed divorced and will stay that way. I need to find a place to live and then put the houses on the market."

Rose owned and ran a real estate company that bought and sold high-end housing in Georgia, Alabama, and Louisiana. She was planning to expand to other states. Her daddy had plenty of money, but she'd turned her back on that and was a self-made woman. I respected the hell out of her. Of all my relatives, Rose was the one in my family I was closest to, maybe because she wasn't just fooling around with family money and doing something she was passionate about.

"Is that why you wanted to meet for lunch?"

"That and I haven't seen you in a while." I was also free this Sunday since my parents were traveling and Rafe was *otherwise* occupied with a woman, hopefully, *not* a student.

"I wondered when you agreed to meet here. Not your kind of place."

No, it wasn't. But it was Rose's.

We ordered, and I watched Aurora and Bianca leave the restaurant.

"You look like a hungry dog," Rose commented.

"What?"

"You have your tongue all but hanging out, Gabe. Are you still in love with her?"

"Madly," I confessed. I leaned back in my chair, heaved my head back and groaned. "Fucking hell, Rose, I fucked this up."

"I think your ex helped," Rose murmured. "You want her back?"

I sighed. "More than my next breath, but I was cruel to her. She told me she forgives me but cannot forget."

"The woman hasn't gotten over you either."

I crushed the small blossom of hope inside my heart. I'd been wishing that she'd come back and tested it by calling her to find that she'd still not unblocked my number. "It's my fault. I obliterated every possibility of her giving me a chance."

I told Rose what happened at the ball, and she smacked my hand. "That was such a dick move, Gabe."

"I know," I admitted. "I was jealous and drunk. Beau almost punched me."

"He should have," Rose muttered.

"So, I don't think there's much chance of me getting her back, which means I'm going to die with blue balls."

Rose chuckled. "There are other women in Georgia."

"I don't want anyone else." I rubbed a hand over my face. "I tried when Beau and I were in Miami Beach, and I couldn't. I want her. I love her. I lost her."

Rose tapped her fingers on the table. "What if you could at least give her a chance to forgive you for real?"

"This is the first time I've seen her in two months, Rose."

"What if you could see her more regularly?"

I narrowed my eyes. "What are you suggesting?"

"Aunt Betsy is friends with Nina Davenport. I'm sure if you used her to push Nina, you could convince her to put Aurora as the lead architect on your Miami Beach hotel project."

"What if Aurora doesn't agree?"

Rose waved a hand to dismiss that. "She will. She'll tell herself she's being professional, but she's not over you either. It's pretty obvious."

I let hope blossom a tiny little bit this time. "Tell me why you think so."

"She looked like her heart was breaking because you are here with another woman."

"You're my cousin."

"She doesn't know that," Rose reminded me.

"You really think there's a chance in hell I can win her back?"

"Abso-fucking-lutely."

CHAPTER 20
Aurora

I was in my office when Nova walked in. "Hey, Aurora."

"Hi. Has Callum arrived yet?" I had a meeting scheduled with Callum Pierce in about half an hour, but he sometimes showed up early.

She shook her head. "Not yet. But there is someone here for you. If you say you don't want to be disturbed, I can handle it."

I waited.

"It's Sophia Rhodes."

I didn't want to see Gabriel's daughter, but on the other hand, if he was dating again, maybe it would help for me to talk to Sophia, and hopefully, she'd be less of a brat to the new girlfriend.

"It's okay, Nova. You can send her in."

I looked down at myself and noted that I was dressed nicely and professionally. Sure, I couldn't compete with Sophia's mother's designer labels, but I looked like an architect. This was my office, my domain, and I was in charge.

I felt like an idiot for being nervous about meeting a thirteen-year-old, but our last meeting in her father's house had been, as Luna had called it, a clusterfuck.

Sophia looked demure as she knocked on my open door and waited.

"Hey, Sophia." I rose. "Come on in." I gestured at a guest chair.

She sat down. She looked adorable in a blue summer dress with sneakers and a backpack slung on one shoulder. Her blonde hair was tied into a ponytail, and she was fresh-faced and gorgeous. My heart hurt a little that we couldn't have gotten to know each other better. I loved Gabriel, which meant that I loved his child, no matter how she'd treated me.

"Thanks, Aurora." She set her backpack on her lap, clutching it.

"Do you want something to drink? A Coke, water?"

She shook her head. "I'm good, thanks."

She wasn't looking at me, and I felt bad for her. She looked so forlorn and sad. "How are you doing, Sophia?"

She looked up then, and I saw her eyes were wet. "Daddy doesn't know I'm here. I...he said that he'd talk to you and then set it up, but...I felt like I had to do this on my own."

I couldn't stand it and walked around my desk to sit next to her. I put an arm around her shoulder. "Hey, what's wrong?"

She looked at me. "I'm so sorry. I was such a bitch to

you. It's been eating at me. I hate that I broke you and Daddy up."

"Honey, you're not responsible for the breakup of our relationship," I immediately said.

She gave me a watery smile, her eyes clearing a little. "Daddy says the same thing. He says he messed up."

"It takes two people to mess up in a relationship."

"I'm sorry, Aurora, for saying the things I did, for lying to my father about you. It was a horrible thing to do. I know you can never forgive me, but I wanted—"

Oh god, I couldn't let a kid carry such guilt.

"Honey, I do forgive you. Don't even think about it. It's in the past, it's done."

Her eyes filled again. "Why are you being so nice to me when I was so mean to you?"

I sighed and pulled her into a sideways hug. "Oh, baby, you're a child, and there are no mistakes that you can't walk away from." I wiped her tears. "It's alright. It really is. I've let it go."

"My therapist said I should tell you why I did what I did. Would you like to know?"

I didn't because I could guess, but it appeared like she wanted to explain, so I assented.

"First, this is *my* fault and no one else's," she began. "I did the wrong thing no matter why. This is an explanation and not an excuse."

I smiled. She had a good therapist.

I pulled away from her, and she sat straighter.

"My mother has never been happy about the divorce. My

father was so happy after the divorce...well, he was when you were there. He hasn't been happy since."

I didn't need to hear that, especially since he was dating again. Maybe Sophia didn't know, and he'd tell her when he was ready.

"I was under a lot of pressure to bring my parents back together, and I caved. I was weak and—"

"No, you weren't," I interrupted. "You're a child, and like I said, we all make mistakes, and we learn from them. Don't belittle yourself."

Her mouth trembled. "Now I feel even worse. You're so nice, and I was such a bitch. My mother told me yesterday that I was weak, and that's why I'd told Daddy everything."

Telling her that her mother was a royal bitch wasn't going to help. "You're not weak," I repeated. "The fact that you're here, talking to me, tells me you're very strong. It takes courage to admit our mistakes."

She sniffled.

"I wanted to ask if you and Daddy can get back together," she paused and smiled, "but, as he has told me several times, and as you just did, I'm not responsible for your relationship with him or his with my mother."

I smiled back. "He's absolutely right."

"Do you really forgive me? I did a very bad thing."

"It's already forgotten. Don't carry it with you."

"Did you love Daddy?"

That killed! Damn it. "I did." I do, I always will.

"But not anymore?"

"Didn't your father tell you that you're not responsible for his relationships with other people?" I cajoled.

She nodded. "He did. I'm so sorry, Aurora."

"And that's the last time you say that to me. Okay?"

"Okay."

"Now, do you want some hot chocolate? I know it's summer, but we have a bakery next door that makes the best." I looked at my watch and saw I had ten minutes before Callum arrived. Well, he'd just have to wait. I'd tell Nova. Right now, this child was in crisis, and I wanted to be there for her.

Damn it! I'd have to tell Gabriel about this visit. I'd blocked him on my phone, and I was glad I did because that meant I didn't wait for him to reach out to me.

I dreaded talking to him, but I was also excited that I'd be able to.

"That would be great." Sophia got up and picked up her backpack.

"Come on, kiddo."

I picked up my wallet and let Nova know that I might be late for my meeting with Callum and took Gabriel's daughter for hot chocolate.

CHAPTER 21

Gabriel

"Gabe, she's your wife," my executive assistant for a decade, Kate French said as she scrambled to defend herself.

"Ex-wife," I corrected her. "Sharing my calendar with her, especially my personal calendar...Kate, I can't understand why you'd do that."

Kate was in her mid-thirties and had always been efficient and good at her job. She was *not* part of Savannah high society but was fascinated by it. I could guess that Iris had seduced her with a few tears, high teas, and cocktails to get her to reveal things that she shouldn't have.

"It was just once in a while, Gabe," she stuttered, "just... she'd ask where you were and things like that."

"And you'd tell her?"

She licked her lips. "Ah...yes. She's your wife."

"Ex-wife," I tried again. "And you didn't think to ask me if that was okay?"

I looked at her, the Savannah bridge behind her, through the large windows of my office, where three walls were glass. Corner office on speed!

She looked nervous. "It won't happen again."

"No, it won't," I assured her. "You're being transferred to the temp pool of assistants."

This pool of assistants was utilized by director and senior director-level executives at Rhodes Hotels, and they didn't work with one specific leader. Kate was transitioning from being the CEO's executive assistant to a role she was overqualified for—merely an assistant. However, I had no choice; trusting my executive assistant was paramount.

"Gabe, I said I'm sorry," she said nervously. "I was only trying to help bring your family together."

"By telling Iris whenever I had an appointment with Aurora?"

"I...she just wanted to know when you were seeing her. I didn't see anything wrong with that," she said defensively.

"Every time you told her I was seeing Aurora, she manipulated Sophia to call me with a crisis," I revealed softly.

Kate gasped.

"Are you surprised?"

Kate licked her lips and shook her head.

"You knew Iris would do anything to break up any relationship I was in, didn't you?"

Tears filled her eyes, and she nodded. "She just wanted her family together, Gabe."

And since Kate herself had just gone through a divorce

that her husband had asked for because he'd fallen in love with another woman had made her an easy mark for Iris.

There was a knock on the door, and I asked the person to come in.

Kate's eyes widened when she saw our head of human resources, Willa Acker, walk in.

I rose. "Thank you for everything you've done for Rhodes Hotels, Kate. Willa will walk you through your next assignment." I looked at Willa and nodded. "I have a meeting, so please feel free to use my office."

"It won't take long," Willa commented.

I knew she was pissed as hell with Kate for what she'd done. Her recommendation had been to fire her, but I hadn't had the heart. If it had been anyone else, I'd have followed her advice; but Kate had been at Rhodes since she'd graduated from university, and we'd had a good working relationship.

I walked out as I heard Kate's sob. "God, Willa, I'm so sorry."

I'd been sitting for an hour in a meeting about the plan to have solar panels put across all Rhodes Hotels around the world, a project that was near and dear to me when my phone flashed with a message.

As soon as I saw Aurora's name on my phone, I got hard. Just her fucking name.

I excused myself and stepped into my office as I answered the phone.

"Aurora."

"Gabriel, hello. Am I disturbing you?"

"No." Never. "Is everything okay?"

"Yes...ah...I wanted to let you know that Sophia came by this afternoon to my office."

Fuck! I hadn't heard anything about this from Sophia.

"She's fine," Aurora rushed, "I didn't say anything to hurt her."

I closed my eyes when I heard the panic in her voice. I'd wounded her so much that she was worried I'd think she was mean to my kid.

"I know you wouldn't," I said gently. "Are you okay?"

"Yes."

My phone beeped, and as I suspected it was a message from Sophia.

"Aurora, I'd like to talk to you about how your conversation with Sophia went. Would that be okay?"

"Of course."

She said *of course* in that tight-assed way of hers when she was doing something, she didn't want to. I was fine with that as long as she'd talk to me.

"I'd like to not do this over the phone. I have a meeting that I just stepped out of to take your call, and I need to get back."

"Oh, I'm so sorry to disturb you, that wasn't my—"

"Baby, I took the call because I wanted to talk to you," I cut in gently, "I *wanted* to talk to you."

This proved to me how one-sided our relationship had been. She'd made all the allowances, and I'd never given her permission to reach out to me, never let her feel she had any rights to me. She'd been there for me when I needed her; I'd never allowed her to need me.

"Okay. Thank you."

"No, baby, thank you. Can we meet to talk?"

"I'm at work," she said. "I...I have a...I'm at work."

She was rattled that I asked for us to meet, but holy hell, she'd finally called, and I wanted to prolong this contact.

"How about around six today? I can come by your place, or...we can meet—"

"Six thirty at the Peacock Lounge," she said hurriedly.

"I'll see you then."

After I ended the call, I checked the message from Sophia; she simply said: *I talked to Aurora. It's all good. I'll tell you everything when I see you.*

I replied: *You want to talk now?*

Sophia: *I'm fine. Really. She was very nice. We had hot chocolate at the bakery next door.*

I smiled and typed: *In this weather?*

Sophia: *It was really tasty. The whipped cream was cold.*

I smiled: *I'll talk to you tonight. Might be out for dinner.*

She was with her mother this week.

She sent back a thumbs-up emoji. I returned to my meeting feeling like I'd won the lottery. I was going to meet Aurora at a bar, and I couldn't wait.

CHAPTER 22
Aurora

L ike a teenager who was wet behind the ears, I got to the Peacock Lounge nearly a half hour before we were supposed to meet. I didn't want to fuck this up.

I felt like an idiot. Aurora was a sweetheart, no way would she have been nasty to Sophia or anyone. Seeing her with Bianca had been a knife through the heart. They met every other Sunday, and Aurora was mentoring a teenager the same age as Sophia. They seemed close, and it just showed me what a moron I'd been.

Every time I recollected how I'd ridiculed her difficult childhood and what I said to Pierce at the ball about Aurora not being maternal, it crushed me. She'd trusted me with her past, not to the depth of what Luna had revealed, but I knew enough, and I'd taken that information to hurt her.

The fact that she was even giving me the time of day was a miracle, one that I was going to take full advantage of.

She looked like a vision when she came into the Peacock

Lounge. She wore a black suit dress with a jacket, very proper, everything covered. Her heels were sensible. She liked comfort. Her hair was scraped away from her perfect face into a tight ponytail.

She used to leave her hair loose when she came to me because she knew how much I liked to wrap the silky strands around my hand, especially while she sucked me off.

Christ! One look at her and I was sporting an erection like I was a fucking teenager who got a hard-on because he saw a skirt.

I rose when I saw her, and when she came close, I leaned and brushed my lips across her cheek. I couldn't help myself. I almost moaned out loud at the smell of her, at her nearness.

She hurried away and sat down on the armchair across from me. I should've found a table where we'd have to sit closer, I thought, but the lounge was still empty, and it would've been patently obvious I was being a lecherous asshole.

"What would you like to drink?" I hadn't ordered anything, wanting to wait, wanting to have a clear head, unlike at the ball when I was drunk enough to screw up my life.

"Ah...a martini."

I waved, and a server came by. I ordered a Macallan 12 neat for me and a vodka martini for Aurora.

"How are you?" I asked.

"Good," she smiled tightly. "And you?"

I missed my Aurora, the one who didn't have her

guard up, the one who let me see her. I knew now that I'd lost that in the later months of our relationship when she'd become more and more reserved with me. It had started after she met Sophia, and now I knew why. My daughter had begun to act up, and Aurora hadn't said a word because she didn't want to come between Sophia and me.

"I'm getting through," I told her truthfully. "I miss you something fierce."

Her face fell. "I just wanted to talk to you about Sophia, and that's it."

"I know," I soothed. "I know, baby."

"Don't call me that."

The server came with our drinks, and we waited until he left to speak again.

"Sophia said you were very nice to her."

"She told you?"

I shook my head. "Just a text message to say you had a good talk, and you took her to the bakery next door."

"Bianca raves about their hot chocolate," she explained, "I thought Sophia needed a treat. It was hard for her to come to me. She apologized, Gabri...Ga...."

"Call me Gabriel," I urged.

Most people called me Gabe, but she always called me Gabriel. I liked the intimacy of it, how she said my name, especially when I was inside of her.

Idiot, stop thinking about fucking her right now, or you're going to embarrass yourself.

She took a sip of her martini. "And that's it. She apologized, and I told her it was all forgotten. I really think she'll be fine with your girlfriend."

I raised both eyebrows. "My girlfriend?"

She nodded. "Ah...I assumed. The woman you were with when...anyway, that's your business."

She was flushed, and Rose was right; she'd been jealous. "The woman I was with when I saw you with Bianca is Rose. She's my cousin, Aurora. My father's sister's daughter."

Her eyes went blank. "Oh."

Now, my Mama had raised no fool, so I went in for the kill. "How am I supposed to date any other woman when I'm still in love with you?"

She gasped. "Gab...damn it, you can't say things like that to me."

"Gabriel. Say my name."

She shook her head. "I should go."

"Finish your drink, Aurora," I ordered gently. My god, she was spectacular. How had I let her go?

"This is too hard." Her mask dropped.

"Why? Because you love me too?" I was pushing it, but I didn't know what the fuck else to do.

"Stop. Please."

I leaned forward, and she literally pushed back into her chair.

"Baby, I'm not going to hurt you," I whispered.

"You already did, Gabriel." There was pain in her eyes, and it devastated me. I'd done this to her.

"I know. Let me make it up to you. Give me a chance...a last chance? I'll never ask for another."

She shook her head. "I can't. I...just can't."

"Why?" I coaxed.

She looked at me with clear eyes then. "Because I'll never trust you with myself again." She said it so calmly that I knew she was telling her truth.

"I'll earn back your trust."

"It doesn't work like that. I can't...I won't let you back in."

"Don't let fear hold you back, baby. We were so good together."

"No, we weren't. We had an unhealthy relationship where I was always scared of losing you and you...treated me like a mistress."

"No," I groaned. "No, baby. You were, *are* the woman I love. Not a mistress. Don't think that."

"How can I not?" she demanded, fresh hell in her eyes. "Think back and tell me you treated me fairly."

"I didn't," I admitted. "Give me a chance to show you how it can be."

"No."

"You're just scared, I get it but if—"

"My fear protects me." Her chin jutted out, and there was a fire in her voice. "When you grow up alone, because as you said, no one, not even my parents wanted me, you learn quickly who to trust and who not to. I made a mistake with you, one I won't repeat."

She got up then. "Your daughter is wonderful, and I think the therapist she's seeing has helped her a lot. And... you're a really good father."

"Just a shitty boyfriend." I hadn't given her the best of me, I realized. I'd been so comforted by her love that I'd turned selfish. I became like Iris, taking and not giving back.

"Yes," she agreed, and then she was gone.

She'd not finished her martini. I'd barely had a couple of sips of my own drink. I downed the rest of my whiskey and paid the tab.

When my car and driver came to pick me up, I directed him to take me to my parents' place.

The one thing meeting Aurora again had made clear, I wanted her back and I would get her too. I'd make her trust me again and never ever give her a reason to fear that I'd hurt her.

She was my forever; the certainty of that seeped into me. I just needed her to believe that I was hers as well.

CHAPTER 23

Aurora

"Y ou want me to lead the Rhodes Miami Beach hotel project?" I asked, my eyes wide as saucers when Nina told me that Nola Jolly could not take the project on because she was working on a new corporate park development in Las Vegas, which was her expertise.

"Can you work with Gabe?"

Nina Davenport wanted me to be the lead architect on a project! I was going to be promoted; that's what this meant. I wouldn't be a junior architect who supported a senior one; I'd be *the Senior Architect.*

"I can work with him." I can work with Satan.

"Excellent. Obviously, you know this means you're now a lead architect." She slid a file in front of me. "Here's your amended work contract."

With shaky hands, I opened the file and felt my throat close up at the raise. It was substantial. I'd never expected to make this much money so soon.

"Your work is impeccable, Aurora; that's the only reason you're getting this project. You earned this," Nina pressed.

"Thank you. I won't disappoint you," I promised.

"You never have."

There was a knock on the door, and Luna peeked in.

Nina sighed. "Yes, I told her. Y'all are so impatient."

Luna barged in, followed by Nova and Stella Hunt, a landscape designer who'd been with Nina since the start of Savannah Lace, screeching, "Congratulations."

Lyla Cruz, our indomitable Chief Financial Officer, came in and flung her arms around me. "I'm so happy for you."

Nina hired mostly women at Savannah Lace with pride —and the fact that we were considered the best boutique architecture and design firm this side of the Mississippi meant that we were competing with the big guns with their old family names and good ol' boy network.

I grinned when they opened champagne and threw confetti around my office and on me.

Nina took us all out for dinner to celebrate. Since I came to Savannah Lace, I'd slowly started to let my guard down and allow people in. Luna was difficult to resist. She was so open and vibrant that I fell in love with her. But sitting here with these women, toasting my success, I felt like I'd found my tribe. These women were supportive of one another, not tearing each other down as I'd experienced in my previous company. Here, I felt genuinely appreciated for the first time in my life.

I was going to lead a project. I was going to build a hotel. I couldn't believe it.

"This is a full-service project, so you need to put your team together," Nina told me as we drank coffee after our meal. "Construction, interior design, restaurant design, spa design...lots of things to bring together."

"I know. I can't wait." I could hardly contain my excitement.

"Rhodes already has a hotel in Miami Beach, and I believe the family has a home there. You can stay at either place when you're there for the project."

"The hotel," I blurted. No way was I going to stay in the family home where Gabriel had probably been with his ex-wife. I didn't need that juju messing me up.

"Your call," Nina suggested. "I'm always here for you, so if you need anything, you have a question, just reach out."

"I know. Thank you so much, Nina."

"Hey, it's my pleasure, and trust me, I may be CEO, but I don't promote on my own; it's a team decision, and the team thinks very highly of you."

The team she was talking about was her leadership team. Lyla Cruz was on it as the chief financial officer, Nina was both CEO and head of interior design, Luna was the recently promoted head of architecture, Stella was responsible for landscape designing, and Ginny Montague who was head of construction. Ginny was away on a project in Huntsville.

We were a small company with about twenty-five people, and we were close knit despite the fact that many of us were out of the office for days and weeks on end at times when we worked on a project.

"Nina, does Gabriel know that I will be heading this project?" I asked.

"No," she said. "I don't need him to approve who I appoint to a project."

"I just...you think he'll be okay with it?"

"If he's not, he can go fuck himself."

I grinned; for a prim Southern lady, Nina had one hell of a potty mouth.

"You're going to be alright." She put her hand on mine. "You're a tough cookie."

"I am that."

"You have reserves most people don't have, Aurora. Keep that in mind. And remember to have fun."

"I will."

I loved working at Savannah Lace.

Nina had built a company where management genuinely cared about employees. When Luna was promoted and became my boss, I'd been thrilled. She deserved to lead the architecture team. She was highly skilled and a great leader. Best of all, she was one of my closest friends, and she always had my back. For someone who hadn't grown up with many people who cared about me, Savannah Lace had given me a work family that supported me and was there for me when I needed them.

"You're going to be okay working with Gabe?" Luna asked as we walked to the parking lot outside the restaurant to get to our cars.

"I think so. I hope so."

She patted my shoulder. "In any case, you'll probably be spending a lot of time with his Vice President of Brand."

"That's Devon Parker," I recollected.

"Yeah. He's responsible for the Rhodes Hotel brand, and this is his baby. He's good people and a whole lot of fun. And definitely not the society set that you don't like."

"I don't know; I did date Gabriel for a whole year, who's the epitome of Savannah society," I remarked.

"Devon is down to earth. Would rather go surfing and kayaking in the Keys than attend a party," Luna told me. "He wasn't born with a silver spoon in his mouth like the rest of us."

"So, you don't think I'll be seeing Gabriel much?" I asked and kept the disappointment from my voice.

Luna laughed. "I have a feeling he's going to be very involved, so don't worry, you'll see plenty of him if that's what you want."

"I don't know what I want," I grumbled.

CHAPTER 24

Aurora

I was nervous as I waited for the Rhodes Hotel team to
come to Savannah Lace for the project kick-off meeting.

Gabriel had a new executive assistant, Eldon Wu, and
he'd worked with Nova and me to set up the agenda for the
meeting as well as the participant list.

Gabriel Rhodes would be attending the meeting.

I'd met Gabriel's previous EA, Kate, a couple of times
when I'd waited for him in his outer office before we were
going out. Just like all the other women in Gabriel's life, she
hadn't liked me much either. I wondered what happened to
her. From what I knew, she'd been with Gabriel for over a
decade.

Eldon came an hour before the scheduled meeting to
Savannah Lace so he could meet Nova and me in person. He
was of Asian descent, in his late twenties, and very fashion-
able. He was also charming and professional. He was not
from the South; definitely a Yank.

"Gabe is so excited about getting this project off the ground," he told us as I went through the slide deck we'd be presenting at the meeting.

The project was taking an existing hotel and using the bones but renovating it to become a five-star resort on Miami Beach. Rhodes Hotels & Resorts was known for its opulent and environmentally friendly design, high-end restaurants and bars, and distinctive Southern charm. I had all kinds of ideas for how we could make this a Rhodes flag-ship resort. I wanted Gabriel to be proud of what I would design for him. I was already selecting the team I wanted on board for the project. I couldn't wait to get started. I also had to admit that seeing Gabriel again was giving me a few extra butterflies.

Since Sophia had apologized, she'd been texting me regu-larly—and I liked it. She was a good kid who was working hard to make amends. I hadn't seen her father since our conversation at the bar when he told me he still loved me. I didn't believe him, not really. I wanted to, but trust was such a fragile thing, and people had failed me all of my life, so much so that I mostly waited for people to disappoint me, and when they did, it was almost a relief to not wait any longer.

Normally, it took me a long while to trust someone, but with Gabriel, everything happened so quickly. I found myself head over heels before I could consider the risks.

And I'd paid for it. I had his words running through my head on a loop.

"Now I can see why your father and mother walked away

from you. All this calm and quiet is an act, isn't it? I can't believe you're so selfish."

I'd always wondered what was wrong with me, why no one could love me, and I was afraid that Gabriel had spoken the truth. I was selfish and cold...which was why people left me.

"Well, be careful with this one; she didn't grow up with parents, so she's not particularly maternal."

And there was some truth in what Gabriel had said. I wasn't particularly maternal. I was, in fact, afraid of having children, scared that I'd do to them what my mother had done to me.

"Oh, please, Aurora, when you grow up and have children, trust me, you'll be just like me," my mother used to tell me.

I looked so much like my mother, and I sometimes could hear her intonations in how I spoke, which was why I'd never thought I'd have children.

Maybe that was another reason I was attracted to Gabriel. He already had a child, and if our relationship actually managed to get past me being unlovable, it would be fine if I didn't have children. I hadn't *actually* thought that far though. I'd felt fortunate and giddy that a man like Gabriel, successful, handsome, charming, and sophisticated, was interested in Aurora Turner, the girl who'd had to have two jobs in high school, one bagging groceries and the other cleaning toilets at the local gym to pay her way through living at her aunt's house.

The Aurora Turner who looked like a mongrel, and everyone wanted to know, *"Where exactly are you from?"*

And when I'd say I'm from Savannah, they'd say, *"No, really, where are you from?"*

My skin color was a mix of my heritage, and though it was clear I wasn't white, the question always was, *"So, what are you?"* I had no idea how to respond to that.

Gabriel hadn't asked me that; he'd simply said that he thought I was one of the most beautiful women he'd ever seen. Like they say, beauty does lie in the eye of the beholder. But in the end, my beauty was only surface deep, and when he went a little beneath my skin, he found a cold, selfish, and unmaternal woman.

I wanted to be warm and sweet like Stella, passionate like Luna, and caring yet professional like Nina, but I knew I came off more like Ice Maiden than the girl next door. I couldn't help it. It was my armor, and I'd been wearing it for so long that I didn't quite know how to be without it. I was an introvert to boot and was more comfortable with silence than conversation, with listening than talking, with blending into the wallpaper, than standing out, being in focus.

I gathered my thoughts as I heard Gabriel's voice from the lobby. My hands were clammy. Luna walked into the meeting room and smiled at me. I simply nodded, telling her silently that I was ready for this meeting.

My first project as a lead architect would be kick-ass, I promised myself. I wouldn't let Nina or Luna down. I wouldn't let myself down.

Gabriel walked into the meeting room with a blond whose hair was ruffled, his tan was distinct, and he looked absolutely *not* corporate because he wore jeans that had rips in them, leather sandals, and a Hawaiian-style t-shirt. He, I assumed was Devon Parker, Rhodes' head of brand. He appeared to be the complete opposite of Gabriel, who was in a dark teal linen suit, ideal for the Savannah summer and the perfect foil for his tanned skin.

He introduced me to Devon, who shook hands with me. Gabriel didn't touch me, just nodded.

"Aurora, I've heard great things about you from Gabe. You and I are going to become good friends working on this project."

I smiled. He was friendly and not in a flirty kind of way. He immediately put me at ease.

"I can't wait," I told him as I inhaled Gabriel's cologne when he walked past me.

He rattled me by just being there.

He sat across from me and listened intently as I went through the agenda and discussion points for the meeting.

Devon did most of the talking along with Eldon from Rhodes, while I was the point person as the lead architect and project manager from Savannah Lace. Luna was there to support, and Nova helped with the presentation.

I was nervous, though I knew it didn't show. I wanted Rhodes Hotels & Resorts to be happy with me as their lead architect. I wanted to seem competent and professional to Devon and Eldon. I wanted to impress Gabriel. I wanted him to think, *wow, she's something* instead of *she's cold and selfish*.

As the meeting progressed and I started to become

comfortable, Gabriel leaned forward, interlocking his hands, and directed his first question at me.

Look away from his hands, Aurora, I told myself because I could remember how it felt to have those hands run over my body.

"Baby, you're so responsive, so hot. I could just spend my day touching you, feeling you. Fucking hell, I need to be inside you. Let me in, open wide, now."

My eyes heated, and I couldn't stop myself from swallowing hard. Could he see, I wondered? Could he see that I was aroused? That I wanted him. Good god, what had happened to the nice Southern girl who hadn't ever been passionate about a man? Now, all I needed was to look at him, and I was wet.

"Aurora," he said my name, and I licked my lips.

"Baby, you suck me so good. Take me all the way to the back your throat. Fuck, Aurora! You're gonna swallow everything I give you, aren't you?"

I really, really needed to focus on the meeting and not wonder if my nipples were poking out of my bra, and everyone could see that I wanted this man.

His lips curved, and I again wondered if he could see how I felt. It took everything inside me to not let tears fill my eyes. I missed him.

I loved him, and he'd crushed me.

His eyes shuttered. The smile disappeared, and he looked almost angry. "Considering the unique history and aesthetic of Miami Beach," he continued, "How do you plan to integrate the Rhodes Hotel's signature Southern charm without clashing with the local vibe?"

I took a sip of water as an excuse to get my heartbeat down and tamp down the fever racing inside me.

"Miami Beach has a vibrant, Art Deco aesthetic that's iconic." I nodded to Nova, who pulled the right slides on the monitor, ones that showed the Art Deco buildings I was referring to. "The Rhodes Hotel's Southern charm offers a warmth and hospitality that's equally distinctive. Our approach is to create a fusion that respects both."

The designs I'd created were on the screen, and I held my breath. What if he hated them? What if he scorned them? Did they look cold?

"Wow," Devon exclaimed. "These are stunning, Aurora. How long have you been working on these?"

"Ah...not long," I mumbled, not sure what he was asking.

Luna chuckled. "She's been on the project for exactly three days."

"And you did this in three days?" Eldon muttered, impressed.

Buoyed by their praise, I went on. "We'll incorporate Art Deco elements in our design motifs and color schemes, blending them with the elegant, lush landscaping and interior design elements that evoke the welcoming, genteel atmosphere of the South. Think of it as marrying the glamour and vivacity of Miami Beach with the comfort and elegance of a Savannah estate. This way, the hotel doesn't just exist in Miami Beach; it belongs there, adding a new layer to its rich cultural tapestry."

Everyone was silent while Nova went through the designs that showed some of the elements I'd been thinking about for the exterior and the interior. I glanced at Gabriel, and his expression was blank as he looked at the screen. I knew that look. He was not happy.

Damn it! I so wanted him to be impressed.

I was about to ask him directly what he thought, when he spoke again.

"Let's talk about sustainability. We're known for our commitment to the environment. How do we ensure this project aligns with those values?"

Devon gave him a puzzled look, and Luna rolled her eyes. Nova was surprised that Gabriel had not said one nice thing about what I'd put together. I knew they were preliminary, and I wondered if I should've waited. Gabriel Rhodes was known for his high standards, and maybe I just didn't measure up.

Well, I'd done my best, I consoled myself. If he wanted to talk to Nina about getting someone else on the Miami project, that would be his call, and I'd accept it. The client, after all, was always right, even if they had their head up their ass.

"Slide 25, Nova," I told her, and she switched to what I wanted to show. "Sustainability is at the core of our design philosophy for this project. We're incorporating green roofs, solar panels, and energy-efficient lighting and HVAC systems to reduce the hotel's carbon footprint. Here are some of the calculations that I have put together. Please note, these are preliminary and will be refined once we have an approved building design."

Again, Devon and Eldon were pleased with what the numbers told them, Gabriel didn't say anything.

Panicked, I spoke hurriedly, hoping to answer all his unasked questions. "Our landscape design will use native plants to reduce water consumption and support local wildlife. We're also exploring innovative materials and construction techniques that minimize waste and environmental impact. Our goal is to achieve LEED certification for the hotel, making it a beacon of sustainability in Miami Beach."

That was the end of the presentation, and I nodded to Nova, who turned the monitor off and made the lights in the meeting room brighter. I poured some more water into my glass from the carafe, aware that I was expending energy to make sure my hands didn't shake. I was nervous as hell.

"I have to say, Aurora, you've given us a lot to think about and start to work with," Devon grinned. "I can see why you're so impressed with her, Gabe."

Gabriel looked at me, and his eyes softened, but he didn't say anything. His jaw was still tight. He was still annoyed about something. I wish Nina had checked with him before putting me on his project. Maybe he didn't think highly of me as an architect.

All my insecurities were clamoring for attention, and my

inner critics were so loud I couldn't hear anything besides the jabs and taunts that I was not good enough.

"Let's talk next steps," Gabriel prompted sternly.

The meeting went on for another half hour, and again, Gabriel was silent while Devon, Luna, Eldon, and I started to put together a preliminary project plan.

At the end of the meeting, everyone was amazed at how much we'd gotten done in such a short time.

"I think you may be the best-prepared architect and project manager I've ever worked with," Devon remarked. He looked at Gabe, "Anything from your end?"

"I'd like to see a firmed-up project plan by the end of the day tomorrow." He rose then. "Thanks, team."

He looked at his watch. "Can you guys find your own way back to Rhodes HQ? I have an appointment I'm late for."

"Sure, boss," Eldon said puzzled.

Gabriel all but stormed out of the meeting room.

"Don't know what bug he's got going up his ass," Devon muttered and then looked around the room and winced, "Sorry, I keep forgetting I'm in Savannah now. Excuse my language."

"I personally think he has a stick up his ass," Luna dead-panned.

Devon laughed. "And here I thought I had to be careful with the genteel Southern lady."

"Hey, watch out who you insult by calling genteel." Luna cocked an eyebrow. "Aurora, amazing work. I can't believe you pulled this together in three days. Bravo."

"I agree," Eldon added. "I've been working on hotel projects for many years as Devon's EA before Gabriel stole me, and I have to say...wow. I think this is going to be one hell of a hotel."

CHAPTER 25
Gabriel

"You wanna tell me why you were such an asshole at the meeting?" Devon asked me when we met for dinner at Alligator Soul on Barnard Street.

I ran my hand through my hair. Devon and I had been friends before he'd even come to work for Rhodes Hotels & Resorts. At work, we kept it professional and maintained a boss-employee etiquette, but when it was just us, I was not his employer.

"I hated how nervous she was," I confessed.

Devon frowned. "Aurora?"

"Yeah."

"She wasn't nervous, she was fucking confident and amazing," Devon was incredulous. "What the fuck, Gabe?"

"She was nervous," I stated. "And she was remembering things I said to her, hurtful fucking things."

"Okay, back it up here, dude. Is this the woman who you fucked up with because of Iris?"

"Yeah."

"And you didn't think to tell me before this meeting?"

I shrugged and was relieved when the server came to take our order because Devon, I knew, was going to rip me a new one.

I'd asked my mother to talk to Nina Davenport and put Aurora on the Miami Hotel project. "I'm delighted to help you get her back, even though you don't deserve her after what a dickhead you've been."

I didn't want anyone to ever know that I had a hand in getting Aurora her promotion. If she ever found out, it would devastate her; she'd think she'd gotten ahead on her back and not her abilities. Nina had assured my mother that she was planning on promoting Aurora anyway, and this would be a great project for her to work on, and all she wanted was the promise that I'd treat Aurora professionally and fairly.

"Did you get her on this project because you want to get into her pants?" Devon demanded.

I glared at him. "You know Nina Davenport? She look like the type who'd dabble in nepotism?"

Devon paused at that and nodded. "Hell, no. And in any case, Aurora knocked it out of the ballpark, dude. Were you not impressed?"

"Yes," I admitted, "absolutely. Why?"

"Because you didn't say anything positive at the meeting. In fact, you were a bit too severe almost to the point of being rude," Devon explained. "Don't get me wrong, no one expects Gabriel Rhodes to hand out compliments but usually you do more than grunt."

I waited to reply until the server left our drinks.

"I was afraid that I'd...slip."

Devon scowled. "What?"

I sighed. "I was way too impressed, and...I...didn't want it to be too obvious."

"Don't worry about that. It wasn't obvious at all. In fact, we all thought you were angry."

"This woman has got me in knots," I muttered. "How the fuck am I supposed to function with her around?"

Devon leaned back, amused. "Wow! Never seen you like this before."

"Like what?"

"Heartsick."

"Fuck you."

"No, it's kinda cute."

"You know what, let's keep the personal shit out of bounds and talk to me about what the fuck is going on with the Munich hotel."

Devon knew when not to push, and this was one of those times. I was not just impressed; I was mesmerized. I also had a hard-on that could drive nails into walls. I could see she was aroused. I could feel her heartbeat all the way from across the table. I wanted her. For a minute, I wondered how it would be if I *asked to see her in her office, laid her on out her desk, and took her hard from behind.* We could then go back to the meeting. We'd both be relaxed and be able to focus on the fucking agenda.

She wore a pale pink sheath dress with nude heels. I wanted so badly to slide my hand between her slender legs and...fuck me!

And while I was trying to get my libido under control, I saw pain flash in her eyes. I knew the instant she remembered some of the horrible shit I'd spewed at her—and I wanted to howl in anger, which was mostly directed toward me. I'd caused her pain, and I was continuing to do so. Maybe it was a mistake to be in proximity of her. She'd keep remembering what an asshole I'd been, and it would hurt her. I didn't want to hurt Aurora; I wanted to love her. I wanted to heal her, have her heal me.

That night, as I lay in bed, I texted her after losing a fight with myself on restrain.

Me: *You were amazing in the meeting today.*

I knew she'd unblocked me, but I didn't know if she'd respond. She did, it took ten minutes, but she did.

Aurora: *Thank you.*

Me: *Devon said that I looked angry. I wasn't angry with you.*

Aurora: *But you were angry?*

Fuck this. I called her. She picked up the phone.

"I was angry with myself. I saw the moment you remembered something I said, and I could see the pain in your eyes and...I'm so sorry," I blurted.

"I thought you were angry with me," she whispered.

"No, baby. Never. I was amazed at your work. Your drawings. Everything. I was angry with myself and then afraid that everybody would see that I was in love with you, and that would embarrass you. I don't know what the fuck I'm doing, Aurora."

I heard her soft laugh. "This might be the first time I've heard you say you didn't know what you were doing."

A smile spread on my face. She was talking to me.

"You reduce me to a spluttering moron."

"Gabriel, I—"

"I could also see when you were aroused. Could you see that I was?" I stroked myself. Having her over the phone reminded me of all the times she'd let me see and hear her come when we couldn't be together. It was almost Pavlovian; she was on the phone, we were both in bed, and I was hard as stone.

"Gabriel," she breathed.

"I wish I'd been sitting next to you, darlin'. I'd drop something on the floor so I could smell you. You were wet, weren't you?"

"I'm going to hang up."

"No, baby. Give me this much. I'm fucking lost without you."

"Gabriel, I can't be some phone whore for you," she raged.

I stilled my hand. "Aurora, you never ever fucking reduce what we had to that. *Got it?*"

Hell, now, I was angry with her.

"Baby, talk to me," I pleaded.

"I was aroused," she breathed. "I looked at your hands and...I can't do this."

"You remembered how I touched you?" She was feeling

vulnerable, and I was enough of a ruthless asshole to press my advantage. "Do you remember how I'd hold your thighs apart when I came inside you?"

She paused for a long time, and I could hear her breathing heavily like she used to when she was excited, wet, and wanting me. Triumph blazed through me.

"I have to go." Her voice was unsteady.

"Come for me instead."

"I can't do this. *I won't do this.*"

I could hear the tears in her voice, and I hated myself for pushing her so hard. "Hey, hey, no crying."

I heard her sniffle.

She hardly ever cried, and it was a testament to how upset I was making her that she even got there. Unlike Iris who used tears to manipulate, Aurora was always controlled and took pride in that.

"I just wanted you to know that I was impressed with you and your work. I can't wait to see this hotel. I know you're going to make it amazing."

"You really think so?"

For the Ice Maiden she portrayed, I knew Aurora had so many self-doubts. She used to confide in me before I'd shattered us by not seeing what Iris was doing to Sophia and my relationship with Aurora.

"Yes, I do. The Art Deco idea is ingenious. I think it'll be a great fusion between styles. Authentically Miami with some Rhodes Southern charm."

"What did you think about the water feature? I was

watching this movie called *A Little Chaos*, and even though I'm not a landscaper, I got the idea from there."

"You want to bring a piece of Versailles to a Rhodes Hotel?"

"You've seen the movie?"

I laughed softly. "Tell me how you'll go about doing it."

She went on excitedly talking about her plans. She came alive. We talked for nearly an hour, and it was the best day I'd had since we broke up.

CHAPTER 26
Aurora

"Aurora?" A woman called out to me while I browsed clothes at Custard Boutique, which specialized in environmentally-friendly clothing.

I turned around, and it was the woman I'd seen Gabriel with, his cousin he'd said. Was she? I pushed that thought aside. Gabriel had never lied to me, and I shouldn't add to his sins.

She held out a hand. "I'm Rose Dixon, Gabe's cousin."

I shook her hand. She knew my name. Why did she know my name?

"I love this place and it's very much your style, I can see," she remarked.

I looked at my white sundress with blue flowers. "Yes, they have some great clothes here."

It was a beautiful Saturday afternoon, and I'd decided to treat myself to some shopping, especially since I was going to Miami Beach soon. I wasn't trying to dress up for Gabriel, absolutely not; I was just upgrading my closet. That was all it was.

Yeah, I didn't believe that either.

"Gabe's told me so much about you," she continued as she pulled out a dress and looked at it critically.

I froze. I wanted to ask what he'd told her, but I decided to keep my mouth shut.

"Oh, honey, he can be a complete git, bless his heart. The family knows that about him." She put the dress back on the rack.

I stood still like a moron for a few seconds and then decided to do what I was here to do, shop.

I looked through the next rack, and Rose kept talking like we were friends.

"I hear you're working on his Miami Beach hotel project. It's going to be amazing. I'm so excited about it."

"Me too," I managed to squeak out. This woman was in my personal space. She was loud, and she was crowding me. It was disconcerting.

"I've been trying to find Gabe a new house." She looked at a sheath dress and handed it to me. "More your style than mine."

I took the pale yellow dress from her. It certainly was.

"A house?"

"Oh, I'm in real estate, honey. And Gabe is selling his place...well, his and hers, which, of course, I'm selling for him."

"Selling his place?" I was now repeating things like an idiot.

She smiled. "Yeah, honey. He doesn't want to live so close to his ex. Don't blame him, she's such a bitch, bless her heart."

I just stared at her, not sure if I could believe that Gabriel was taking such a big step. I never thought he'd do it. He'd always been clear that he wanted his daughter to not choose which parent she spent time with.

"He still wants to stay in The Landings, and I have no idea where Iris will move to and don't care."

We walked around the boutique, looking at clothes while she chattered away.

"He wants a place with a pool, and big enough for Sophia and him and any guests who may come by. He wants room for a studio."

"A studio?" My pulse raced.

"You can work here while I'm out, Aurora."

"No, I need my studio. I've set that up in my second bedroom. I need my draft table to design, and supplies to make models."

"Damn it, I was really hoping you'd stay, and I could come back to you."

"Come back to my place."

"I have Sophia tonight."

"Next week, then."

"I'm going to set up a studio for you here so you can work from my place whenever you want."

We never had the chance to make that happen.

"Yes. Natural light. Room enough to store materials and

make models. I'm assuming that's got something to do with architecture?"

I stopped walking and looked at her. "Why are you talking to me about this, Rose?"

She grinned. "Lord, I thought I was losin' my touch, honey. Cause I'm talkin' away here, and you're not even throwin' me a bone."

"I don't understand."

"He wants to make sure you can work at his new place. What's there to understand, honey?"

I took a deep breath. "We broke up."

"Oh, I think he's hopin' to change that."

"I...I don't think that will happen," I told her sadly.

"Why not? You obviously still love him."

I raised both eyebrows. "Excuse me?"

"Oh, come on, at the restaurant, you were just about ready to poke my eyes out because you thought I was goin' with him. Don't deny it. Woman to woman, I know that look." She put her hands on her hips and looked saucy as hell when she spoke.

"I can't trust him again. He...I...it doesn't matter."

"It does," she replied softly. "I know what he did. I know he's ashamed of himself for hurtin' you. Of taking your childhood, which sounds like it was hard as hell, honey, and usin' that to hit at you."

I hung the sheath dress that she'd given me on a rack. "I don't trust easily. I *never* trust a second time."

She nodded. "Well, why don't we try some dresses and if

you have time, I'd love to have lunch with you. What do you say?"

"Lunch?"

"Yeah. Come on. Let's have some fun."

I bought two sheath dresses, and she bought half the store. Rose was fun and funny, interested, and interesting.

"Why don't you drive me, and I can ask my driver to pick me up at Husk Savannah?" she suggested.

"You want to go there for lunch? It's going to be impossible to get in without a reservation," I warned her.

"They'll seat me regardless," she chuckled with the same confidence Gabriel had. It was their last names and status in society; reservations during lunch hour rush were not an issue.

CHAPTER 27

Aurora

Rose was texting and talking to me while we took the short drive to Husk Savannah. I left my Nissan Leaf with the valet, and we walked inside the exclusive establishment.

She was good company. She spoke of the city, its people, and its architecture with a fondness that was infectious. I found myself warming up to her, her elegance and Southern grace was unmistakable, yet she wore it as lightly as a summer dress.

The restaurant, nestled in the heart of historic Savannah, exuded a charm that was both rustic and refined. Its walls were adorned with contemporary art that somehow felt at home among the antique fixtures. The air was filled with the aroma of Southern cooking, reimagined with a modern twist, a hallmark of Husk Savannah.

I'd been here with Gabriel once. He'd had to leave right after dinner because Sophia had called him. I'd told him to go and had ordered an Uber to drive me back home. One of the many times our time had been cut short by his daughter. I had to keep remembering that and realize that no matter what, Gabriel would never be able to balance being a father with being in a relationship. He'd want his girlfriend to be the one to make allowances and be flexible. I couldn't go back to that—I deserved better.

"Have you been here before?" Rose asked.

I nodded but didn't elaborate. I really didn't want to discuss Gabriel with his cousin. I didn't know why I was here in the first place. She'd just swept me away, and now I was having lunch with a veritable stranger.

"Table for three," she told the maître d'.

"Who is the third person?" I asked as we were shown to our table. We were seated in a cozy corner with a view of the lush, private garden that was a green oasis in the urban landscape.

"Oh, I already had an appointment with an aunt of mine. You don't mind, do you?"

I shrugged. What was having lunch with two strangers instead of one?

A woman dressed in an elegant linen pantsuit walked up to our table, and Rose squealed. She jumped up and gave the woman a hug. She was a stunning woman. I guessed, she was probably in her fifties. She had a fit, petite body. She didn't dye her hair, and it was platinum blonde, cut into a sleek bob. Her makeup was minimal, and she wasn't wearing pearls like most of the women around us were. Instead, she had diamonds, big ones on her ear lobes and her wrists. The rings on her fingers could probably light up a city.

"Hello, dear," she said to me. I stood up. I felt like I should because there was something regal about her.

She held her hand out. "I've been dying to meet you, Aurora."

Her smile was warm, her handshake firm, and her demeanor as inviting as a gentle Southern breeze. I smiled uneasily at her. I had no idea who this woman was.

"I'm Betsy Rhodes. And I hear you're the reason my son these days is as prickly as a patch of briars in a cotton field."

I snapped my mouth shut because I knew it had fallen open.

"Mrs. Rhodes," I managed to say through the constriction in my throat.

"Betsy, please. Mrs. Rhodes was my mother-in-law who's now thankfully passed, bless her heart."

I let out a nervous laugh at that.

"Now, before you think this was some sort of conspiracy to bring us together, let me assure you it most certainly was." Betsy sat down and set her Christian Dior purse on the table.

"I texted her that you and I were having lunch, and she insisted on joining," Rose explained.

"Please tell me that meeting me was perchance, and that you weren't stalking me?" I tried to lighten the mood with some humor because I really needed it.

"Total coincidence," Rose declared.

Gabriel's mother looked at the menu. "Let's eat first, and then we can hash out the other stuff."

What other stuff? This woman was intimidating as hell. I wanted to desperately text Gabriel that I was having lunch with his mother and cousin and that it had nothing to do with me; I'd been maneuvered into it. I doubted he'd be happy that I was meeting his family like this. He'd kept me away from them long enough.

"We must try the shrimp and grits," Betsy suggested, her voice carrying the melody of a life well-lived. "And the catfish is simply divine here, not to mention their take on collard greens. It's like a hug from the inside."

Rose nodded in agreement. "Please, let's not forget the peach cobbler. It's a little slice of heaven."

When the server arrived to get out drinks, Betsy asked for a Ruinart bottle of champagne.

"We must celebrate," she announced, "After all, I'm meeting Gabriel's first love."

"Mrs. Rhodes, I—"

"Betsy, darlin'," she cut me off and winked at me. "Come on. You must know he's in love with you. Don't get me wrong, the idiot fucked up, big time, and I think you should make him crawl on broken glass, but the fact is that he's in love with you."

"I agree," Rose mused. "Never seen him like this."

I closed my eyes for an instant. "I should go," I said and rose.

"Sit down," Betsy ordered. "Now."

I didn't want to be rude, so I sat back down. And the truth was she was a little scary.

"He told me how he treated you. And I want you to

know, Rafe, Rose, and I have been telling him to get rid of that trash he married for years."

The server brought our wine and made a production of opening it and filling our glasses before setting it in a silver ice bucket.

"To women who know how to make men pay." Betsy raised her glass.

"Amen." Rose raised her glass.

"Cheers," I said, resigned.

After we ordered food, Betsy looked pointedly at me. "I didn't want you to think that his family was okay with how he behaved. We're not. And truth be told, neither is he. But he's made his bed and blah blah."

"I don't know what you want me to say," I sighed.

"Tell me about the Miami Beach project," she urged.

"Oh, yes, Devon told me that you gave an amazing presentation," Rose added. "He absolutely loved your sketches."

"Are you still sleeping with Devon, Rose?" Betsy tilted her head to look at her niece.

Rose grinned. "Now, Auntie Betsy, you know, a good Southern girl doesn't kiss and tell."

These women reminded me of Nina, Luna, Stella, and the other women I worked with. They were strong and confident. They believed in doing something meaningful with their lives. Betsy talked about her charities with passion, and I found out that Rose had turned away from her father's money and never touched her trust fund because she wanted to make it on her own, which she had.

Our conversation flowed effortlessly, touching on art, architecture, and the subtle beauty of Savannah. They asked about my work, genuinely interested in my vision and experience.

As an introvert, I tired quickly in social settings, but not this time. I was engaged and enthralled. So, after dessert, when we dawdled over coffee and petit fours, I didn't mind.

Betsy shared stories of her move from Boston to Savannah, the cultural adjustments, and the love she had grown to feel for this city. "It's about finding beauty in the new, in the unexpected." There was a twinkle in her eyes. "It's about building bridges, between places, between people."

Rose chimed in with tales of how she navigated the Savannah society set. "Honestly, Auntie Betsy is a breath of fresh air. I'd be dyin' if it was just my mother and other aunts all tryin' to get me to become a Southern belle."

"The rest of the family doesn't like me, darling," Betsy informed me.

"But since she's Mrs. Atticus Rhodes the Third, she's the top society matron, and everyone genuflects to her," Rose chuckled.

Betsy snorted in a most unladylike manner. "It's the Rhodes name and the money. The thing is, I come from money, so I didn't really care about how much Atticus had."

"Yeah, but you also didn't care about the status you got as becoming Mrs. Rhodes."

She laughed. "Sometimes I wished he had no money, then it would've been easier because his family was a nightmare."

"Uncle Atticus told them all to fuck themselves," Rose said proudly. "You should see them even now, madly in love."

Betsy blushed a little, and I was charmed. "Well, I don't know about that. We've been together for forty-five years now. It's been like all long marriages. There were ups and there were downs."

"Gabe thought he'd have that with Iris," Rose told me softly.

"We warned him," Betsy shook her head.

"But she was pregnant." Rose poured some more tea for Betsy and me. "He tried to stay married, and when he couldn't, he thought he'd at least give Sophia the best of both worlds."

I looked from one woman to the other. They were trying to help me understand Gabriel's behavior. They didn't have to. I understood just fine.

"One of the things that appealed most about Gabriel to me was how dedicated he's to Sophia." I made a pattern on the tablecloth with my finger as I spoke, feeling emotional and not wanting to look at anyone.

Betsy put her hand on mine and squeezed. "I'm sorry about how your parents treated you."

I looked at her in shock. She knew. Gabriel had told her about me. He'd told her about us. He'd told her how badly he'd behaved. He hadn't hidden a thing. And even though I didn't want to, I felt something warm run through me at that validation.

"I'm friends with Nina Davenport, and she thinks very highly of you." Betsy turned my hand and clutched it, palm to palm and smiled warmly at me. "And Rafe was ready to steal you from Gabe, but he said he couldn't. You are too much in love with my older son. You were kind to my granddaughter when you didn't have to be. She's a good kid, but it's not easy with that mother of hers."

I pulled my hand away from her, not wanting to let her in. She was after all Gabriel's mother. I'd probably never see her again after this lunch. "I really liked meeting Rafe, and Sophia was *very* courageous to come and talk to me."

Betsy looked me in the eye, and I saw sincerity on her face. "He messed up, no question about it. But if you care for him, I implore to you, please give him a chance to make it up to you."

"Betsy...I..." I shrugged because I didn't know how to respond.

She patted my hand. "Just think about it. And whether you get back with him or not, I'd like to propose more lunches like this. What do you say, Rose?"

"Absolutely."

"Now, I hear you sold that monstrosity the Deluca's built," Betsy stage whispered to Rose. "Do you know that building, Aurora?"

"Yes, and I agree it's a monstrosity."

Smoothly, we went back to talking about everything and nothing. I was shocked to find that I spent nearly three hours in the company of two women I didn't know well, and the kick of it was that I wanted to do it again.

CHAPTER 28

Gabriel

"Stop flirting with her," I warned Devon.

Aurora had stepped away to use the ladies' room while we were having dinner at Forte dei Marmi after a long day of meetings and walk throughs of the existing hotel in Miami Beach that we were going to convert into a Rhodes property.

"You've got your head up your ass." Devon didn't hide his amusement.

"And what the fuck was that about how you'd like to show her your suite?" I demanded.

"Because she's staying in a single room, and she could see the layout of a suite in a Rhodes Hotel. For Pete's sake, Gabe, get a fucking grip, will you?" Devon shook his head as if disgusted with me. "She's being professional. I'm being professional."

"And what am I being?"

"Insufferable."

I drank some of my after-dinner espresso. It *had* been a long day. I wasn't involved in the type of meetings I had today—but I did it to spend time with Aurora. I loved seeing her in work mode. She was smart, intelligent, and charming. She was also tough as nails. When one of the hotel directors had been rude to her, making a veiled sexist comment, she'd neatly and nicely put him in his place without breaking a sweat or alienating the rest of the room. I was ready to punch him while she'd been the fucking epitome of grace.

"I want Nathan out on his ass as soon as possible. He doesn't get to talk to women like he did with Aurora," I told Devon, whose team Nathan was in.

"On it."

My phone beeped with a calendar alert. "Fuck, I have to go. I have a meeting with the Bangkok team in thirty minutes."

"What I don't understand is what you're doing here in the first place? I've never seen you get involved in a project this early on," Devon commented.

"Fuck if I know," I replied honestly.

Aurora came back then, and I felt my heart stutter. She'd been working all day, and even now, while I was so tired, I felt like a creek bed in August, all dried up and cracked; she looked fresh as a daisy.

Her dark hair was tied up in a ponytail with a few wisps of hair around her face. Her lips were devoid of lipstick, but she'd put something glossy on them when she'd gone to the restroom. Her face looked dewy. And her brown eyes were full of energy.

"Thank you so much for dinner." She smiled at me, it wasn't one of the smiles she used to give me when we were together; this was her professional smile.

We'd reached a sort of détente after we'd talked the other night on the phone when I'd told her she'd been amazing at the project kickoff meeting. I'd stopped apologizing for being a jackass to her and stopped telling her that I was still madly in love with her, and she was treating me like a client. I fucking hated it.

Aurora had chosen to stay at the Rhodes Hotel on South Beach, whereas I was at the family home. Although I extended an invitation for her and Devon to join me, they politely declined. Devon preferred to maintain a suite at the hotel during week, going to his home in Key Largo for the weekend.

"Your car picking you up?" Devon asked as we went out of the restaurant.

"Yeah." It was a good thirty-minute walk to the house, while the Rhodes Hotel was only a couple of blocks away.

"Well, goodnight then," Aurora said to me.

"I can drop you both off," I offered when the car and driver arrived.

"It's a short walk Gabe, and I need it." Devon patted his stomach. He was wearing shorts, leather thongs, and a Hawaiian shirt. He had that whole beach bum vibe going for him. The way Aurora looked at him made the green-eyed monster inside me roar.

Was she into him? No fucking way!

"Actually, I need to talk to Aurora for a minute, so I'll

make sure she gets back." I had no idea what I wanted to talk to her about.

Devon looked at Aurora as if waiting for her to assent, and when she did, he walked away whistling Air Supply's *Lost in Love*.

Aurora folded her arms.

"Should we get into the car?" I gestured to the Cadillac.

"I prefer to walk."

"It's late, and I said I'll drop you off."

"I'll walk," she said stubbornly.

"Get in the fucking car, Aurora." The woman was driving me up the wall.

"No," she replied calmly. "What do you want to talk about?"

"Stop flirting with Devon. He's a total man whore."

The shock on her face was almost comical, and I knew she wanted to knee me in the nuts.

"You're out of your ever-lovin' mind, Gabriel Rhodes."

You have no idea, darlin'.

"I'm just saying that—"

"What is wrong with you?"

"Me?" I leaned to bring my face close to her. "I'm fucking jealous of every man you talk to. And working with you is driving me crazy."

She swallowed. "That sounds like a *you* problem."

"I want you," I admitted.

She closed her eyes and when she opened them, the fight was gone. "You can't do this. Is this why you're here today?

Devon mentioned you never get involved in a project this early on."

Son of a bitch. He had to tell her.

"Baby, I have a chance here to see you on the regular and you think I'd let that opportunity go?"

"Why? We're never happening. Don't you get that?" The pain and desperation in her voice all but killed me.

"Baby, give me a chance." I was ready to plead. To beg. Hell, I'd do anything if she'd just let me try again to show her how much she meant to me.

"Why?"

"Because I love you," I snapped. "And you love me."

She shook her head. "I'm not walking into the kind of pain you subjected me to."

"I've sorted things out with Sophia and—"

"This isn't about your daughter; this is about *you*," she cut me off. "You didn't respect me, Gabriel. I didn't see it then because I didn't want to, because I was so blinded by how much I felt for you. I don't have blinders on anymore. You ignored me when it wasn't convenient for you. You came to me when it was. The minute I didn't conform to whatever it was you wanted, you dumped me. You don't deserve a second chance. You didn't even deserve a first."

A group of people came out of the restaurant, and I took her hand in mine, leading her silently to the car. I opened the door and waited.

She got in, obviously exasperated, but understanding that we were not going to hash this out with an audience.

"Carlos, we're going to the house," I said to the driver before I raised the privacy screen.

"Gabriel, it's late, and we have early meetings, so—"

"You think I don't know that I don't deserve you? Fuck, Aurora, I was just as blind as you. But I don't have blinders on now either, and what I know is that for the past ten years, the only happiness I've had is with my daughter and you. Real happiness. The kind of joy that makes me want to get the fuck out of bed in the morning."

"Like I said, Gabriel sounds like a *you* problem." She was looking out of the window.

I put a hand on her chin and gently turned her face to look at me. "Say you don't love me."

Her eyes went glassy. "Fuck you, Gabriel."

She hardly ever cursed, and the fact that she was, told me the depth of how much pain I'd caused her.

"Baby, say the word," I joked.

Her eyes flashed anger. *So*, maybe my timing was off.

"We're done. Don't you get that?"

"Say you don't love me," I challenged again.

She licked her lips. Her arms were still crossed as if she was holding herself together. "I don't."

"Say, Gabriel, I don't love you."

She closed her eyes. "Stop it," she hissed.

"Say it, god damn it, because I haven't slept in months because I ache for you. Whenever I fucking smell lavender, I get hard. I pick up my phone at night and want to call you, talk to you. I want to fuck you, make love to you, be with you. So, say you don't love me or say you'll give me a fucking chance," I bellowed.

The car stopped. We were at the family house. I didn't know how I was going to maneuver her inside. I knew there was no chance I'd get her into bed, and the truth was, regardless of how much I wanted her, sex wasn't going to solve our problems. It would feel damn good, but I wanted her to trust me again, believe in us again. That meant I couldn't just take advantage of her desire for me.

Her eyes were wide, and I knew she was holding back tears. "What does giving you a chance mean?"

Her voice was so low that I almost wasn't sure she'd said what she had. My heart, which had all but stopped, began to slam against my ribs.

"I'd like for us to date. Go out. Spend time with one another."

She just kept looking at me.

"No sex," I added, "Not until you trust me again." I was an idiot. I wouldn't be able to last with her smelling like she did. Even now, the need to bury myself inside her was debilitating. But I'd just have to curb my libido and rebuild what I'd destroyed.

"Why are you doing this? You can have any woman. Just—"

"I don't want any woman. I want you. Only you."

"How do you know?"

"Because I tried. Last time I was here with Beau...Beau Bodine," I explained, and she nodded, "I tried."

The flash of jealousy in her eyes made me feel better, made me feel there was hope.

"You tried?" The words seemed to have been choked out of her.

"Yeah. I didn't want anyone, not even for a quick fuck. I can't see anyone but you."

She looked at her hands. "I wanted to fall for Callum."

"Pierce?" *The son of a bitch!*

"I couldn't. I tried as well."

I wanted to ask how far did it go. Did he kiss her? Touch her? Where did he touch her? Jesus! I'd never been a jealous or possessive man. Even when I was young and dating, I wasn't an alpha male asshole. But with Aurora, I had this Neanderthal inside me, beating his fucking chest and roaring, *"My woman."*

"Give us another chance, baby." I was enough of a businessman to know when I had someone where I wanted them.

She looked at me. "What will dating do, Gabriel?"

"It'll show you that you can trust me. That you can believe in me. Give me this one chance, and you'll never have to give me another."

She licked her lips, and I had to stop myself from pulling her into me and devouring those glossy, cupid bow lips.

My phone beeped with a calendar alert, and I sighed.

"You have a meeting." She knew the different sounds my phone made.

"With the Bangkok team."

"Go for your meeting. Your driver can drop me off."

I stroked her cheek with the back of my hand. She didn't move away, but she didn't give me a sign that she wanted more. Usually, she'd nuzzle my hand and kiss my knuckles.

"Goodnight, Aurora."

"Goodnight, Gabriel."

As the car drove away, I felt the band around my chest that I'd been wearing since we ended, become just a little looser. She was giving me a chance, and I wasn't going to fuck it up, come hell or high water.

CHAPTER 29

Aurora

"I'm an idiot," I told Luna and Stella as we lounged by Stella's pool in her incredible garden on the Friday evening a week after I came back from Miami.

The three of us were each holding a spoon as we indulged in a tub of rocky road ice cream.

It was a gorgeous day; and we'd spent the afternoon by the pool, yakking as we drank colorful drinks with umbrellas in them.

"We're all idiots when we're in love," Luna announced, licking her spoon.

"When were you in love?" I asked, curious.

Stella guffawed. "She's been hung up on Dominic Calder for years."

I raised an eyebrow. "*The* Dominic Calder who won the Pritzker Architecture Prize a couple of years ago?" It was only one of the most prestigious awards in our business.

"First, I'm not *hung* up on him. Dom and I sort of grew up together."

"As in, Dom's mother was the help at the Steele Estate," Stella explained.

"Oh my god, this is so juicy. I want to know more."

"Nothing to know," Luna snapped. "Dom lives in New York, and I see him maybe once a year. He's condescending, and I'm rude. His mother and my brother, who's, for some reason, Dom's best friend, try to keep the peace between us. Miss Abigail all but raised Lev and me."

I knew Luna's parents weren't the cuddly sort. Her mother was a proper Southern lady who wore pearls and pantyhose at eight in the morning; and her father the proper Southern gentleman who played golf now that he was retired. Luna's brother Lev ran the family business, which was forestry. The core of Steele Corporation was managing vast tracts of Southern pine and hardwood forests sustainably since Lev had taken over and supplied raw materials to various industries.

"She's hung up on him," Stella assured me.

Luna growled at her and dipped her spoon into the ice cream.

"And how about you, Stella?" I asked.

Stella was in her late twenties and single like me. "I've dated but never fallen in love."

"She's waiting for Prince Charming," Luna mocked.

Stella sighed. "That's true. I want someone who is warm and funny, loves to go dancing, wants to have a house in the country with a big garden, and wants to fill that house with children."

"Add a white picket fence to that, and we're set." Luna patted her friend's shoulder.

I arranged my sundress around my thighs. "I don't think falling in love is all that it's cracked up to be. My heart hurts all the time. Every time I see him...I want to climb him like a tree."

"I don't blame you. Gabe Rhodes is hot." Stella fanned herself with her hand.

"He's been a dick to her," Luna pointed out.

"A dick who's all but on his knees apologizing," Stella reminded her. "And I hear he's put his and his ex-wife's house on the market and is looking to buy something new. She's apparently telling the world that Gabe is screwing her over."

"What nonsense," Luna muttered. "Everyone knows that he gave her a shit ton of money, and it's not like she's running low. Her family has got plenty."

"But not her." Stella waved her spoon. "She apparently blew through her trust fund and she's basically living off of Gabe. If he takes the house away, she's going to have to buy one. She's gonna fight tooth and nail."

"How do y'all know so much about everyone?" I gasped.

"Honey, this is Savannah; gossip is the lubricant that oils the machine of this city," Luna grinned. "And the social circuit we're a part of is incestuous. Everyone knows everyone's business."

"Tell me about it. Remember when Nina got divorced?

Everyone knew that her husband had cheated on her with that tramp Angela." Stella shook her head.

"When was this?" I asked. I knew Nina was divorced, but I didn't know for how long.

"Six years ago, somethin' like that," Luna recollected. "That was a clusterfuck, pardon my French. Angela was his physical trainer. Talk about a cliché."

"Nina kicked him out," Stella continued.

"But he screwed her on money in the divorce. Which was why Stella asked her father to invest in Savannah Lace," Luna mentioned.

I knew that Stella was a partner; I didn't know how she'd become one.

Stella's father was Senator Baron Hunt.

"That was nice of your father." I scraped the last of the ice cream and then set the empty carton on the table next to my lounge chair.

Stella, who was sitting across from me on another chair, picked up the carton to look in it.

"Baron Hunt is anything but nice," Luna snorted. "In return for the money she now has to go to all the Hunt family events; and her father decides who'll escort her."

"Your father is setting up dates for you?" I chuckled.

"All asshole men who want to marry the *sweet* Hunt girl," Luna laughed.

"Until they find out that maybe I'm not so *sweet*," Stella smiled and fluttered her eyelashes.

But Stella *was* sweet. She wasn't exactly as introverted as me, but she wasn't bold and audacious like Luna either. She was a loner though—and even though I knew she and Luna were close, I always felt that Stella kept to herself, didn't let anyone in to deep. I could relate.

I knew that Stella's mother, who'd passed when she was a baby, was from Venezuela, and she, like me, was more brown than white. She wasn't close to her father's second wife or her half siblings I'd deduced from the ways she spoke of her family.

Despite Stella and Luna having grown up with one or two parents, they, like me, felt abandoned by them.

Maybe that's why I felt this kinship with them, because we all understood what it meant to make our own way in this world.

"So, when's your *give-me-a-chance* date with Gabe?" Luna wanted to know.

"Tomorrow. Lunch. That's if he keeps it." I was keeping my expectations low. He'd canceled so many dates that I was certain he'd do the same again, or he'd keep this one and go right back to it soon enough.

I was convinced that Gabriel saw me as someone he'd failed and wanted to right the wrong to soothe his ego. I didn't think he loved me because if he did he'd never have treated me the way he did. I'd said yes to giving him a chance because I knew in my heart that he'd blow it, and when he did, I wasn't going to let it crush me as I had that first time. This time, I'd be ready for it.

"Where's he taking you?" Stella leaned back on her lounge chair.

Luna took her robe off and dove into the pool. They'd

both been swimming by the time I got to Stella's place. She'd said she'd lend me a swimsuit, but I was not in the mood for a swim, regardless of the heat.

"He didn't say." I watched Luna do the breaststroke gracefully. "Just said, dress casually."

"Hey, are you giving him a real chance or a pity one?" Stella asked.

"A real chance, but I know he's going to screw it up, Stella. I have no doubt about that."

"That's not giving him a real chance," Stella protested.

"That may be so, but it's the best I can do," I admitted sadly.

CHAPTER 30
Gabriel

"I t's going to be fine, Daddy," Sophia told me as I got ready for my lunch date with Aurora.

A dinner date could convey post-dinner sex pressure, so I'd asked her out to lunch.

"I don't know, Sweetpea, she's pretty pissed with me." I put on my watch and looked at my daughter, who was sitting on my bed, holding a pillow on her lap.

"And the biggest, most positive thing will be that I won't be calling you in the middle of your date." Her blue eyes swarmed with guilt.

I sat down next to her and took her hands in mine. "You can always call me. Just because I'm on a date with Aurora or at work or anywhere doesn't mean that you can't. You need me, you call."

"I know. Dr. Ryan talked to me about the difference between calling you when I need something versus when I want to mess up your date."

I sighed. "Sweetpea, I don't want you to carry this guilt around."

"Because Mama manipulated me?"

"I'm not going to badmouth your mother in front of you," I said emphatically. "We can discuss this if you want in our next session with Dr. Ryan. But you have no reason to feel guilty. Whatever went wrong between Aurora and me had to do with me. I messed up, big time."

"Because of me." Her eyes filled with tears.

I pulled her into my arms and hugged her. "No. Not because of you. I can be an asshole all by myself with no help at all, Sweetpea."

She let out a watery laugh. "Language, Daddy."

I pulled away so I could look at her. She was gorgeous, this child of mine and I was so incredibly proud of her for owning up to her mistakes. To make amends. It was something I was learning from her.

"You're going to be okay with Nana and Grandpa?" My parents were taking Sophia to a summer party at Hilton Head, and she was excited about it.

Neither Iris nor her parents would be there, which I think was for the best so Sophia could freely enjoy herself. During therapy, I'd discovered that it wasn't just Iris who put pressure on Sophia to bring her parents back together; Iris's parents, Doug, and Cindy Cook, had also been urging her to convince me to scrap the divorce.

I'd met with Doug and Cindy and told them that Sophia would not be visiting with them unsupervised from now on.

"Gabe, she's our granddaughter," Cindy protested.

"Who you've been messin' up, Cindy. Asking a kid to save her parents' marriage that's been dead for over four years? I mean, come on."

"This is all because you began dating that woman," Cindy snapped. "Iris told us how you and she were all but living together, you were a family."

"We were never living together. We lived in separate homes."

"That were connected," Douglas interjected, "Come on, Gabe. Enough is enough. Get back with Iris and reclaim your family. This is not helping anyone, especially Sophia."

"You're right. Living so close together is not good for Sophia, which is why I've put the houses on the market. Rose is looking for something for Sophia and me."

"What about Iris?" Cindy asked.

"Iris needs to find a place too."

Cindy and Douglas looked at one another. "I'm assuming you're paying for this house, son?" My former father-in-law used his condescending tone.

"No. I gave her a lumpsum, more than the prenup even required, so she's on her own."

"But she doesn't have any money. You have to pay her alimony," Cindy blurted out.

I didn't know about Iris's money problems, but I knew she spent easily, and it hadn't mattered when we were together. But now, her problems were her own.

"I paid her a lumpsum in lieu of regular payments," I explained. They knew all this. Iris knew all this, and yet I couldn't help but feel that I was being gouged for money.

"But you have so much," Cindy insisted.

"So do you, Cindy." And on that note, I'd ended the conversation.

But it started to make sense to me why Iris was so persistent about getting back into the marriage. She'd probably gone through the lumpsum as she had her trust fund. How she'd gone through that much money wasn't a surprise, considering how she spent on clothes, jewelry, and travel.

She wasn't in love with me. I don't think she'd ever been. She'd been in love with the Rhodes name and money, the social status that came with being Mrs. Rhodes.

"It's all set with Harrison," my mother told me when she and my father came to pick up Sophia.

"Thanks, Mama." I gave her a quick hug.

"Oh, and I don't know if Rose told you, but I had lunch with Aurora."

I gaped at her. "Excuse me?"

"Yes. Several days ago," she said nonchalantly.

"Mama," I warned.

"She bumped into Rose, and they decided to have lunch at Husk Savannah, and I joined them. She's nice."

"Your mother said she's very beautiful," my father added.

"She's *very* nice." Sophia leaned into my father, who had an arm wrapped around her.

I ran a hand through my hair. "Christ, Mama."

"It's fine. It was fun. She's smart and sharp. I liked her very much. Try to not fuck this up, okay?"

"Language, Nana," Sophia teased.

"Honey, *you* are not allowed to swear, but I'm in my sixties, and I'll say fuck if I want to."

"But it's not ladylike." Sophia winked at my father.

"That's true. Very unladylike," my father agreed.

"You like it when I'm unladylike," Betsy Rhodes, who didn't have much of the South in her, said in front of her son and granddaughter.

"*Eww*, Nana," Sophia protested.

"I really didn't need that image in my head, Mama." I kissed her cheek. Even though Rafe and I made faces when they used to (and still did) get affectionate, I absolutely adored how my parents loved each other. I'd wanted that. I'd never had it.

I called Harrison, my mother's cook, and checked for the third time that morning that everything was set the way I wanted.

"Honest to god, Gabe, you're pushin' it with all the nagging. So, cut it out. It's all set. Bring your lady over, okay?"

"The champagne and—"

Harrison hung up on me. He'd known me since I was a teenager when he began to cook for my parents, and he was, in many ways, family. I'd told him what I'd wanted for my first date with Aurora, and he'd promised to deliver.

CHAPTER 31
Aurora

I wore linen pants with a linen blouse and sandals. There, that was casual enough. The fact that half my closet was out on my bed was another matter. I was nervous about seeing Gabriel again. It felt like a first date with crazy baggage.

Since our talk in Miami Beach, he'd pretty much disappeared from my professional setting, leaving me to work with Devon and his team. But that didn't mean we weren't in touch. He sent text messages. He wished me good morning and goodnight like he used to when we were dating. But we didn't talk on the phone in the evenings because that had always been a precursor to phone sex.

"Can you tell me now where we're going?" I asked after we'd been driving for fifteen minutes.

He was in jeans, a T-shirt, and moccasins. He glanced at me, his eyes covered with sunglasses. A rush went through me. That was the other problem with this relationship or whatever this was. How did a man who looked like Gabriel find me interesting? Don't get me wrong, I knew I was nice enough looking, but Gabriel was handsome. The kind that gets noticed. He walked into a restaurant, and you could all but hear half the female population their sigh. Added to that, he was successful in his own right despite having inherited his wealth. He was hardworking. He was a dedicated father. From what I could see, he was close to his family and had authentic relationships with them. A man who was all this would obviously want someone better than me, wouldn't he? Even my parents didn't want me, as Gabriel had reminded me.

Again, all my insecurities started to bubble up. I couldn't help myself. It was one of the reasons why I let Gabriel get away with so much the first time we were together. I was always afraid of losing him. I was scared that if I made any demands or didn't give in, he'd walk. I mean, why shouldn't he? Everyone else had.

"I'm taking you to my family estate," he murmured.

I looked at my clothes. "Gabriel, I'm not dressed to—"

"My parents are not at home. Don't worry. I know you've already met Mama, so—"

"How do you know?"

"She told me."

Of course, she did. "It wasn't a secret or anything. I just... I didn't know how to bring it up without it sounding weird."

He laughed, and there went my panties. I should've brought a spare.

"She told me she liked you very much and that I shouldn't fuck this up."

My heart hammered in my chest. I so much had wanted to meet his parents and have them accept me and that it was already done was oddly satisfying, so I couldn't understand why I felt bereft.

"My father is looking forward to meeting you, and I promise we'll make that happen, but not on our first date." He put a hand on mine, which was resting on my thigh.

"So...why are we going there?"

"Now, that's a surprise." He stroked my hand. "Hey, let the worries go. It's a beautiful day in Savannah, and, for a change, not hotter than Hades. So, let's enjoy ourselves, yeah?"

I was wound up so tight that I didn't know how to relax. I didn't know what to expect. I didn't know how to handle this Gabriel, the one who was solicitous and...wait, he'd always been like this. When we were together, he was warm and affectionate. He laughed a lot and made me laugh. This was the normal Gabriel, the one I knew. But breaking up the way we had made me distrust everything he did and question how he behaved.

"You know what? You should just take me home," I blurted out.

Gabriel stroked my hand. "Why, baby?"

"I...I don't think this will work. I'm just winding myself

up, and I don't trust you. And I keep wondering what you're up to and how I'll get hurt. It's just too much."

He removed his hand from mine and turned on his blinker as he turned right. We were in front of a gate, and it opened automatically.

"I know you have doubts," he continued as if I'd just not had half a meltdown. "But let's just have lunch. And then see how it goes, yeah?"

As Gabriel's car rolled down the winding driveway of the Rhodes estate on the Isle of Hope, my heart thumped in a rhythm that mirrored the uneven cobblestones beneath us. The sprawling oaks, draped with Spanish moss, created a canopy that whispered of old Savannah's elegance and secrets.

"I feel like a scared filly that's ready to bolt," I confessed.

"I know," he whispered.

"I'm sorry."

"Don't say that, Aurora. The fault here is mine and mine alone. Let me show you how it can be?"

"That's the problem," I wailed softly, "I know how it can be. I was there."

He parked in front of a mansion that looked like something out of the movies. I got out of the car, gawking and thinking about Tara from *Gone with The Wind*.

Gabriel joined me. He put his arm around me and kissed the side of my head. "I promise, baby, it's going to be different...better this time."

I leaned into him, feeling miserable. "It was fine last time."

"No."

I turned to face him. "What do you mean? You were always like this when we went out. You were nice and charming and fun and funny. While I was...well, me."

He smiled. "And what does that mean?"

I shrugged. He put a hand behind me and yanked the hairband off my ponytail like he used to. When my hair fell, he ran his fingers through the tresses.

"You're sweet. You're loving. You're affectionate. And so fucking sexy that I'm always hard or semi-hard around you."

I looked down at his crotch, and he chuckled. "I've got my hands in your hair; yeah, I'm turned on."

I looked up at him. "I don't know how to do this."

"Don't worry about doing anything. Just have lunch with me. It'll be fun."

"It was always fun when we were together," I admitted.

"May I kiss you?" he asked.

I licked my lips automatically and saw raw desire flicker in his eyes.

"Bad idea?"

I shook my head. I couldn't form words. I was so scared. If I let him in, he'd hurt me again.

He leaned and brushed his lips against mine, gentle as a whisper.

"Come on, let me show you your surprise."

He held out his arm, and I slid my hand through it. "It's a short walk."

"This house...mansion...palace...whatever...is stunning."

"Yeah? We can go inside after lunch, and you can tell me all about the style of the building."

"You already know." He was a hotelman; he knew his architecture.

"I love seeing things from your perspective."

He guided me through the garden on a cobblestone path, which brought us to a grassy knoll.

The riverside setup took my breath away—a beautifully laid-out picnic on the lush banks overlooking the gently flowing Skidaway River. Under the canopy of an old Chinquapin oak tree, on a large carpet with cushions spread around for comfort was a spread that looked like it had leaped out of a gourmet magazine.

"I wanted to do something special," his voice was laced with a mix of nervousness and excitement, "something intimate, to show you how much I've missed us."

How was I supposed to resist him?

"This is beautiful, Gabriel." I was genuinely touched by his effort.

I took my sandals off and sat down on the soft carpet, and Gabriel did the same.

I couldn't stop the smile from taking over my face.

His eyes reflected the clear blue sky above us. "I may not cook, Aurora, but I know how much those dinners you made meant to both of us. This is my way of saying thank you."

"Ah...you didn't cook this?"

He laughed. "This is courtesy of Harrison, my parents' cook."

Of course, this was a world where people had cooks and lived in palaces.

Harrison had outdone himself, I thought, or maybe this was just a regular Saturday afternoon for him. There were delicate sandwiches with a variety of fillings, from classic cucumber to shrimp remoulade. A salad of mixed greens, edible flowers, and a light vinaigrette sat beside a platter of assorted cheeses and fruits. Fresh iced tea, garnished with mint and lemon, sparkled in crystal glasses, promising refreshment.

A bottle of white wine and one of champagne rested in an ice bucket.

Gabriel opened the champagne, and I held our glasses so he could pour the golden liquid into them.

"Thank you for giving me this chance." He touched his glass to mine.

"Thank you for wanting the chance," I replied and saw the relief he felt at my words.

I realized then that he'd been as nervous as me. Maybe this wasn't some 'let's make it right' endeavor. Maybe he meant it when he said he loved me.

I drank the champagne, leaning against a pillow, watching the river flowing quietly, its movements a subtle reminder of time passing, of moments to be cherished.

"This is very serene."

"Mama loves to spend time here. This is her and my father's picnic spot. I told her I was borrowing it. She approved."

"And how many picnics have you had here?" I teased.

"You're my first, and I hope my only."

My breath caught. "You have to stop saying things like that."

"Even if they're true?"

I nodded.

"Why?"

"Because I can't believe you."

"Yet."

"What?"

He brushed his lips against mine, gently, softly, no pressure. "You can't believe me yet."

"I liked meeting your mother," I changed the topic. "She's not what I expected."

Gabriel laughed, a sound that seemed to make the very air around us lighter. "That's one way to describe her. She's definitely not your typical Southern matriarch."

"No, she's not."

"What did you expect?" He was leaning lying on the side, his elbow holding him up.

I shrugged.

"Someone like Iris?" he guessed.

I nodded.

"My family never liked her."

"I gathered."

"I married her because she got pregnant. We'd been dating for a few months, and if she hadn't gotten pregnant, we'd have broken up. I didn't love her. I liked her fine enough. I thought love would come."

I set my glass down and picked up a sandwich, so I'd

have something to do. I set it on a small plate. "You want one?"

"I'll get one shortly. I want to finish my champagne."

"I haven't had breakfast," I confessed. "I was too nervous about today to eat."

"I was nervous too. But I can eat through anything. I have an iron constitution."

"I remember." Nothing interfered with Gabriel's appetite...for food and sex.

"I never fell in love with Iris." He watched me as he spoke. I ate one sandwich and then started another. The bread was homemade, and I had no idea how something as simple as a sandwich could be so delicious.

I set a half-eaten sandwich down and filled first his and then my glass with more champagne. "Did you become friends?"

"Not really. She isn't my type," he said blandly. "She cares too much about status, money...appearances. Maybe it's Rhodes arrogance...probably is, but Rafe and I were raised to not give a shit about those things."

"That must've been freeing."

"Very. Rafe didn't want to join the company and my parents were cool with that. I did, and they were happy about that as well. Dad didn't hang around long after I took over. He retired and barely pays attention to what I do, not even showing up for board meetings."

I couldn't stop looking at him, wanting him. We'd talked about his life and his wife before, but this was a more intimate conversation that included the rest of his family, which hadn't been the case earlier. I knew he was divorced and the issues he faced currently with her, but not the past.

"What does he do now?"

"I thought he'd play golf but instead he got involved with the Rhodes Charitable Foundation. My mother has always been."

I picked up a cherry tomato from the salad bowl and popped it into my mouth. "Do you want me to put a plate of salad together for you?"

"Yes, please."

He sat up, and we ate as we talked. We finished the bottle of champagne and then the bottle of Chablis that had been resting in the ice bucket.

The conversation flowed as easily as the river beside us. We talked about everything and nothing. It felt like we were rediscovering one another, peeling back layers with each shared laugh and look.

I lay down on my back as the sun started to flirt with the horizon. "I'm tipsy."

"Me too."

"How am I going to get home if you can't drive?"

"We'll get a driver to take us."

He cleared the remnants of our picnic, putting them in a wicker basket that had been resting by the carpet. And then he lay down next to me. We lay, staring up at the skies.

He reached out for my hand, and I let him hold it.

"Gabriel," I began, my heart finding courage in the beauty of the moment, "I was scared...still am. Afraid of being hurt again. But today...this feels right."

His hand squeezed mine. "I know I've made mistakes, Aurora. But I want to build something with you, something lasting. And I'm willing to work for it every day if you let me."

"I'm going to need time," I warned him.

"Take all the time, baby. I'm not going anywhere."

"What if you get tired of waiting for me?"

He turned and put a hand on my waist, so I'd face him. He stroked my cheek and smiled at me. "You're the love of my life, Aurora Turner. I will wait for you until eternity if that's what it takes."

My eyes filled with tears. "You have to stop saying things like this."

"Don't cry, baby." He pulled me closer and kissed me. I opened for him, and he tasted me, his tongue touching mine, invading me, taking me over.

I moaned softly and felt his hand on my waist clench. I thought he'd move the hand to get more aggressive, but he didn't. He just kept kissing me like we had all the time in the world.

After the picnic when he dropped me off at my doorstep, he hugged me, and I clung to him, wanting more kisses.

"I'm going to come in my jeans, baby," he said hoarsely.

I looked down at the bulge in his pants and couldn't help myself.

"Eyes up here, darling. Stop looking because then I will come and embarrass myself," he joked.

I smiled shyly at him and went on tiptoe to brush my lips against his. "Thank you for today. I had a really good time."

"Me too, baby."

That night, I texted him before he could: *Goodnight, Gabriel. Thank you again for a lovely lunch.*

He replied immediately: *I love you. Sleep well, baby.*

CHAPTER 32

Gabriel

Rafe leaned over the table, his cue stick a smooth extension of his arm, as he took the break shot. The satisfying crack echoed through the room, signaling the start of the game, even if it meant he was likely to pocket a solid or two.

It was a sweltering July Friday at Congress Street Social Club in downtown Savannah, our unofficial hangout for catchups and leisurely games of pool.

The atmosphere was always just right—lively but not too crowded, with a perfect blend of locals and the occasional tourist. The scent of spiced wings and fried pickles mingled in the air, a backdrop to the clack of pool balls and the low hum of conversation.

"I thought you'd be with Aurora." Rafe began lining up his next shot.

"She's out with friends. Luna and Stella."

Rafe laughed. "Luna is probably corrupting her."

"No doubt. Have you seen Lev around lately?" Luna's brother Lev, his friend Dom and Rafe had been the three musketeers growing up.

"Yeah, but he's busy working all the fucking time."

"How's Dom?" I asked.

"He's moving back to Savannah," Rafe stated, "it's going to be interesting."

"No doubt."

Dom was the son of the housekeeper at the Steele Estate, and sure, there had been those who scoffed at Rafe and Lev for allowing him into the "elite" circles, but they never gave a shit. Dom was a close friend and continued to be.

I chalked my cue, watching Rafe miss sinking a solid into the corner pocket.

"How's it going with your second chance with Aurora?" Rafe rested his cue on the rack and picked up his beer.

I leaned over the table, focusing on the cue ball and lining it up with a stripe. The shot was clean, the ball rolling smoothly into the side pocket. "One step forward, ten steps backward."

"What do you mean?"

I moved around the table and lined up my cue again.

"She's scared I'm going to be an asshole again."

"It's a legit fear." He took a pull of his beer.

I pocketed another stripe.

"I don't know how to convince her that I love her. She doesn't believe me." I looked at the pool table critically.

I leaned again to take a shot. "Have you had sex yet?"

I missed the shot hearing his question, which rattled me as he'd hoped it would. "Fucker."

Rafe grinned, setting his beer down. "Have you?"

"No. I...I told her we wouldn't until she trusted me again. I have the worst case of blue balls."

"Mama said the picnic was a success."

"Yeah." I got to kiss her that night. Since then, we'd gone out twice, both times to a restaurant. She used to invite me home for dinner, but she didn't anymore. It bothered me that she thought that if she asked me over, I'd take her to bed. I wanted to, but I wasn't going to fucking seduce her when she looked at me like I was going to break her heart.

"But?" Rafael took a shot and pocketed another solid.

"But...she's cautious. I asked her to come over for dinner with Sophia and me; but she turned me down. Said, she doesn't want to confuse Sophia since she doesn't think we're going to make it."

Rafael paused, straightening up. "Ouch."

"Tell me about it." I took a long pull of beer.

"Can I ask you something?"

"Sure."

"Is she worth it?"

I looked at Rafe, and he was watching me, I knew, to assess how I really felt. We were close, and he knew me as well as I knew him. "Yeah. I love her, Rafe."

"You really fucked up. Don't get me wrong, Iris and Sophia pulled a number on you, but...fuck, Gabe."

"I know," I snapped. "You don't have to tell me again and again."

"Tell you what again and again?" I heard Beau from behind me. Great, another person who was going to bust my chops about Aurora.

"That he fucked up with Aurora."

Beau slapped me on the shoulder. "Fuck yeah, he did. It was *epic*." And then gave Rafe a hug. "Been a long time, brother."

"I know. How are things with you? I hear Trevor is getting married soon."

"Yeah. Mama is running around like a chicken without a head planning the wedding. I steer clear of all that shit."

A server came by, and Beau gave her his *'drop your panties, baby'* smile. "Darlin', I'll have whatever IPA you have on tap."

"We have Stone Hazy and Voodoo Ranger." She smiled wide at Beau. They all always did.

"Well, darlin', what do you recommend. I like my beer real bitter."

She flushed. "Voodoo Ranger, then."

"Thanks."

"Jesus, she's a kid, Beau," I muttered.

"She's a full-grown woman," Beau replied. "And I was only flirtin' with her."

"You're a pig, you know that?"

"I'm not the one who got drunk and told the love of his life that she's bad mama material," Beau reminded me.

"Fuck, here we go again." I shook my head.

"We playing or what?" Rafe asked.

"Why don't you just trounce my ass, and we can drink

beer while Beau reams my ass about my lousy choices?" I suggested.

"Since you ask so nice." And then Rafe expertly cleared the table of his remaining solids, setting himself up for the eight-ball.

"I hear Dom's coming home," Beau remarked.

Rafe lined up his last shot. "Yeah, in a few months."

"He visiting or...?"

"He's coming to stay." Rafe moved his cue, and the eight-ball rolled smoothly into the pocket.

"Yeah? Lev didn't mention it. I saw him the other day at some charity nonsense that Mama dragged me to so I could give them a boatload of money."

"Dom just told me yesterday," Rafe remarked when his phone buzzed. He smiled when he looked at the message. "Gabe, your woman is down the street at Tree House Savannah."

"Who messaged you?" I asked.

"Luna."

"Now that's a hot woman," Beau commented.

"Don't poach, man." Rafe cocked his eyebrow.

"Yeah, Dom will fuckin' kill me if I look wrong at her."

"They still doing that dance?" I mused.

"Oh yeah. Every time we talk, there's a lot of, so is she dating someone without asking if she is. He asks about everyone's love life like he gives a shit. I just stopped playing the game and told him to ask Luna." Rafe set our cues away and finished his beer.

"So...should we go to Tree House?" I suggested.

"After I finish my beer and maybe get that cute server's number," Beau chuckled.

I checked my phone to see if Aurora had sent me a message by chance. She'd started to once in a while initiate conversations, which made me believe we were making progress. But she was still skittish about it. It was as if she was always waiting for the other shoe to drop.

"I'll buy you another beer at Tree House, asshole."

"Son of a bitch, she's got you by the short and curlies," Beau shook his head in disgust *and* awe.

"Afraid so," I confessed.

CHAPTER 33
Aurora

"Hey, baby." I felt Gabriel's breath against my neck and then his stomach and chest against my back.

My lungs felt like they had shrunk. I couldn't get enough air. I turned and looked up. "What are you doing here?"

"Y'all are here having such a good time that we just had to come."

"Hey, gorgeous." Rafe, Gabriel's brother dropped a kiss on my cheek.

"Yeah, that's enough." Gabriel pushed his brother, to my amusement.

"We met at the infamous ball." Beau also leaned and brushed his lips against mine. I gasped at his boldness.

"Fucker," I heard Gabriel mutter.

They all knew each other.

Naturally, they did. All these rich people had grown up attending the same gatherings. Nova, much like myself, wasn't accustomed to this echelon of society. However, she was well-versed in who was who and effortlessly mingled with the crowd, being friends with Beau's brother Trevor.

"Come sit next to me," I requested Gabe.

Instead, he pulled me off my bar stool. We were sitting on the rooftop at the Tree House, and the music was loud, the drinks aplenty, and the mood upbeat. I'd had two martinis and was nicely tipsy.

"I want to hold you." He wrapped himself around me and leaned down to kiss my mouth.

I let him in, and he groaned into my mouth, licking, tasting, hungry. He looked up at me, and his eyes were hooded, his breathing shallow. I was no better.

"Get a room," Beau called out.

I flushed with embarrassment. Gabriel just wrapped me close to him and said, "You're just jealous."

"Fuck, yeah. That's a damn nice-looking woman you're giving a tonsillectomy to."

"Stop embarrassing her, Beau." I heard Luna say.

"Come away with me," Gabriel pleaded when I pulled away a little to look at him, my eyes wide, my lips unable to stop smiling.

"Ah...." I looked behind us at our friends.

"I want to be alone with you," he hissed.

I licked my lips and, like always, saw his eyes drop to them. I didn't do it on purpose...well, not always, but when I did do it, I knew he wanted me. He bent and sucked my lower lip. I trembled.

"Okay," I agreed.

"Rafe," Gabriel called out.

"Yeah, yeah. I got it."

"What did he get?" I asked as he ushered me out of the bar without even letting me say goodbye to the girls.

"The check."

"Oh, I should pay for my drinks and—"

He kissed me again roughly. His hands cupped my ass and pulled me into him so I could feel him hard. "I want you. I know you don't trust me yet, and we won't make love, but I need to touch you, or I'm going to go crazy."

We were standing in the middle of a bar in downtown Savannah, and he was basically making love to me with his words.

"Where do you want to go?"

He kissed me again, and people jostled us as they moved around us. "I don't care."

He took my hand in his, and I let him lead me out. We were out on the street now. It was summer, and downtown was busy and alive on a Friday night.

He pushed me against a wall, and his lips went to my neck, nibbling, finding that sensitive spot right below my ear, and I moaned.

"Are you wet for me?" His hands were cupping my ass again.

"Gabriel, get a grip," I managed to say. And I need to get a grip as well.

Someone whistled, and he rested his forehead against mine and gave a short bark of laughter. "Fuck, Aurora. You make me feel like a teenager who's shaking like it's his first time."

"You make me feel the same way." I stroked his cheek, and he leaned his face into the palm of my hand, telling me he loved it when I touched him.

"I love you," he said simply, looking at me with such affection that right then I was having trouble doubting the sincerity of his words.

"My place is close by," I whispered. I was afraid to take him home and give myself to him, but I was also not willing to turn him down when he was being so sweet, so indulgent.

He smiled then and stepped away. He held out his hand, and I slid mine into his. "How about a walk?"

"A walk?"

"Yeah."

"You don't want to go to—"

"Fuck, yeah, I do, Aurora. Are you kidding me? I want to make love to you so badly it's torture. But you're not ready."

"No, I'm not ready," I admitted, a little sadly.

"Let's go for a walk."

"You don't mind?"

"I've got my girl with me; nothing can make this moment better."

"Well...if we didn't have our clothes on, and you were inside of me?" I deadpanned.

He gave out a choked laugh. "Stop teasin' me, darlin'."

Hand in hand, we made our way to Forsyth Park, a gem within Savannah's historic district known for its expansive green spaces, majestic oak trees draped with Spanish moss, and the iconic white fountain at its heart.

We strolled along the meandering paths of Forsyth Park. The noise and chaos of downtown faded into the background, replaced by the gentle rustling of leaves and the soft, ambient glow of streetlights, casting long shadows. The park, spanning thirty acres, was a world apart, a tranquil haven where time slowed down.

"How are things at home?" I asked.

"You mean with the shitshow my ex is?"

I didn't reply; I just held his hand, enjoying him. Enjoying this quiet intimacy.

"Therapy is working. Sophia is in a really good place. Iris is not. It's getting to a point where I'm worried I'm going to have to fight her for full custody," he ground out.

"I'm so sorry."

"I have something to tell you."

"Okay."

We came up to the fountain, a focal point of the park, which was illuminated by surrounding lights, its water dancing gracefully in the air before cascading back into the basin below.

We sat down on a bench, and I leaned my head on his shoulder.

"You wanted to tell me something," I reminded him.

He let go of my hand and slid his arm around me, holding me close. "I have you to thank. You and Luna for getting my daughter and my family the help we need."

I raised my head in confusion.

"Don't be annoyed with Luna."

I narrowed my eyes, and he chuckled. Kissing my nose.

"She recorded the scene Sophia made when you went to pick up your stuff and drop mine off."

I gasped.

"She showed it to me after the ball. She also recommended a therapist. That's who we're seeing. If that had not happened, I don't know how long Iris would've continued to fuck with Sophia's head."

He kissed my mouth softly.

"I...she never...I didn't know." I manage to sputter out.

"I know. But thanks to that video, I talked to Sophia, and she came clean."

"She has a lot of courage," I remarked. "The way she came to my office. You know she said that she had no excuse for what she did, and what she wanted to give me was an explanation."

"Yeah. She's a good kid. But for you, Iris would've...I don't know how she'd turn out and how long it would've taken for me to get my head out of my ass and realize that I was fucking up."

I put a hand on his cheek. "No, you're not."

"I don't know, Aurora. Everyone told me that the way I was living so close to Iris wasn't healthy, and I just didn't want to hear it. You tried to tell me that Sophia was acting up, and I just bulldozed over you."

"Stop it," I said sharply. "No one's perfect. You were doing what you thought was best. It isn't your fault that Iris decided to be a complete bitch—" I shut up as I realized what I'd said. "Oh god, Gabriel, I'm so sorry."

"She *is* a complete bitch."

"It's not my place."

Suddenly, he picked me up and put me on his lap. I slid my hand around his neck for support.

"I love you," he whispered against my mouth. "I love you so fucking much."

I used to say the words back to him, but now they were clogged in my throat. I couldn't bring them out into the open, give him the keys to my happiness again.

"No, don't feel guilty. There's no pressure, baby."

I kissed him softly then. It was what I could give right now.

"I'm selling the houses," he told me.

"Rose mentioned."

"Ah, the infamous lunch."

I chuckled.

"I'm looking for a new place, but it's taking some time. I may have to just buy something temporarily, and then...I don't know."

"Rose told me you want a studio at your new place."

He let out a long breath. "I want you in my life. I want a home that is right for Sophia and you; and us."

That was such an enormous commitment, and my heart stuttered. He was making all these plans, and I wasn't even remotely ready.

"Hey, hey, no. No panic."

He could read me so well, I thought, and it made my heart ache some more. I wasn't being fair to him.

"You're a good man, Gabriel. You should leave me and move on." I pulled away from him, and he let me go. I stood in front of him. "I don't know if I can...the thing is, the way I grew up, I'll always be waiting for you to leave. You understand?"

He rose and put his hands on my shoulders. "I'm not leaving."

"Someday you will. They all do. And you already left once."

"And I'll try to make up for that every fucking day of my life to you."

"But I don't want you to," I cried out. "I want you to be happy. I'm not the kind of person you can be happy with. I'm damaged. I...I'm not relationship material."

"I can't leave you even if I wanted to."

"What does that mean?" I exclaimed at a loss for words.

"That I want to live my life with you. I'm here. I'm going to be here until I fucking wear you down."

"Wear me down?" Anger came like a raging inferno.

He grinned. "Yeah. Wear you down. You're afraid. You love me, but you're scared. I have given you reason for that. I fucked up; I'll give you that. But even if I hadn't, we'd be here if I said, hey, let's move in together, or asked you to marry me."

I took several steps away from him. "You're out of your ever-lovin' mind."

"Scares you, huh? To think about marriage?"

"We...we're not together. Get it through your thick skull."

"I know. But we're going to be."

"Are you on drugs or something? I'm telling you, there's no us. Look, this whole second chance thing was a mistake."

I marched away from him, walking away from the light of the fountain in the darkness of the pathway that would take me out of the park, away from Gabriel.

I could feel fear roil through me. Marriage? This man was out of his mind. I didn't want to get married and have children. Women like me didn't. No one wanted me. He'd tire of me soon enough. And then where would that leave me?

I knew he was walking behind me. He caught my arm and stilled me. "No, it wasn't a mistake to give me a second chance. It's okay to be scared. I was as well." He turned me around to face him. It was dark where we stood, but I could still catch the determined look in his eyes from the lights around the park. "I still am that I won't be able to convince you that we're meant to be together, that you're going to look at the shitshow my life is with an ex and a kid in therapy, and nosey fucking parents, and you'll bolt. But, baby, my love for you is bigger than my fear."

"That's such a fucking line."

"I've never heard you drop the F word so often."

"I had two martinis."

He embraced and kissed me. This time, he didn't hold

back. He ground his hips against mine so I could feel how hard he was. And there, right by the fountain at Forsythe Park, he put his hand underneath my blouse and cupped my breast, squeezing my nipple.

"Gabriel, I—"

"Shh. Just let me touch you."

We were in the middle of a park and granted it was late, but people could be walking around. This wasn't the place to be making out.

He dragged me away from the pathway and pushed me against an old oak tree in the dark. He leaned into me, kissing me, his hands now skin against skin, against my stomach, my back. He pulled up my skirt and stroked my thighs as he plundered my mouth.

"Gabriel," I whispered when he cupped me.

"So, fucking wet."

I couldn't think, couldn't process. I was angry with him, wasn't I? I was—. All thought left me when he slid a finger inside me.

"Ah, god." He groaned.

His mouth started to bruise mine, and I didn't care, didn't mind. My hands were under his T-shirt, touching his skin, bringing him closer.

He began to circle my clitoris, and I whimpered.

"You like that?" he gritted.

I couldn't speak because my entire world was between my legs, where he was touching me.

"You're drenched. You want me so much, don't you."

"Yes," I hissed when he left my clitoris and stuck two fingers inside me, pumping in and out.

I moved my hips, wanting him against my clit so I could come. God, nothing was more important right now than release.

"You want to come, baby."

"Yes, yes."

He went down on his knees, and I panicked. "No." We were in a public place. We could be arrested for public indecency.

He didn't seem to listen and raised my skirt. Before I knew it, I heard my panties being ripped, and his tongue was on me. I leaned against the tree, my hands in his hair as he tasted me.

I didn't care if someone saw us. I didn't care if anyone heard me moan. I was lost in Gabriel.

"You smell like fucking lavender," I heard him say. "You taste like heaven...like you're *mine*."

He suckled my clit at the same time he jammed three fingers inside me. I erupted and began to shake. My knees could barely hold me, and I would've fallen, if not for the tree supporting me, his fingers inside me holding me upright.

"Just like that, baby." He lapped at me, and my orgasm extended, pain and pleasure warring against each other.

"Stop."

"No," he growled. "I want another."

"I can't," I whimpered.

He suckled my clit, and I began to sob softly because my

body wasn't mine anymore. When I came again, I slumped a little and lost time and place. When I could get control of my faculties again, Gabriel was holding me close, stroking my back, murmuring softly into my hair.

"*Wow*," I whispered.

CHAPTER 34
Gabriel

I was shaking from my need for her that was all too familiar and still brand new. I was burning up for this woman, physically and emotionally.

I was greedy for her and wanted to grab her with both hands, especially when I held her close, her chest heaving as she caught her breath. I could smell her release on my breath, and it made me want to let the animal out and hammer her into the tree, see if I could make her come again with my cock inside her. I wanted her to beg for me again, scream for me, moan for me, come for me.

"Gabriel," I heard her low voice.

"Yes, baby." I looked down at her face. I put a hand on her cheek. This beautiful woman had been mine and I'd fucked it up. I was a goddamn idiot!

"Come home with me."

She was so hot for me that she'd let me do whatever I

wanted. I knew that. Fuck me! Being a Southern gentleman was just not how I was feeling right now.

"Baby, I want to bury myself deep in that tight pussy of yours so badly, you have no idea. I'm hard for you, and no matter how often I use my hand thinking about you to find release, I'm aching for you twenty-four-seven."

She smiled then, a sexy and sultry smile. "I want you."

"Aurora, I love you."

She stiffened, and I continued to stroke her back. Arousal cleared her eyes, and I felt sadness engulf me. I'd destroyed something inside this wonderful and kind woman. She'd fought a childhood that had been difficult and lonely to become this strong and amazing person, and I'd crushed some of that spirit by being someone she couldn't trust.

"When you can say that back to me, I promise we'll make love."

Her eyes filled with emotion. "Then what was this." She tried to push me away, and I didn't let her.

"This was me losing control."

She licked her lips, and I groaned.

"You've got to stop doing that." I ground my hips against hers. "Can you feel how desperate I am for you?"

She nodded.

I rested my forehead against her, panting. "I want to make us...rebuild us."

"I'm sorry for being so difficult," she whispered.

"No, baby, you have nothing to be sorry about."

"Don't I? I don't know if I'll ever get past what happened."

"Tell me how it made you feel," I asked because I wanted to understand. I wanted her to tell me what was deep down inside her, the fear of being left behind, of being abandoned.

We heard laughing around us, and she buried her head in my chest. "No one can see us here," I whispered, nuzzling her ear. "I promise. I'd never expose you like that."

"Can we walk?" she asked.

We held hands again as we strolled around the park. There were a few teenagers hanging out, their presence being made known by the smell of weed wafting around us.

"My mother was...flighty. She moved around a lot. It was hard because I'd be in a school for a few months, and then she'd pull me out in the middle of the night and drag me to a new place. Usually, this was all centered around some guy who dumped her, or some guy she stole from, or some guy whose wife found out that he was cheating on her and came after Mama...you get the picture?"

I hated that she didn't want to look at me when she spoke, that this was a story she wasn't comfortable telling me. But she was talking to me, and I would take whatever I got.

"Yeah, I do."

"I'd call my father and beg him to take me. He lived in Memphis. In the beginning he picked up the phone but after a while I didn't even have his phone number or address, no way to contact him."

I wanted to stop and hug her. There was such acceptance, such resignation in her voice for how she'd been treated.

Our steps were slow as we continued to walk. The wide-open spaces of the park offered a sense of freedom, while the encircling trees provided a sense of seclusion and intimacy.

She kicked a small pebble in front of her with the tip of her blue sandals.

"I was getting pretty desperate because now I was older and my mother's men...well, you can imagine."

I squeezed her hand. "Tell me anyway," I coaxed.

"Why?" She seemed baffled that I wanted to know.

"Let the fear out."

She scoffed. "Are you playing therapist, Gabriel?"

This wasn't the sweet Aurora I knew, yet she was still present beneath the surface. Her defiance was merely a facade, a survival tactic to shield her vulnerabilities and appear stronger than her haunting memories.

"No, just your lover and friend."

She stopped walking and yanked her hand away from me. "Damn it, Gabriel. Do you have to be so nice?"

"Hell, Aurora, I've been a complete asshole to you, so I'm hardly nice." I held my hand out again, and she slipped hers back in if a little begrudgingly.

"You are nice. Don't get me wrong, you also have a mean streak. I've heard about it. Angry Rhodes, isn't that the nickname?"

"Yeah."

Around us, the park was alive with the subtle movements of nature—the occasional night bird calling out, the breeze whispering through the branches of ancient oaks, and the distant sound of other late-night wanderers enjoying the peace of the park. The air was fresh, carrying the scent of blooming flowers.

"Some of my mother's boyfriends started to...make advances," she continued as we walked. "I hid. I locked myself in the closet. I mean, things get complicated when you're in a one-bedroom motel room, and your mother wants to...."

I didn't know how to comfort her. After Luna had come to my office, I'd pieced her history together from things she'd told me and my own extrapolation. I wasn't surprised, but I was still horrified.

"I did some research and found my father's contact information on LinkedIn. He was working for FedEx in Memphis. I called him, and he talked to me." She was silent for a long moment, and I didn't push her. I felt like she hadn't told anyone about this. Luna knew, but not in this kind of detail.

"What did your father say?" I asked gently.

"He had a family, and I was on my own, and I shouldn't call him again."

Fuck!

"So, when I see how you love your daughter and are there for her, I just can't hold it against you, and I never will."

"I know." She had the biggest fucking heart. Sophia had been mean and cruel to her, and yet, she was ready to forgive and forget everything my daughter did to her.

"Finally, I had two choices, the system or find a relative. I managed to convince Mama to come to Savannah. I met my aunt and told her I'd keep her house, I'd sleep on the couch, I'd take care of her, cook and clean everything. She agreed to let me stay as long as I paid her rent."

"How old were you?"

"Thirteen."

I wanted to howl. I'd grown up on a fucking estate and inherited my fortune. She had been thirteen and had to pay rent? But my getting angry and throwing a fit wasn't going to help her, so I just listened and felt my heart break for the kid she'd been. How different her life had been at the age of thirteen versus Sophia's.

"How did you pay rent?"

"I got a newspaper route, and I mowed lawns. I cleaned houses and offices. I bagged groceries. I worked in a diner. I cleaned bathrooms in a gym. I did anything and everything I could, that they'd let me do."

"That must've been hard."

"It was, but I didn't notice. I was just happy to go to the same school every day, not worry about who was going to stick their hands up my...." Her breathing was rough now, and I knew she was remembering.

Had she been sexually assaulted? My heart clenched.

"Then my aunt died, but I was already eighteen. I figured my life out."

"You did more than that." I stopped her so I could let her see how I felt under the light of a streetlamp. "You're a force to be reckoned with, Aurora Turner. You are amazing, and I'm so fucking fortunate that you're here with me. I'm so fucking proud of you and all that you've achieved."

She swallowed. "You mean that?"

"Mean what?"

"That you're proud of me?"

Her voice was small like she was begging for a scrap of affirmation.

"Yes. So, so much. Everyone who works with you thinks you're awesome. Can't you see, baby? You overcame hell to become an amazing person. A warm and loving woman when you could've become bitter and cold. I'm not just proud of you, I'm in awe."

How had I not seen this? Known this? She needed validation. She needed someone to see her. Isn't that what she'd told me? All I needed to do was be with her, spend time with her, and not buy her jewelry or gifts.

"I see you, Aurora," I whispered and brushed my lips against hers. "I see you, and I love you."

CHAPTER 35
Aurora

That walk in the park was a turning point in our relationship. Oh, we weren't back to where we were, but we were spending time together...always fully clothed.

Were we both frustrated? *Absolutely*. Was I the one who was putting the brakes? *No*. Gabriel was firm that sex would happen when we were back on solid ground.

"Baby, come on," he pleaded when I stroked him over his pants. "Don't do this."

We'd just come back from dinner, and we were in my condo.

"Please, Gabriel."

We were sitting on my couch, and we'd been drinking coffee when he kissed me, which led to more.

"Aurora, *baby*." His breathing was ragged as I went on my knees in front of him. He put his hands in my hair. "We can't."

"Why not?" I unzipped his suit pants.

"Because...fuck...," he groaned as I freed him. "You're making this very hard for me."

I stroked him the way he liked it. "I can feel that."

He let out a laugh as he watched me with eyes that were unfocused. "Taste me," he hissed.

I licked his tip where precum glistened. He watched mesmerized. But before I could take him in my mouth, he pushed away. He got up hurriedly, moving away from me.

"You're dangerous," he muttered.

I stayed on my knees, watching him zip up his pants and take in big gulps of breaths like he'd just worked out.

"How long are we going to do this?" I demanded, rising. I was throbbing. Desperate for release.

"You and me?" He quirked an eyebrow and when I nodded, he grinned, "Forever." My eyes widened, and he chuckled. "Not the not having sex, that we will get to hopefully sooner than later. But you and me? I want forever."

I slumped on the couch. I didn't know what I needed from him to move past my fears and insecurities. I didn't know what else he could do. We were doomed. I wanted him, he wanted me, and we were at an impasse because I wouldn't give him my commitment.

"We used to have sex before," I sulked.

He sat down next to me and kissed my nose. "You're adorable when you pout."

I glanced at him with irritation. "What do you want from me?"

He stroked my cheek. "Everything."

I sighed. "You didn't have that before, and you had sex with me."

"I was an idiot before."

"Why can't you be an idiot for a little while now?" I demanded, suppressing the urge to cross my arms and stomp my feet.

He put his hands on my thighs, and I pushed them away. "No. You can't just me off anymore. I wanted to suck you off."

"*Jesus*, do you have any idea how difficult this is for me? You say the word *suck*, and I'm ready to come in my pants."

"I feel like you're keeping sex off the table as a way to make me compliant," I threw at him.

He leaned back and laughed. "I can't believe you just said that." He pulled me into his arms, and I rested my head on his shoulder.

"I can't believe I said that either. I must be desperate for you."

"You must be."

"What are we doing, Gabriel?"

"We're trying to build trust."

"I trust you to give me an orgasm," I muttered.

He stroked my hair. "I really fucked up, didn't I?"

"You've made up for it." He had. For months now, he'd been an attentive boyfriend. He'd taken me home and introduced me to his parents. I was half in love with his father. Atticus had a raw sense of humor and, like his wife, an irreverent attitude towards life. I'd met Rafe, his brother, a few times as well.

Sophia had been away at camp for part of the summer, but we'd spent some time together. The one person who I'd managed not to see, *thankfully*, was his ex-wife.

He'd set boundaries with his ex-wife, which were working. She couldn't just walk into his house, and he never walked into hers. He talked to her at her doorstep if he needed to, and it was always only about Sophia.

She was pressuring him for money, and he was happy to give it, but his lawyer had counseled him against it.

He was open with me, transparent. He spent time with me. He'd not interfered anymore in the work I was doing with Rhodes Hotels. He was doing everything right, but I felt it wasn't real, that he'd go back to who he used to be.

Even though it left me frustrated, I was, in some ways, happy we were not having sex. Before, I'd sometimes felt that I was a booty call for Gabriel.

It was at the start of fall when the other shoe dropped as I was waiting for it to.

"Baby, I'm so sorry but I have to cancel." He'd called me while I was getting ready for a dinner date. It was Friday evening and every other week when he didn't have Sophia, we were together.

"Of course. It's fine." I could feel my heart ready to jump out of my chest.

"Fucking hell, Aurora," he roared. "Don't you even want to know why?"

"Sure. Why?"

"Because I'm needed in Houston. We had a shooting at our hotel there."

"What? God, I'm so sorry, Gabriel."

"Yeah. I have to go, baby. I'll call you soon."

He hung up, and I felt like the world's worst person. How could I have been such an ass to him? He had a life, and it wasn't like he was the only one who sometimes had another commitment; I had things like that happen as well. I had an emergency on a project just a couple of weeks ago due to a water leak on a project in Atlanta. Luna had been unable to go because she wasn't well, so I'd had to take care of it.

Why was I doing this? Was it because each time Gabriel groveled, it felt good? It felt like I was important? Was I afraid that the minute we became a real couple, he'd show his true colors again, and I didn't want to lose this attentive Gabriel? It was all kinds of messed up.

I called Luna.

"I thought you were on a date with Gabriel."

"He canceled."

"Not again."

"Why would you say that?"

"Because that's what he used to do."

"There was a shooting at the Rhodes Hotel in Houston."

He was trying so hard to be the man I needed him to be, and I couldn't stop waiting for him to screw up so I could say, I told you so. It was petty and sad. It wasn't the kind of person I wanted to be.

"Fuck. Is he okay?"

"I don't know," I told her how our conversation had gone.

"Aurora, hell, I was ready to blame him too without hearing him out," she confessed. "This is going to take time."

"It's been months. How long am I planning to punish this man?"

"Maybe your reluctance has less to do with Gabriel and more to do with you?" Luna ventured.

"I want him. I love him. I don't trust him."

"Have you ever trusted any man you've been in a relationship with?"

I thought about it. I'd not been in that many relationships, but the truth was that I'd never trusted anyone. Even the wonderful people at Savannah Lace. Luna was a good friend, and if she disappointed me, it would hurt, but I would survive the damage. If Gabriel hurt me again, it would destroy me.

I used to trust blindly, but that changed after my father had refused to help me even when I'd told him what the men Mama was spending time with tried to do to me. He'd been impervious.

"You should call 911 when you're in trouble. Look, I have a family now, and I don't have the space and time to take care of you. You just have to stay with your mother, Aurora. I'm really sorry. And...ah, don't call me again."

Had it started then?

I probably needed therapy to unravel all my insecurities. But that was a long-term solution. Right now, I knew what I had to do. I'd hurt Gabriel, and I needed to fix that.

I called the only person I knew who could help me.

"Aurora, darling, how wonderful to hear from you."

"Betsy, you know what happened in Houston?"

"Yes, Gabriel let Atticus and me know. He's at the airport waiting for a chartered flight."

"I messed up...and now I need a favor."

CHAPTER 36

Gabriel

"Mama, the pilot is delayed, so we're still waiting," I told her over the phone as I looked through my email on the plane. "Look, I need to go. I have calls to—"

"Take care of yourself, son."

"Yeah, Mama."

I immediately called the Rhodes Hotel, Houston's general manager to get an update on the three people, two employees, and one guest, who were in the emergency room being treated for life-threatening gunshot wounds.

I felt helpless, and worse, I felt alone. I wished I hadn't had to cancel on Aurora. I knew how she'd feel, but this was a legitimate fucking emergency. I'd make it up to her, I told myself. I just didn't know how.

"Any news?" I barked on the phone.

"Still waiting," my GM said. "Hey, Sandy from PR has been calling me and—"

"I'll handle that. You stay with your people. Don't worry about anything else. I'm on my way."

I hung up and called my head of PR, and as soon as she answered, I pounced on her. "Gareth has two people who may die, so you don't call him to do a fucking press conference," I said tightly.

"Mr. Rhodes, we have to do damage control and—"

"I need to take care of my people first. How is everyone at the hotel doing? The staff? The guests?"

"Mr. Rhodes, the media is—"

"Fuck the media. It will be what it will be. Are my people okay?"

"I—"

I hung up and called Willa Acker, my head of HR.

"I'm on it with my person in Houston. We're getting counselors in place."

"You have anything on the gunman?"

"Disgruntled husband, certain his wife was cheating on him."

"Was she?"

"Yeah. She was in a suite with her latest boy toy."

The gunman had shot a bellboy, twenty-two-year-old Dennis, and thirty-year-old Kim, who worked the service desk. He also managed to hurt a guest, Staff Sergeant Nichols, who was there with his wife for a night out on the town away from the kids while he was on a week-long break from deployment in the Middle East. Thanks to Staff Sergeant Nichols, who had tackled the gunman, the casualties had been low, but the gun went off and now he was fighting for his life.

"You're making sure Mrs. Nichols is taken care of?" I asked.

"Yeah."

"Thanks. I'll be there soon." I hung and heard sounds outside the plane.

"What's going on?" I asked the steward who was at the front of the plane.

"Ah, you have a guest."

I raised an eyebrow. The steward stepped back, and I saw Aurora.

I put my laptop aside and walked up to her and pulled her into a hug. God, it was good to hold her. I needed this. I needed her. I'd never needed anyone before. I could work through any crisis, no matter how bad, but it was infinitely better to have her soft and warm in my arms and her scent filling me up.

"What? How?"

"If you want to be alone, I'll go back, but this is going to be hard, and I didn't want you—"

"I don't want to be alone," I whispered. "But we're taking off in a bit and—"

"I have a suitcase," she smiled at me. "If you want me to come with you."

I rested my forehead against hers. "Yes, I want you... period."

I raised my head and looked at the steward. "Can you make sure Miss Aurora Turner is added to the flight plan?"

"Yes, sir."

"You'll have to give him an ID." I couldn't stop looking at her, couldn't stop feeling this immense joy of just having her with me.

I held her hand as we were about to take off. "How did you know where I was?"

"I called your mother."

That explained why my mother had wanted to know where I was.

She looked at me as the plane soared into the night sky. She put her hands on her my cheeks and said softly, but clearly, "I love you."

"Thank God," I said gratefully.

CHAPTER 37

Gabriel

Aurora supported me while I managed the horror of what had happened. She didn't make a single demand. Held me whenever I managed to get a couple hours of sleep. Made sure I had coffee and food from room service.

I'd never had this kind of support before. Sure, I had people who worked for me, but never this intimate holding of hands. Someone saying, I'm here; just go do your thing.

I'd had crises before when we were together, but I'd never let Aurora in, never given her permission to be there for me. I didn't know what I'd been missing.

"I have work tomorrow." She stroked my cheek as we lay in bed facing each other.

"The plane will take you back."

"I booked a flight," she said amused.

"A commercial flight? Why?"

"Because that's what normal people do." She laughed. "God, you're cute, you know that?"

"Excuse me?" I growled. I liked it very much that she thought I was cute, no matter how untrue it was. No one who knew me would say that about me. Angry, yes. Asshole, yes. Grumpy, yes. Bossy, yes. Cute? No.

"The rest of the world doesn't have private jets flying them around."

"You're mine; you're not the rest of the world."

"It's more environmentally friendly. And I know you care about that." There was a lightness in her eyes since she'd stepped on that plane, one that I recognized from when we'd first gotten together.

"Thank you for being with me this weekend. You made it so much easier to handle this shitshow," I told her sincerely.

"I know you have to stay here for a few more days."

"Yeah. I need to talk to my mom. Sophia is with me next week, and I don't think I can get out of here until Tuesday."

"I can take care of Sophia."

She surprised me by saying that. "Really?"

"Sure."

I sighed. "It'll be complicated with school and everything if she has to go from your place, Aurora. I'm grateful and so glad—"

"I'll stay at your place."

After what had happened the last time she was there and how studiously she'd avoided being at my house, I knew this was a big deal. This was her way of saying she was all in.

"You'd do that?"

She nodded. "She's your daughter, and we're getting along well, don't you think?"

"She adores you." Now that Iris's hold on her had weakened, Sophia saw what I saw in Aurora, a kind, gentle, and loving woman.

"I like her very much." She sighed then. "The truth is Gabriel, loving you means loving your daughter. I love her. I know I don't have the right. I barely know her, but it doesn't matter; I just do and...."

How could a man get so lucky? I rolled her onto her back and lay on top of her, kissing her mouth. "You're amazing, you know that?"

"Gabriel?"

"Yeah, baby."

"Make love to me."

After months of wanting and not having, the invitation this time was from her heart and not only desire. I nuzzled her nose with mine. And without hesitation I leaned into her, pressed my mouth against hers, tasted her. I felt like a drowning man having been given a lifeboat.

Her soft lips parted, letting me in, and the tip of her tongue touched mine. We dueled with our tongues. A part of me wanted to hurry and remove her tank top and panties, get rid of my boxers, and enter her so the world would start to make sense again—but another part wanted to take it slow, indulge myself, feel her, soak her in.

Her hands tangled in my hair, pulling me down, and I bit her bottom lip gently, tugging it between my teeth. I couldn't stop kissing her.

Her hips rose as I ground into her, letting her feel what she did to me.

Her moans became more urgent, and she pushed me, so I fell on my back. I laughed softly. She had never been the aggressor before.

"What do you intend to do with me?" I asked.

She kissed me and slid down my body, kissing my chest and then my stomach. Everything inside me tightened as she stroked me over my boxers.

"Gabriel."

"Yeah, baby."

"What do you want?"

"Right now?" I wrapped my hands in her silky hair.

"Yes."

"Right now, it would be very nice, darlin', if you could bring me out of my shorts and let me feel the back of your throat."

She tried to move down, but I pulled the bottom of her body and arranged her thighs, so she straddled my face.

"God," she groaned when I nuzzled against her pussy, smelling her.

"Baby, I'm not going to get you off until you suck me dry."

Her thighs trembled, and I loved how sex with Aurora was always passionate and hot. I loved to see the Ice Maiden melt when she was with me. I felt her hands on my erection, and I slid the crotch of her panties aside so I could lick her.

"Gabriel," she gasped.

I smacked her bottom. "Get to work, woman."

She half laughed, and half moaned at that. I felt her take me inside her mouth, and I lost control. I ripped her panties because they were in my way and latched onto her pussy. She was soaking wet, and I began to fuck her with my tongue, avoiding her clitoris as I held her thighs still so she couldn't get what she wanted until I was prepared to give it to her.

I loved to edge her, and I used to until she was begging for me to let her come. I'd never done that with any woman before. They got off, and I was ready to go. But this woman made me want things I'd never wanted. I wanted complete submission from her. I didn't want just her desire or passion; I wanted it all, heart, and soul.

She began to bob her head, as she tried to move her hips, but I wouldn't let her. I knew it was driving her crazy because she was getting wetter.

As she brought her mouth down on me, I lifted my hips and pushed into her. As I hit the back of her throat, I suckled her clit.

She exploded and began to pump me faster with her hands and her mouth. I lapped at her, holding my orgasm off. I didn't want to come in her mouth, and if I didn't let her go, it would be too late.

I released her thighs and maneuvered her mouth away from my cock. She looked at me with hooded eyes, her mouth swollen. Fucking sorceress. I was under her spell.

"What?" she asked, half drugged on passion.

"The first time after all this time, I'm coming inside your pussy."

I loved to take her from behind, but not this time. We'd

do that for round two. This time, I settled atop her and pushed inside. I loved feeling her bare; it was more potent than any sex I'd ever experienced. The intimacy of not having any barriers was erotic as fuck.

She had an IUD that she'd gotten when we first began to have sex because pills didn't work for her. Except for my ex-wife, I'd never been inside a woman without a condom and not for many years even with Iris, but I'd not wanted that with Aurora, even in the beginning when I didn't know what we were. I'd asked her if I could not use a condom. To make her even more comfortable, I'd gotten tested and emailed my medical results to her, so she'd feel safe. She'd done the same for me, even though I hadn't asked. I knew she hadn't been with many men—considering the life she'd lived, she hadn't had the time to date. I knew she'd had one long-term boyfriend in university. I hadn't had indiscriminate sex, ever, unlike Beau—but I'd had my share, and yet I'd never felt this way before.

Maybe it was true that when you made love with a woman you loved, it was different—like fucking *'blow your head clear off'* different.

I moved inside her almost painfully slowly, driving both of us a little crazy. She was more patient because she'd already come once, but I wanted it again; I wanted to feel her release when I was inside her. I wanted to feel the ripples of her cunt, wanted to hear her soft moans. I wanted it all back with her.

"Gabriel, more," she whimpered, her hips rising every time I pulled away, chasing the fullness I gave her.

"Yeah?"

"Please," she sobbed.

I was with her, every step of the way. I didn't have any more control than she did.

"Harder, damn it," she yelled.

She was always so soft-spoken that her cursing spurred me on. I lifted her hips and slammed into her. "Like that, baby?"

"Yes," she grunted.

"No one would ever believe the woman they see in meetings unravels quite so beautifully," I muttered as I pumped in and out, knowing that it would end soon because I'd been dying for her for months. "Fucking hell, Aurora. Say you love me."

She smiled then, that sultry vixen smile that was mine and only mine. She never gave that to anyone else—and only in bed with me.

"I love you."

I couldn't hold it off any longer. "Aurora, make yourself come. I can't...."

I was losing control.

I felt her small hand encircle me so that each time I moved, I felt both her cunt and her hand, and each time I did, we jostled against her clitoris. We'd started to do this when I'd fuck her for a long time, wanting to be inside her. It made her wetter, hotter.

I felt her release moments before I lost control and let go.

I dropped like a bag of wet sand over her, unable to have a coherent thought. The first time this had happened with her, I had wondered how I'd lived my whole life without having sex this good, this incredible. Only with Aurora had I found this utter calm that came after release, this sense of belonging, of home.

I kissed her neck as I felt myself throb inside her, felt her aftershocks.

Her hands stroked my back, soothing, loving.

When I could, I raised myself on my elbows to look at her. She looked fucking amazing. Her hair was mussed. Her eyes were drowsy. Her lips were full and pouty. Her face was flushed.

"You look stunning," I breathed. "And thoroughly fucked."

She giggled. She never did that ever except when she was with me. So many things we did together that were just for each other, because of one another. I'd almost lost this.

After I cleaned her up, we slept holding each other close, secure in the knowledge that I loved her as much as she loved me. It was almost too beautiful to bear.

CHAPTER 38

Aurora

"Okay, these may be the best eclairs I've ever eaten. And I was just in Paris. How about you, Aunt Rose?" Sophia warmed my heart by appreciating my cooking.

It was one of my love languages. I liked to cook, and I liked to bake; and since I was staying at Gabriel's place with Sophia, I was having some fun cooking with her. We'd just finished dinner in the kitchen at the breakfast nook. I'd made jambalaya when Sophia mentioned how much she loved spicy food, and since she'd gushed about all the baked goods she'd eaten in Paris, I'd decided to bring a taste of France to Savannah.

"These are amazing," Rose, who joined us for dinner, agreed.

"Well, just so you know, I helped Aurora make them," Sophia showed off.

"You should make some for your father when he comes back," I suggested.

Sophia grinned. "He's going to lose his ever-lovin' mind. I've never cooked."

"How come?"

"We've always had a cook. Miss Kayla cooks for us," she explained and then fell silent.

Rose and I both noticed.

"You okay, honey?" I asked softly.

She shrugged. "Yeah. I...Miss Kayla used to cook for all of us, and most of the time, we used to eat together."

I didn't quite know how to handle that. Even though she'd come to terms with the end of her parents' marriage, I was certain a part of her wished it wasn't so.

"Is that something you miss?" Rose prompted.

"Oh, god no," Sophia exclaimed and then looked at Rose and me and shook her head. "You should see both your faces."

"What's wrong with our faces?" Rose demanded.

"Just that you're thinking I'm going to go off again and say I wish my parents were together."

"Do you?" I asked, my heart hammering.

"No," Sophia said sincerely. "The reason I was...well, I was just wondering how it's going to work when we move, and Miss Kayla comes with us."

"Your Mama is capable of feeding herself, Soph." Rose licked some chocolate off her thumb. "These eclairs are amazing, Aurora. You know, if you ever want to invite me over again when you're cookin', please don't hesitate."

I laughed. "I won't."

"The dinners when it was the three of us were not fun," Sophia suddenly said. "I just want you to know that, Aurora. Daddy did it for me. I did it for Mama. There were a lot of strained conversations. Mama pretended everything was fine. Daddy focused on me and me alone. I didn't want to see how things were...that they make each other miserable."

Sophia had come a long way since she'd called me a gold digger. I knew it hadn't been an easy road; how could it be to come face to face with the notion that your own mother tried to manipulate you.

But then I knew all about manipulating mothers.

"Oh, please, stop complaining about everything, Aurora. Gavin wasn't interested in touchin' you. He wants a woman and not some dried up kid."

"So, he wanted to cop a feel. Do you have to be such a bitch about it? He bought dinner that you ate, didn't you?"

"So, you'll just leave me to take care of my sister, is that it? You like her better than me?"

"I hear your precious aunt is dead. Did she leave me anything?"

Sophia went to her room to study for a math exam.

Rose and I settled on the front porch with a glass of wine. I preferred it to the backyard, where there was a pool. It was shared with Iris, and I really didn't want to see her. But it was now fall in Savannah, and after the heat of the summer, it was lovely to enjoy an evening out that wasn't stifling for a change.

"When's Gabe home?" Rose asked.

"Late tomorrow."

"I'm so happy to see you both back together," she said, smiling at me.

"Why? You don't even know me."

"I know *him* and everyone who loves Gabe could see how happy he was when he was with you and how miserable when he wasn't."

It was really nice to hear that, especially since I still wasn't sure what a man like Gabe was doing with a woman like me. He said I was amazing. I wish I could feel that inside me.

"I don't know if it's me who's making him happy," I demurred.

Rose groaned. "Oh, come on, honey, you can't be believin' that!"

"I...I just...." I drank some wine. This conversation was going off the rails.

"What's goin' on with you?"

"Nothing."

"You can't see what you do for him?"

We had great sex, but I didn't know if that was going to be enough for...*forever*.

"Ah...we get along," I replied lamely.

"Well, butter my butt and call me a biscuit," Rose clipped. "Honey, you're havin' what women pray to have."

"And what's that?"

"An honest-to-god love affair."

I sighed. "We broke up, and now we're...I don't know what we're doing."

"You're stayin' here with his daughter, honey."

"I know," I groaned. "And we're getting along."

"I'm so fuckin' confused right now," Rose admitted.

"So am I," I agreed. "Have you seen Gabriel?"

"Yeah."

"He's handsome, smart, rich...and...I just don't get it. In the beginning, I thought he was attracted to me, and when the newness of me wore off, he'd on go his way. Then he introduces me to his brother like it's a test."

I'd been so nervous the first time I met Raphael. Gabriel had told me he was a professor, and I'd been expecting a geek, and here was a funny, charming, and good-looking rich man who was close to his brother. He was nice to me and down to earth. I didn't know what end was up.

"Rafe thinks you're as hot as all get-out."

"I don't understand that." I looked at Rose in exasperation. "I usually blend into the wallpaper."

"What the hell kind of wallpaper are you used to?" Rose scoffed.

"And then I met Sophia, and I'm thinking this is a real relationship, and I need to get my shit together. But you know how that worked out."

Rose put a hand on mine. "That's Iris."

"I know, but what the hell am I doing getting involved with a married man?"

"Divorced. Single. Free."

"I feel like it's all going to blow up in my face soon enough," I confessed. "I went to Houston because I couldn't stand for him to go through that alone. I gave myself away again."

"And now you're scared."

"Yeah."

"I don't think I can say anything that'll make you less afraid," Rose said sadly. "Your fears have nothing to do with Gabriel or Sophia or even Iris. You do know that, don't you?"

Tears pricked my eyes. I did know that. My fears came from within. But when you've been unworthy your whole life, it's hard to believe that someone as wonderful as Gabriel would see me as worthy...at least not in the long run.

CHAPTER 39
Gabriel

Something was wrong.

After I came back from Houston, Sophia started to act strangely again. Not like before. She was more withdrawn. She stayed in her room and didn't go out with friends as much as she used to. She didn't want me to stay home either—she was fine with the housekeeper being there; and also indicated she didn't mind being alone.

I hated that even for a moment, I wondered if something had happened between her and Aurora that has caused this, but I reined that thought in. I trusted Aurora. And Sophia had told me that she and Aurora had a great time. She talked about the baking they did, and all in all, it sounded like everything was fine. And yet, I knew it wasn't.

During our weekly session with Dr. Ryan, Sophia seemed almost like herself and talked mostly about school and friends; studiously avoiding discussing her mother. After the time when Iris had run out of a session, Dr. Ryan agreed that bringing Iris into these sessions would do Sophia more harm than good. She'd also warned me to keep an eye out for Iris striking back now that Aurora and I were together again.

I was keeping Iris at arm's length, but I had no choice but to let Sophia go to her every other week.

And every time my daughter came back from Iris's place, she seemed more and more forlorn. It was killing me.

"She's a teenager, and you've got to let her come to you," my mother told me when I was there for Sunday lunch without Sophia because she was with Iris.

Before the shit had hit the fan, Iris used to come along to these lunches with Sophia regardless of whose week it was. But since I'd dis-invited Iris from all Rhodes family affairs, she'd said that she wouldn't let Sophia attend the lunches during her weeks. This was what I'd been trying to avoid since we got divorced. This is why I'd set up our household the way I had so that we both would have our daughter without disrupting her life.

"I just know something is going on with her, I wish she'd tell me."

I watched Aurora talk to my father and Rafe at the other end of the porch where we'd congregated for post-lunch tea and coffee.

"How are things with Aurora?"

I sighed. It was better, but I knew something was off there as well. "All the women in my life seem to be giving only parts of themselves to me."

"What do you mean?"

"She and I are together again. We have sex. And yet, I can feel she's waiting for me to fuck up so she can end us."

"She loves you, Gabe."

Aurora wore a long black skirt with a sexy silk cream-colored blouse that covered her arms. The outfit was almost old-fashioned and looked chic on her.

"But she still doesn't trust me."

"Why do you say that?" My mother poured tea into her cup and squeezed some lemon into it.

"It's a feeling. I promised myself that we wouldn't have sex until she trusted me again."

"And?"

I chuckled. "And she came to Houston, and it seemed like we were back, really back again...but now I just don't know what the fuck to do, Mama."

My mother leaned back on the wicker sofa she was sitting across from me. "From what you've told me about her childhood, this is someone who has had everyone who was supposed to love and care for her let her down. And I think she finally thought she'd found someone to lean on."

"Me?"

My mother smiled. "Yes, you."

"And I fucked up when I dumped her ass because I didn't trust her."

"She forgives you for that because you trusted your daughter over her, and I'd do the same. My kids always come first."

"Then what?" I asked, frustrated.

"But you broke her trust, and she's gun-shy."

"And what if she never learns to trust me?"

"Then...I don't think you and she will work out."

That sounded so final that it hurt. "How do I make sure she trusts me?"

Aurora turned to look at me right then and gave me a bright smile.

"Keep doing what you're doing so she'll keep looking at you like that and you'll get there."

"How does she look at me?"

"Like you hung the moon, son."

Aurora walked up to us, leaving my father with my brother. I held my hand out to her and when she slid hers in, I brought her close and pulled her onto me, so she'd sit on my lap.

"*Gabriel.*" Her cheeks flushed with embarrassment.

"I like having you close."

She tried to get up, but I wouldn't let her. "Stay," I murmured.

Rafe and my father joined us. Rafe sat on the armchair next to me while my father got comfortable on the sofa next to my mother.

"The hotel in Miami seems to be moving along nicely," my father said. "Aurora has been giving Rafe and me an update."

"Aurora is an amazing architect." My chest swelled with pride. She was a remarkable woman.

"Nina thinks very highly of you," Mama added.

"You know Nina Davenport?" Aurora asked.

"Yes. For many years now. Her ex-husband used to know Atticus quite well."

"Until he cheated on his wife with his trainer...I mean, the man is reduced to a cliché," my father remarked. "Nina got us in the divorce."

"And her husband got someone nearly two decades his junior," my mother commented dryly. "What's with men and need for a younger woman?"

"I don't want a younger woman, darlin'," my father drawled, "I can barely keep up with you as is; a younger woman would give me a heart attack."

"Depends upon the woman," Rafe mused. "I know several *mature* young women."

"Please tell me you're not sleeping with any of your students, Rafe," my mother admonished.

"There is no school policy saying that I can't," Rafe defended himself.

"Oh god, he's sleeping with a teenager," my mother said in mock horror.

I hugged Aurora close as my family bickered in good humor.

"You okay?" I whispered in her ear, nuzzling what I knew was one of her erogenous zones.

She shivered. "I'm good."

"I'm getting hard, baby," I murmured, low, just for her. "I want you."

She squirmed.

"What do you think, Aurora? You want to join us when we go to London next month?" my father asked, what felt out of the blue because we weren't following their conversation.

"Ah...," she managed to say when I interrupted her.

"If she can get time off. Right, baby?"

"Yes," she replied flustered.

I smiled. She had no idea what she'd committed to. It was a wedding that we were going to London for, and it charmed me that she'd trusted me enough to say yes. Or maybe I'd gotten her so hot that she'd say yes to anything. Did I want that?

Fuck. This woman had me in knots, and I didn't quite know how to unravel them.

CHAPTER 40
Aurora

I was drugged on sex. There was no other way in which I could explain what had just happened in my office. *My office!*

Gabriel had come in early for a meeting where I was, along with Devon, presenting the final plans for the Miami hotel.

"You're early," I muttered as I looked through the printouts I was putting together for the presentation. "I'm not ready. You have to—"

He shut the door and locked it. He prowled...that was the only way to describe it.

"You look good enough to eat."

I'd dressed carefully and wore a burgundy sheath dress with black high heels.

"I'm busy. *Shoo.*"

He came to my side of the desk and kissed me. And that's when I lost my mind.

He had his hands on my ass, squeezing, feeling me while his tongue fucked my mouth, his erection pressed against my stomach.

"Gabriel, this is my place of—"

He spun me around and pushed me, so I was face down on my desk. "Hold on to something, baby."

"Oh god." I was scandalized.

"This is your fault." I heard his belt buckle release. "You didn't come to me last night, and I'm hungry as hell for you."

I had wanted to work, so I'd stayed at my condo and told him to leave me alone. This meeting was important.

He pushed up my dress and groaned. "I love your lingerie."

I'd worn La Perla lace panties in hope that after the meeting, we'd go to my place.

"And you're wet. I've been in your office for two minutes flat, and you're soaked for me."

He pulled aside my thong and ran a finger over my slit.

I wanted to stop him. I was lying on top of printouts and papers, and for some reason, I didn't care.

"Come inside me," I pleaded.

"I will, baby, but let me look at you." His hands went up and down my thighs, and then suddenly, he was inside me. I groaned. "Shh, baby. You're gonna have to be quiet."

His fingers never left my clitoris as he pumped in and out of me. "You're gonna leave my cum inside you, aren't you, while you sit prim and proper in that meeting room?"

He was pounding into me now, and my senses were as scattered as the papers falling off the table.

"You'll be flushed, and I'll know you're still wet for me. Still wantin' me. You'll smell like me, and I'll smell like you."

He kept thrusting, as his breathing changed and I knew he was about to come, he pinched my clitoris hard, and I unraveled right before he did. I felt him leak out from inside me onto my thighs.

I leaned on the desk now for support because my legs were shaking. I felt a finger wipe out his semen, rolling down my right thigh. And then he brought that finger to my mouth.

"Open, baby."

I did and cleaned his finger. "Yes, like that. Will you suck me off tonight?"

"Yes," I breathed.

He used tissues to clean me up; pulled my panties up and pushed down my dress. He patted my ass gently and helped me stand.

I turned to face him and watched his smug expression as he fixed his clothes. There was a flush on his high and sharp cheekbones. His eyes were still lit with arousal. There was a sensual lift to his lips. There was no doubt he'd just gotten laid.

"How do I look?" I asked, panicking suddenly, smoothening my hair.

"Thoroughly fucked, darlin'," he drawled.

"Oh god. We have a meeting and..."

"You have my cum inside you."

"Stop it," I admonished. "Now get out so I can get

ready." I looked at my watch. "I have just fifteen minutes. Damn it, Gabriel."

He kissed my mouth. "You should touch up your lipstick."

"And you should wipe some off your face." I pushed him as he laughed.

I wanted to be annoyed but what I felt was intense satisfaction that not only had he lost control, but that I had as well. I was trusting Gabriel again, and it felt good to do so.

"You look beautiful," he whispered.

I smiled. "Now, go, get a cup of coffee or something. You're way too distracting."

"The feeling is entirely mutual. No one would ever believe that Gabriel Rhodes was so gone for a woman he was ready to disrupt a work meeting for it."

He seemed surprised by his response to me. Well, join the club. I was just as amazed, and it felt damn good.

Throughout the meeting, I felt a low hum of that euphoric feeling of being in love.

Nina Davenport was at the meeting along with my boss Luna. Stella was going to be the landscape designer on the Miami project, and I knew she could make my dreams of a bit of Versailles in Miami Beach come true. Ginny, our head of construction, asked a ton of questions, which Devon and I answered.

Gabriel had several comments that I wasn't surprised were well thought through and would only enhance the plan. He knew his hotel business well and knew exactly what sold with his clientele and for how much.

"I'm concerned about the budget," Nina said as the meeting was coming to an end.

"Budgets are always a concern," Devon said cheerfully. "But I think we're okay. Did you take a look at the numbers I sent you yesterday, Gabe?"

Gabriel nodded, his fingers steepled. "I'll add my concern to Nina's, Devon. I don't want this project to go over budget by even a cent—we're already at the edge of what the whitepaper for this project recommended."

"Check," Devon said. "Well, Aurora, looks like we need to maybe tweak a little more. And knowing you, I'm assuming you already know what we need to do to keep us on budget?"

"If you can let go of a few things in the lobby area; and agree to the bathroom fixtures to be what I suggested...we can get there." I couldn't keep the excitement out of my voice. This was my first project where I was the lead, and we were almost done with the planning phase.

"Let me think about that," Devon grumbled. "She's tough, Nina."

"Every time I'm thinkin' that stickin' to the budget will be like trying to nail Jell-O to a wall, Aurora here finds a way," Nina said in her mellifluous voice.

"Well, Gabriel, what do you think? You approve?" Devon asked.

"I do. Take it to the branding committee and get their approval—then we can release the funds to get you started on construction." Gabriel gave me a warm smile, and I'd never felt this good about anything I'd ever worked on.

Gabriel told me he'd see me at a restaurant for dinner in an hour as he wanted to talk to Devon.

I was on a high and walked up to Nina's office, wanting to thank her and Luna for trusting me.

"When Betsy said that she wanted Aurora for this project, I can't say I didn't have doubts," I heard Nina say, and I froze at her door.

"You were already planning to promote her, Nina," Luna's voice came through.

"Maybe in six months, I would've started her out with a smaller project. But Betsy was adamant. And it wasn't like I didn't think Aurora can't do the job. I just didn't want to put too much pressure on her too soon."

"But she's handled it beautifully," Luna's voice was filled with pride.

"I know," Nina agreed.

I knocked on their door, not wanting to eavesdrop any longer. I walked in when Nina called out for me to enter.

"Aurora, great work today." Nina waved at the empty client chair next to Luna.

I didn't sit, couldn't. "I'm sorry but I overheard your conversation just now," I blurted out.

Nina raised an eyebrow.

"Did you promote me because Betsy Rhodes asked you to?"

Luna groaned. "Fuckin' hell."

"Sit," Nina urged.

I did, feeling all the joy I'd been feeling evaporate. I was here because I'd been sleeping with Gabriel, or rather not, and his family had manipulated it so I would spend time with him. Be grateful to him for this opportunity. It was all kinds of wrong.

"You really think I'd give you a job if I thought you couldn't do it?" Nina challenged.

"That dog won't hunt, Nina," I felt rage inside me. "I heard what you said."

"And what I said is that I was going to promote you, anyway. I didn't want to burden you with a big project. It was taking a chance. I like taking chances on people I trust." Nina didn't seem a bit fazed by what I was accusing her of. "And believe me, if I didn't want to, Betsy Rhodes, friend extraordinaire she may be, wouldn't be able to make me."

I looked at Luna, feeling small and petty suddenly.

"Hey, you got here on your own merits. Did Betsy help? Sure. But then my connection with Nina got me my job here, doesn't mean I wasn't good enough. Stella's father's investment in Savannah Lace made her partner, you think she's not a good enough landscape architect?" Luna spoke softly, gently, knowing that I was an insecure ninny.

"You sure I'm good enough?" I asked in a small voice, hating that I had dropped my super confident Ice Maiden routine to show Nina who I was though Luna already knew.

"Did you or did you not get approval on a three hundred million dollar project in less than six months?" Nina asked.

I licked my lips. "I did."

"Do you think Gabe approved your plan because you're sleeping with him?"

"Ah...I don't think so," I squeaked, my face burning with embarrassment.

"He wouldn't because he's all business," Nina continued, "I know him and I can tell you, he keeps his personal and professional lives separate."

"He's involved with me both personally and professionally," I argued.

"He demanded the professional."

I looked at her, confused. "I thought it was Betsy and—"

"Come on, she came to me because Gabe asked her to. He believes in your work. He's seen your work. He'd have found another way to woo you back, Aurora. He did this because he saw a win-win." Nina was using her most no-nonsense tone; I knew to let me know that I was worrying for no reason.

"Thank you."

"Now, should we go get a drink?" Luna grinned. "I know Gabe is taking you out for dinner, but we'll tell him where we are, and he can join us."

"Maybe bring Devon along," Nina commented as she looked at her phone.

"We can ask Rose to join," Luna chuckled, "They're keeping it casual...but...you know Rose."

"Do you all know each other?" I asked, surprised.

"Honey, the Savannah society is small and incestuous," Nina explained. "We all know everyone's business. And since you're now part of it, what with your association with the Rhodes family, you're everyone's business. Don't be surprised if you find new clients who bring us pots of money so they can get some gossip about Gabriel Rhodes and his new tart."

"Tart?" I asked, amused.

"Well, yeah. We're all tarts, darling until we get a ring on the finger." Luna fluttered her eyelashes. "That is why so many of us Southern girls get an M.R.S. degree."

The Missus degree!

"Well, that's not any of us who work at Savannah Lace," I gushed.

"We have some married women," Nina said thoughtfully, "but you're right; most of us are single or, like me, divorced. I wonder what that means."

"Means we're independent, kick-ass women who don't think a man is a plan," Luna announced. "Now, let's go clink some champagne glasses together and celebrate the approval of your first major project, Aurora. Because I think there are so many more to come."

"I have to say one thing, Aurora. If you go to Rhodes Hotel as an in-house architect, I *will* kick your ass," Nina warned.

With their banter and sincerity, they'd managed to make my insecurities disappear. I was so grateful to have these women in my life.

CHAPTER 41
Gabriel

I was surprised when Iris was in Dr. Ryan's waiting room for a session with Sophia.

"How are you, Gabe?" she asked silkily, and I felt a frisson of fear run through me. She was up to something.

I had now gotten enough information to know that Iris wanted money. She didn't have a lot, and her parents weren't going to fund her life either. Her lawyer had brought that up with mine, and I'd told him to ask her to go fuck herself. No fucking way was I giving more money to a woman who was hurting our child.

"I'm good, Iris. And you?" I looked at my watch. Another five minutes before Dr. Ryan would ask us to come in and join Sophia.

"I hear you are back with *that* woman." She looked at her nails as she spoke. "Looks like she's got her gold-digging claws into you."

"She's never taken a dime from me, Iris, unlike you, so I don't know who the gold digger is."

"I'm your wife," she ground out.

"Ex-wife," I reminded, knowing it was futile.

Iris used to not be like this. We used to not be like this. But as our loveless marriage had continued, I think we'd both gotten bitter. The fights and arguments had escalated. She became meaner, and I became colder until I reached a point where I just zoned her out. That was the only way I could think to keep the marriage going until Sophia was not living at home. But that had exacerbated the situation, and Iris started to lose her temper at the drop of the hat. Finally, as I lay in an emergency room having someone sew a cut on my foot made by a shard of glass from a broken vase Iris had thrown at me, I realized our relationship was unsustainable.

"I'll always be your wife, Gabe," she said solemnly. "I've only loved one man, and that's you."

I gave out a harsh laugh. "And how did you show me this love, Iris? By yelling at me all day? By fighting with me all the time? By throwing things at me? By slapping me? By manipulating our child into treating someone I care about poorly? How did you show me this love?"

"By staying with you." There were tears in her eyes, and I knew they were manufactured. "By being honest to our vows. Don't tell me you weren't sleeping around while we were together."

"Never," I bit out. "I never ever cheated on my marriage. And if you think that's the kind of man I am, you obviously don't know me very well."

"I know you just fine, Gabe. I think you are under some mistaken notion about who I am. If you think I'm going to let you go be with someone else when we're married, you're mistaken."

"And you're nuts," I replied, honestly shocked, "we're not married, Iris. You do know that, right?"

"Till death do us part, baby."

On that ominous note, Dr. Ryan asked us to join Sophia.

She sat almost huddled in her chair, and my heart went out to her. Something was going on with my kid, and I didn't know how to help her. She'd bounced back during the summer, but since school had started, it was like she was a shell of the person she used to be.

"Sophia has something she needs to tell you, Gabe." Dr. Ryan nodded encouragingly at my daughter.

She looked at me with troubled blue eyes. "Daddy, I want to stay with Mama full-time."

I heard her, but I had trouble processing what she said. I felt like a bomb had exploded somewhere. I turned to look at Dr. Ryan, who showed no emotion, while Iris looked very smug.

"Sweetpea, can you tell me why?" I managed to get the words out of my constricted throat.

"You have Aurora, and Mama has no one. I...feel I should be there for her."

Iris was obviously manipulating her again.

"So, if I wasn't with Aurora?"

Sophia's eyes went stormy. "But you love her; you should be with her. She makes you happy. That's not what this is."

"So, you don't want to stay at our place?" I couldn't believe my heart could hurt quite this much, that it could bleed this way.

She shook her head but didn't look at me.

"At all?"

"We can do every other weekend...when we can see Nana and Grandpa," she whispered.

"Sophia, can you look at me, darling?" I tried to keep my anger at Iris out of my voice and stay calm.

She did, and the pain in her eyes ripped me apart. Something was going on here, and I wish she'd tell me. I'd see my baby girl once every other week for two days. Four days or so a month.

"I mean, you're selling the house and moving. So, I think this will be for the best." Sophia turned away, not looking at Iris or me, just staring blankly at the wall behind Dr. Ryan.

"What if we didn't sell the house?" I asked, knowing that was a recipe for disaster, but it couldn't be worse than this.

Sophia shrugged. "But you've locked Mama out of the house, and...Aurora is there. I mean, you even had her stay there when you weren't at home."

"I don't know why you couldn't just have asked her to stay with me," Iris piped up. "You didn't have to ask your whore to—"

"Iris, you need to stop using that kind of language with your daughter," Dr. Ryan cut in.

"Fine. *Girlfriend*. Is that better?" Iris flung her hands up in the air. "She didn't have to take care of Sophia. She has a mother who is capable and able."

"When do you want this to start, Sweetpea?" I wanted to cry. Honest to God, weep. My child didn't want to be with me. There was really nothing to do anymore.

"Right away," she whispered.

"Okay." I'd talk to my lawyer, but even though I knew that someone her age could choose, I didn't want to drag her to my house and make her stay with me if she didn't want to.

"And...I think I don't need to see Dr. Ryan anymore." This time, she looked at me, and her eyes were clear but in a way that told me she'd practiced it, had fought to put emotion aside.

"Sweetpea, hasn't Dr. Ryan been helping you?"

"She's helped enough, Gabe," Iris sighed. "If you want to keep seeing her, knock yourself out. But Sophia and I are done."

Iris rose. "Come on, Sophia, let's go. She'll pack up her stuff and be outta your hair, Gabe."

Sophia stood up, her shoulders slumped. I pulled her into a hug, and she clung to me for a long moment.

"I love you, Sweetpea."

"I love you too, Daddy." There were tears in her voice.

I kissed her forehead and smiled. "You call me every night to say goodnight and text good morning. Okay?"

She nodded and gave me a pathetic half-smile.

"Sophia, wait outside. I just need to talk to your father," Iris ordered, and my daughter left, her movements hurried.

"What the fuck have you done?" I hissed.

Iris waved a hand. "Our daughter doesn't like it that you're fucking some strange woman in her home. I told you this is how it would end, and you wouldn't listen. Now that she's staying with me full-time, my lawyer will be in touch with you about child support."

"Is that all this is about? Money?" I asked. I'd give her millions as long as she didn't fuck my kid up, didn't take her away.

"No, Gabe, this is about you learning that you shouldn't have broken up our family. When you've learned that lesson, you can crawl your ass back home, and we can all be together again."

With that, she spun around and left.

I sat down, still in shock.

"She's emotionally blackmailing Sophia," Dr. Ryan told me.

I nodded. I got that.

"Sophia wouldn't admit to that. Simply said she loved you both, but her mother needed her more."

"Iris needs money," I clipped.

"I can see that."

I took a deep breath. "What do I do?"

Dr. Ryan shrugged. "It's hard. You can make child support conditional to Sophia's continuing therapy. Even if not with me, then someone. She needs it. Especially now. I don't trust Iris, and I still think you should go to a judge to petition for full custody."

"And how would that work when Sophia will tell a judge she wants to be with her mother?"

"The judge will listen to her," Dr. Rya agreed, "And my testimony will be trumped by a therapist Iris puts on the stand who'll say the opposite of what I will."

"So, I've lost my kid." How the fuck did this happen? After all that I'd done to keep her with me, keep her safe.

"No," Dr. Ryan said firmly. "Sophia needs you more than ever now. Iris is emotionally messing this kid up, and she needs you. So, make sure you talk to her every day, so she knows that even though she wants to be with her mother, you don't hold it against her, blame her for how you're feeling."

"No way do I blame her. She's a kid. She's a good kid. She was getting along so well with Aurora. I don't know what the fuck happened."

"She told me how much she likes your girlfriend, how much she enjoys being with her. She liked baking with her."

"Yeah, and...now I feel like because I have Aurora, I can't have Sophia."

"That's how Iris wants you to feel."

I dropped my face in my hands. I felt like everything I'd always treasured and wanted was somehow slipping away from me.

"What if I broke up with Aurora?" I asked, and the thought made me sick. This would kill her—and I'd be no better.

"Do you want to?"

"I will if I have to."

"And get back with Iris?" Dr. Ryan challenged.

I sighed. "That would only fuck up Sophia more. You see how we are with one another?"

Dr. Ryan nodded. "Sophia will blame herself if you break up with your girlfriend. Your ex won't change her behavior no matter what you do. This will continue even if you were to go back to her. That will destroy both you and Sophia."

And Aurora!

Instinctively, I knew that, but right now, I was losing my kid, and I wanted to do something, anything, to stop that.

"What about the house?"

"Stay put until we clear this up."

"You think we can?"

Dr. Ryan smiled sadly. "Iris's manipulation won't last. This is going to blow up in her face, but the sad truth is it's going to hurt Sophia as well. I just...wish she'd talk to us. But a mother's voice is powerful, and Iris is a narcissist who knows how to twist your daughter up."

CHAPTER 42
Aurora

I was surprised when there was a knock on my door at ten at night when I was working in my studio. I was in pajama shorts and a tank top, ready for bed, when I became distracted, thinking about an element in the Miami hotel, and ended up tweaking the design.

I was further surprised when I saw it was Gabriel.

"Hey, I thought you had Sophia." I opened the door to let him in.

He looked shattered. I'd never seen him like this before, well, except for the time when he'd come over to apologize for his behavior and his daughter's.

He stepped inside, and even before I could shut the door, he pulled me into him and hugged me.

"Just hold me," he whispered.

I hugged him tightly, not sure about what was wrong, but certain something *very* bad had happened.

After a while, we disentangled, and I walked him to the

couch. He was still in a suit, but it was rumpled. His tie was gone. His eyes were red-rimmed.

I cupped his cheek. "What happened?"

He closed his eyes for a moment and opened them. "I lost Sophia."

"*What*?"

"She told me today she wants to stay with Iris full-time and see me only every other weekend."

I couldn't believe it. "Did I do something when I had her a couple of weeks ago? Is that it?"

"No, baby. She loved spending time with you." He stroked my cheek, and I couldn't stand the pain in his eyes.

"Then what?"

"Dr. Ryan thinks Iris is manipulating her. Sophia has shut down. She won't talk to me."

He rested his forehead against mine. "I don't know what to do. I just helped her move a lot of her stuff to her mother's house. I'm putting the sale on hold. I...know that's not what I promised you and—"

"You don't worry about any of that," I admonished, "What's important is Sophia. What did she say were her reasons?"

He sighed. "She said I have you, and her mother is alone."

"Then we break up." I got up, putting distance between us. "Just go home now and say we're done. Say it's over."

He smiled warmly at me. "Come here and hold me."

"No. Just go. It's over. I won't be the reason you see your daughter for just a few days a month." My eyes filled with tears. I'd been so selfish. I'd made him choose between his daughter and me.

He held out his hand. "Come here," he ordered again firmly.

I put my hand in his, and he pulled me onto his lap. "I just need to hold you. *Just hold you.*"

I held his face against my breast and felt his unbearable grief course through me as well.

"I'm so sorry, Gabriel. So sorry."

He nuzzled my breasts and then sucked a nipple into his mouth through the tank top.

He pulled away to look at me. "No, baby, don't cry."

Tears were flowing down my cheeks. "How can I not? Your pain is mine. How could this happen?"

He wiped my tears with his fingers. "I'll talk to my lawyer tomorrow. But Sophia is nearly fourteen, and if she tells a judge she wants to be with her mother then that's that. Something is wrong and that hurts a lot more than her saying she doesn't want to stay with me."

"Did you tell her you and I could—"

"I asked her, and she said that you made me happy, and she didn't want us to break up."

A sob choked out of me. "She said that?"

"Yeah. She loved spending time with you."

"What the fuck has your ex-wife done?" My temper rose. I hated that woman at the moment. How could she do this to Gabriel...her own daughter? Sophia loved her father, and making her choose between parents was heartbreaking and horrible.

"I don't know. Sophia isn't talking. Fuck, Aurora, I fucked up, and my kid is...I have made so many mistakes, and she's paying for them."

I stroked his hair. "No, Gabriel. You're a great father."

"I should never have set up our homes the way I did. I confused her. I gave Iris false hope. She said she wants us back together."

I'd let him go; I realized if it meant he would be able to be with his daughter, care for her, protect her from whatever it was her mother was doing to her. But before I could speak, Gabriel shook his head. "I know what you're thinking. Don't use this as an excuse to end us," he warned.

"But Sophia needs you."

"And I'll always be there for her. She's next door right now and...I'm going to have to keep it that way. I feel like I pushed her away somehow. She doesn't even want to go to therapy anymore."

I stroked his cheek and kissed his mouth. "How can I help?"

"Can I sleep with you tonight?"

"Every night for as long as you want," I vowed. I loved this man, I realized, and I wasn't afraid anymore. If I had just a few months with him, I'd take them. If he'd go back to his ex-wife now to make sure he could keep his daughter close, I'd let him. It would break my heart, but I'd do whatever it took to make him happy. And wasn't that love? That you made those who you loved happy even if it hurt you?

"Yeah?"

"Yes," I confirmed.

"You forgive me?" There was such emotion in his voice that tears choked me again.

"There's nothing to forgive. It's in the past. We move forward." I'd been so foolish, holding on to my fear, afraid to lose him when he was right here, saying that he wanted me even though it had cost him his daughter.

He kissed my mouth gently. "Thank you."

"And if at any time you want to go back to Iris, you just say it, okay? I won't stop you. There will be no drama and—"

"I'm never going back to her. And if I do, can you imagine how horrible that would make Sophia feel?"

"But—"

"And don't I deserve to be happy? Have a chance at it, at least? I haven't been happy for over a decade, Aurora, not until you came into my life. The time we were together was... is the happiest I've ever been, except with Sophia. I have a family, and we're close. I have great friends. I have a wonderful daughter. But my heart... it's been aching to love and *for* love."

He kissed me again.

"I love you," I gave him the words I knew he wanted to hear.

"I love you too, baby, so, so much. I can't do this without you. I...just can't."

"I'm not going anywhere."

God, I hated how hurt he was.

"Have you eaten?" I asked.

He chuckled. "No, but I'm not hungry. I just...needed you."

"Come on then, let's go to bed."

"I need a shower." He looked so tired that I doubted he had the energy for one.

"How about we just get into bed now, and we can take a shower tomorrow morning?"

"Together?" he asked trying to lighten the mood though it wasn't likely right now. Something terrible had happened to him and I didn't know how to fix any of it, how to make it better for him.

"Yes. I'll let you wash my hair."

"And let me fuck you against the wall?"

"Yes."

I helped him undress and he let me like he was too tired to think about things like taking his socks off or unbuttoning his cuffs.

We held each other close as we lay naked in my bed. He lay on his back and held me, stroking my back, cupping my ass. He wanted comfort, I realized, not sex, but intimacy. He was getting hard; I could feel him against my thigh that was nestled between his legs.

We didn't make love that night, just fell into fitful sleep. We woke each other up often and then wrapped ourselves in one another, seeking and finding solace.

"Aurora," he murmured against my hair in the early morning hours as the sun was streaking pink and purple across the Savannah skies.

"Yes, Gabriel."

"Don't leave me."

"I won't."

"Promise."

"Yes."

He fell back to sleep as if soothed by my words, as if he'd woken up just to make sure I wasn't going anywhere.

After all these months of not trusting Gabriel, right now, I had no more doubts. He loved me. And I loved him. And because I did, I was going to find out what the hell happened with Sophia. No way would I let Iris break his heart.

CHAPTER 43
Gabriel

I was so excited for the weekend that Sophia agreed to spend with me. I'd asked Aurora to stay at my house, but she'd told me that I needed alone time with my daughter.

Since the day that Sophia had dropped the bomb on me about living with her mother full-time, I'd spent every night with Aurora. She'd stayed at my place, not complaining about it. She'd brought several of her things along so she could go to work straight from there.

I didn't want to be too far, worried that Sophia would need me. She called me every night but continued to be withdrawn.

I was hoping that Sunday lunch with my parents and Aurora would help open her up. She'd been polite and *reserved*. She was close to my mother but even Mama with her infamous interrogation techniques couldn't get anything much out of Sophia.

She spent time with Aurora. Went for a walk by the river with her. I could feel Sophia's agony, so I put on a front of being okay and madly happy that she was willing to spend the weekend with me.

"Aurora can stay the night even if I'm here, Daddy," she said to me when Aurora went back to her place after lunch at the Rhodes estate, and we were driving home.

"She feels that since you and I don't have a lot of time together, she wants us to have it one-on-one," I explained.

"I like having her around."

"I'm glad, Sweetpea. How are things at school?"

"Okay. Fine."

Our conversations that used to be easy were now stilted. She didn't annoy me or nag me, she was sweet and fucking *withdrawn*.

I called Aurora that night after Sophia went to bed. "How did she seem to you?" I asked.

"I asked her what was going on, and she asked me to promise her that I wouldn't leave you because of this," Aurora told me. "I'm convinced Iris is emotionally blackmailing her."

"Dr. Ryan thinks the same thing, and I agree. But unless Sophia opens up...there isn't much we can do."

CHAPTER 44
Aurora

Gabriel and I fell into a pattern, yet we both keenly felt Sophia's absence. As days transitioned into weeks, Sophia remained quiet and reserved when she was with Gabriel on his weekends. I attempted to give them space, but recently, she began requesting my presence more frequently, prompting me to stay at Gabriel's place more often.

He'd wanted to convert one of his guestrooms into a studio, but I resisted. I just felt like we were waiting for something to happen—and I had the sick feeling that it would mean the end of our relationship...again.

Gabriel was sad; as was his family. It broke my heart, and I kept thinking that maybe if I could just walk away then he could get Sophia back. This was no way to live.

"Iris, it's her birthday, damn it," I heard Gabriel in his office on the phone.

I stood outside, feeling his pain.

"Aurora is my girlfriend. Come on. It's a birthday party,

I can't ask her to...you know, the hell with it. It's my weekend the day after so...what? Iris, we discussed it, it's my weekend."

I heard him curse more and hang up. I waited for a beat and went into his office.

"She won't let me see her for her birthday."

"Yes, she will. You just have to go to her party without me, which is absolutely okay." I kept a cheerful face like this didn't matter. But it did. Iris knew what she was doing. With every such blow, she was hurting our relationship. Gabriel wouldn't admit it, but we were struggling, and I couldn't see the forever he'd been claiming a few months ago.

He put his hands on my shoulder and rested his forehead against mine. "I don't want to be there without you."

"You have to be there for Sophia," I cajoled. "And it's not like I'm going anywhere."

"But it's not fair to you."

"It's fair to Sophia, and that's all that matters."

"You're too good for me, baby."

I knew he thought he was giving me a compliment but what I heard was that I wasn't right for him. The insecurities that I'd managed to banish were back in full force and I was waiting, expecting him to tell me he couldn't keep doing this, staying away from his daughter.

Betsy, Atticus, and Rafe went to Sophia's birthday party with Gabe while I went to my condo. The party was taking place at the pool that was shared by both houses and I didn't want to be sitting in a corner, looking out at the festivities, feeling like the sad girl who I used to be, the one who was alone and had no friends.

The stress of what was happening with Gabriel was taking its toll on both of us. He was getting snappier and even though he apologized, I could feel the tension radiating from him.

He was soon going to start resenting me—and it broke my heart that I wanted it to happen sooner rather than later so it would get Sophia back to him quicker. Losing him would destroy me—but I was a tough bitch, I'd recover, I'd stand up straight again. I knew that. It wouldn't be fun, but I'd get there.

"These are some seriously negative thoughts, Aurora," Stella said to me when I confided in her as I was packing up at the end of the day.

Gabriel and I had dinner reservations, and I was seriously contemplating telling him that we were over.

"He's so depressed. I can't stand it."

"Sophia is still not saying how Iris got her hooks into her?"

I shook my head.

"I'm just...I can't bear his pain, Stella. If we weren't together, Sophia would go back to him. Then, they can go back to their old setup. He'll have his daughter."

"He made his choice, Aurora."

"Choosing me over his daughter is a dumb choice. I won't allow it."

Stella smiled then. "That's not what he did. And I have a feeling Gabe isn't going to let you walk away. He loves you.

He lost you once, and he's not prepared to go through that again."

"Well, my leaving him is not under his control."

But as soon as I saw him in the restaurant and he pulled me into a hug and kissed me, I couldn't say the words. I loved him. Maybe I should let him leave me, which he would when all of this becomes too much. That would be the easier way to do this, I decided like a coward.

"You're so beautiful," he murmured, kissing my knuckles as I sat down across from him. "I can't believe you're here with me."

Right! I couldn't believe he wanted me for any reason.

"How is Sophia?" I asked.

"Good. She called last night, and we talked for nearly a half hour. She's working on a project in school about historical buildings. She said she'd reach out to you about that."

For the first time since Sophia had made her announcement, there wasn't that horrible sadness in his tone.

"I'd love that. Maybe next time I go on a building tour with Bianca, Sophia can join," I replied excited that I could, in some way, bring joy to his daughter.

"Every time I think I know how great you are, you give me more."

There was love in his eyes and I was falling harder and harder every day. When he ended it, this was going to hurt a lot. I stored this expression of his in my memory files to bring out later, on lonely days when I wanted to feel loved.

"What's going on behind those pretty eyes of yours?" he asked.

"What do you mean?" I looked away from him as if to peruse the menu.

"You just thought of something sad or bad."

How am I supposed to defend myself from someone who can see through me so easily?

"It's nothing. How are things in New York?" I changed the topic. I knew he was having some problems at the Fifth Avenue Rhodes Hotel, and he dove in, telling me how he was navigating the challenges.

As we ate, the mood between us lightened and became normal, like we'd been together for a hundred years and would continue to do so for another hundred.

"Coffee?" he chided when I ordered a double espresso after dinner.

"I have some work to get through," I told him. "I've been so busy with your hotel that I haven't delivered a design change for Callum's project."

He scowled. "I hate that you dated him."

"I never dated him," I soothed.

"You were at that ball with him. Why do you think I got so unhinged?"

I loved his jealousy when doled out in small portions. It was perverse, but it made me feel loved and cared for.

"Gabe," a voice called out as a man came to our table.

Gabriel rose and shook hands and introduced me to his acquaintance. They talked for a minute before the man left. It happened often when we were out. People knew Gabriel, and he always introduced me as his girlfriend.

Before my espresso arrived, I excused myself and went to

the ladies' room. I'd finished my business and was about to exit the stall when I heard the front door open and close, followed by the clatter of stilettos.

"Did you see Gabe Rhodes is with that slut of his?" one woman said.

My heart clenched.

"You know, it's such a terrible thing. But he's handsome and is richer than Midas so of course some woman like her wants to get with him," another woman said.

A third woman spoke then, "Poor, Iris. She's going out of her mind with worry. And Sophia is devastated. You know, she said she wants to stay with Iris because Gabe is too smitten with trashy pussy to put his own daughter first."

"How does Betsy Rhodes stand this?" scoffed one of the women.

"Apparently, Betsy is doing everything she can to get Gabe and Iris back together."

"Yeah?"

"Well, it was Sophia's fourteenth birthday party, and guess who was not invited?"

"The slut?" a woman chortled.

"I can't believe he flaunts her like this in public. Usually, when one of our men is taking a ride on the wild side, they have the decency to do it with discretion."

I'd had enough. I wasn't going to hide. I stepped out of the stall and walked up to the sink.

The women made way for me. They weren't embarrassed, they were smug. I realized then that the conversation they had was for my benefit. They knew I was in the stall.

"Some women just don't know the value of family," a blonde in a Coke red dress said as she checked her lipstick in the mirror.

I picked up a towel and wiped my hands.

"They think because they're exotic they can have who they want," another who was in a black dress said, looking straight at me.

Exotic? Was she talking about my skin color? I felt my face and ears go hot at that blatantly racist comment.

The third woman who I recognized as one of Iris's friends. I'd seen her at the ball where Gabriel had lost his mind.

"Someone should let these women know they're good for a while with whatever they have between their legs but that's all they are. They can't compete with class and sophistication."

I walked out of the restroom, hearing the women chuckle. I knew it was just meanspirited nonsense that I should ignore, and I wanted to, but I felt tears prick my eyes.

"What's wrong?" Gabriel immediately asked when he saw my face.

I shook my head, afraid that if I spoke, I'd have a breakdown.

My god, was this how people looked at me? As some brown floozy who'd ensnared a wealthy man with my pussy?

Gabriel put his hand on mine. "Aurora," he insisted firmly.

I looked at him, and he saw my eyes were watery and cursed.

"What the fuck happened?"

I shook my head. "Just...some women who were talking about how I broke up your family. The usual."

"*The usual*?" He raised both his eyebrows.

The women who'd been in the bathroom walked towards us, and he saw me stiffen.

"Gabe, how are you, honey?" the woman in the red dress said, holding her hand out.

"Ladies," Gabe muttered and kept his hand on mine.

"Won't you introduce us to your friend?" the woman in the black dress wanted to know.

I stared at Gabriel's hand, aware that I was about to self-combust with embarrassment and shame.

"No." Gabriel patted my hand and stood up. "I hear that you made unflattering remarks about my fiancée, who you know of because you're all Iris's friends."

The women were shocked, as were the people around us who could hear. Did he just say, fiancée? Okay, what did I miss while I was in the restroom?

"You're engaged?" One of the women stuttered.

"Yes. Aurora Turner has agreed to be my wife. Now, feel free to spread that message around. And before you go down the marrying for money bullshit, Aurora is a career woman with a well-paying job, unlike all of you who've never worked a day in your lives. Now, if you excuse me, my fiancée and I would like to finish our dinner in peace."

He sat down, and I looked at him, certain he was furious; instead, he was smiling.

"What was that?" I whispered.

"Something Betsy Rhodes would do," he grinned. "I should've done this years ago."

"Done what?"

"Hit back and not worry all the time about what people will say when I do. And speaking of things I should've done, I know I dropped a bomb with the F word."

I smiled weakly. "I'm assuming you're not talking about the word fuck?"

He laughed, and I could feel the eyes of many people on us. "You make me so fucking happy, Aurora. Marry me."

I stared at him. I thought he said that to put those women in their place.

"Excuse me?" I squeaked.

"I don't have a ring. I'll get you one, I promise. But who the fuck needs a ring when we have love and commitment and fucking joy. So, Aurora, will you marry me?"

"Yes." The word slipped out of me before I could control it, before I could assess it. It was an answer from the heart.

He stood up with his scotch. "Everyone, I'm so pleased to announce that this wonderful woman, Aurora Turner, today, agreed to marry me."

Gabriel was not for public displays, but he was doing this to shut everyone up. To show everyone how much I meant to him.

The restaurant clapped. The servers immediately brought champagne to our table. People came by and said congratulations. All the while, Gabriel didn't stop smiling, and neither did I.

CHAPTER 45

Aurora

The day after we got engaged, I found out at work that all of Savannah knew where and how I became Gabriel's fiancée. Gabriel wanted to celebrate, but a work emergency forced him to cancel and head to New York.

He wanted me at his place. His reasoning was sound: "If Sophia calls, you'll be next door since I'll be too far away, so I need you here." There was no way I'd be anywhere but his house after that.

The fact that he trusted me to be there for Sophia when he wasn't, took the rest of the reservations I had about us away. I was not going to let him down because of my insecurities. I'd rise above them and embrace my life with Gabriel.

I never expected Sophia to call me but when she did an hour after Gabriel's plane took off late at night, I grabbed my phone hurriedly.

"Sophia, honey, all okay?"

She was crying, and I felt my stomach bottom out.

"Aurora, is Daddy around? I tried to call but couldn't get through."

"He's on a plane, honey."

"Right. He texted. I forgot."

"Sweetpea," I called her what Gabriel did to soothe her, "what's wrong?"

"Everything," she wept. "It's all wrong."

"Talk to me."

"You and Daddy got engaged."

"Yes."

"He told me he was planning to ask you and that he wanted me to pick the ring with him. But...Mama is so angry."

"Oh, baby, that's not on you." I was pacing up and down Gabriel's bedroom. I had my ear buds in, and I was texting Gabriel, telling him to call as soon as he was able.

"But it is. Don't you see? Mama is so...I don't know what to do."

"I'm coming over."

"Where are you?" she breathed.

"Next door."

"Really?" There was such hope in her voice.

"Will you tell me what's going on?"

I heard Iris call out for Sophia, screaming at her, and my blood chilled.

"Aurora," Sophia sounded scared. "Mama locked me up."

"What?"

"She said she was going to kill herself and then locked me in my room. I was lucky I had my phone in my pocket."

Oh, fuck that. "I'm coming over."

Gabriel had a key for emergencies to Iris's place and I knew where it was. I took it with me. The door could be opened with codes and a thumbprint but also the old-fashioned way.

"Aurora, I'm scared."

"I'll be there in two minutes. Don't be scared."

I heard Iris scream. "Who are you talking to? Tattling away already, are you?"

I fumbled as I opened the door. I wanted to hang up and call Betsy and Rafe, anyone who could help, but I didn't want to let go of Sophia. I wanted her to know I was listening to her; I was coming for her.

I walked into Iris's house and followed her voice. God, that woman was screaming at poor Sophia.

"I told you. I told you what to do, and you haven't done it. When I kill myself, it'll be your fault."

Iris was standing outside Sophia's room. She was in some cocktail dress—looking like the perfect Savannah socialite unless you saw into her heart, which I knew was ugly.

"Sophia?" I called out.

"What the fuck do you think you're doing?" Iris turned to me. "Get out before I call the cops and have you arrested."

"This is Gabriel's house," I said easily, "And I have every right to be here." I didn't. This was Iris's domicile, but I didn't give a damn. My girl was in trouble, and I wasn't going to stay home and hope for the best.

Sophia was on the floor, leaning against her bed, sobbing.

"No." Iris stood at Sophia's door, barring me from entering.

"Move," I said.

"Get out," she screeched.

"Mama, please," Sophia was crying now, looking so broken that my heart was crushed.

"Iris, move now," I ordered.

"Fuck off, bitch."

She pushed me then, and I pushed her right back. She was in five-inch heels, and I was in sneakers. I had the advantage. She fell against the wall, and I grabbed Sophia. Before Iris could find her balance, I got Sophia out of the bedroom.

"Mama, I'm so sorry," Sophia was crying, but she was holding on to me like she'd never let me go. She needn't have worried because there was no way I'd leave her.

I didn't want to stay in the house next door and picked up my bag that was sitting in the foyer of Gabriel's house.

My car was still parked up front. I yanked the electric cable out of the socket of the Leaf and opened the door for Sophia to get in.

Iris came running outside. "Where the fuck do you think you're taking my daughter?"

"Away from you." I walked around Sophia's door and got into the driver's seat, my heart hammering hard.

Iris opened the passenger side door of my car. "Young lady, get into the house."

"Mama, I can't do this anymore." Sophia's lowered her head.

"Move, Iris," I demanded.

"This is my daughter, and I'll call the cops on you for kidnapping her."

"Knock yourself out," I said. "Let them know we'll be at the Rhodes Estate. I dare you."

I didn't wait for Iris to move and pushed on the accelerator. She lost her grasp of the passenger door and Sophia immediately closed it and looked at me like we were engaged in a prison break, which in some ways, I think, we were.

CHAPTER 46
Gabriel

I'd barely landed in New York when I had to fly back home.

The Wi-Fi service on the plane was just as crappy on my return flight as it had been on my way into New York, leaving me anxious after my brief conversation with Aurora on the ground. I still didn't know how Sophia was.

My daughter had been hysterical when we talked and kept saying she was sorry.

"Call Dr. Ryan," I instructed Aurora. "I'll text you her number. Ask her to come to my parents' place."

"I got this. You just get home," Aurora said calmly.

"Thank you," I whispered.

"For what?"

"For being there for Sophia."

"I'll always be there for her," she vowed, and I fell in love some more.

It took a few days to figure out what happened, and

during that time, Sophia, Aurora, and I stayed at my parents' estate. It was large enough that we essentially had a part of the house to ourselves, so we had privacy but also family close by when needed.

Iris had threatened Sophia that she'd kill herself if our daughter didn't say she wanted to live with Iris full-time.

"Did you believe she'd harm herself?" Dr. Ryan asked.

Sophia nodded. "She has in the past. You know, she'll put pills in her hands and say she'll take them all, things like that. But the fact that she was threatening told me that she needed me."

"Why didn't you feel you could tell me, Sweetpea?"

"Because Mama needed me," she reiterated. "I know I messed up and—"

"You didn't mess up," Aurora jumped in. She'd joined some of our sessions with Dr. Ryan. "You're a child; fixing the screw-ups and issues of grown-ups is not in your job description."

Maybe it was because of her difficult childhood; and definitely because she loved Sophia as much as she loved me, Aurora had become fiercely protective of my daughter. Sophia was also leaning on Aurora who she said had been a lioness, getting her out of Iris's house that night when her mother had locked her in her room.

I was so grateful that Aurora had been there; and that she'd not hesitated in protecting my daughter. My sweet and loving woman was one hell of a Mama Bear!

Speaking of Mama Bears, my mother was pleased with herself.

"I knew it," she said happily, watching Aurora and Sophia cooking in the kitchen while we sat on the porch outside.

"Knew what, Mama?"

"That she was right for you. For you and Sophia."

I put my hand on my mother's. "I need to buy her a ring. Sophia said she'll help me. Maybe you can as well."

My mother's eyes glinted. "I think I'll do you one better."

She went away for a while and came back with a jewelry box. I quirked an eyebrow. I opened it and smiled. It was my maternal grandmother's engagement ring.

Nestled within an intricate setting of delicate, aged gold, the centerpiece of the vintage ring was a stunning amethyst, its hue reminiscent of soft, serene lavender fields under a dusky sky. Surrounding it was a halo of tiny, sparkling diamonds, each stone catching ambient light to accentuate the amethyst's ethereal glow. The craftsmanship spoke of a bygone era, with ornate filigree details that wove around the band.

"You know, whenever I smell lavender, I think of Aurora." I stroked the precious gem.

"Well, then, this seems like it is fate."

"You sure about this?"

My mother nodded and looked at my fiancée and daughter. They were laughing about something while Aurora taught Sophia how to pipe dough for cream puffs.

"We need a place to stay. I'm selling the two houses now...even if it means losing money," I declared.

"Stay here," my mother suggested and raised a hand

before I could protest, "until you find the right home for your family."

"We may be here for a while...it hasn't been easy finding a place."

"You know, Gabriel, you have an architect for a fiancée; I'm sure she can design something adequate for you."

I grinned. "Yeah?"

"Maybe you can build your house on the estate."

The Rhodes Estate did have enough room for not just another but several homes. It would be good to be close to my parents, especially when Aurora and I added to the family. We hadn't discussed it, but I wanted children with her. The idea of her being swollen with a baby aroused me, which was uncomfortable, considering my mother was sitting next to me.

"I'll talk to her." I dropped the jewelry box in my suit jacket pocket.

"When do you intend to propose for real?" Mama asked.

"Very soon and I won't be proposing alone."

Life didn't turn around immediately. There were sessions with Dr. Ryan where Iris reluctantly showed up to avoid child-endangerment charges.

Sophia felt guilty for not being able to help her mother, but she was also aware that she couldn't let Iris continue to mess with her head.

"You can't do this to me, Sophia," Iris hit back. "I just wanted our family back together."

"That's a lame excuse, Mama," Sophia said wearily. "And it doesn't matter what you wanted. Daddy was honest about not loving you. You were fine with how things were until Aurora showed up. Once you could see Daddy was in love with her and wanted to be with her, you started on this whole I want us to be a family kick."

"Young lady, stop blaming me for everything."

"I'm not, Mama. I blame myself mostly," Sophia had said sadly.

Iris and I met with our lawyers because I'd learned my lesson, and I wasn't discussing anything with her without witnesses present.

"You need to buy me a house," she told me.

"Ms. Rhodes, you were paid a lumpsum after your divorce instead of regular alimony payments. Mr. Rhodes does not owe you any money at this point," Dixie, my lawyer pointed out.

"Come on, Mr. Rhodes is a wealthy man. Does he want his daughter to see her mother living in squalor?" Iris's lawyer argued.

"Hardly squalor. Ms. Rhodes received...," Dixie went through the numbers. I was shocked to learn the amount of money I'd given Iris in the past four years. The number included the upfront payment plus all the living and childcare expenses I'd carried since the divorce. And now that Sophia was living with me full-time, Iris would not receive any child support.

"Come on, Gabe, don't be an asshole," Iris cried out. "I need a few million. You can afford it."

"And I would've given the money to you if you'd just asked. Instead, you fucking tortured Sophia and fucked with her head. No way, Iris. I'm sure your parents will be happy to help."

Aurora had tried to convince me to just give Iris what she wanted and get her out of our lives. I could afford it, but I didn't believe in paying blackmailers. And the truth was that I couldn't have Sophia think that what Iris did was okay. It wasn't. I had asked Sophia if she wanted me to give her mother more money, and she'd simply said, "Your divorce is none of my business."

Seeing Dr. Ryan again had put her on firmer footing. She was letting her mother go, and as painful as that was because I'd never wanted Sophia to choose between her parents, I was also happy to not have to worry about what poison Iris was injecting into my girl's head.

Iris had tried again outside the lawyer's offices.

"Just buy me a place and..."

"No. We're done, Iris. I can't believe you pulled this stunt for money."

"I wanted to save our family."

I shook my head. "No. You wanted money, and you used Sophia. You're on your fucking own."

"My parents would like to continue to see Sophia."

"Not happening."

"Gabe, don't be cruel."

337

I looked at her sadly, realizing she didn't get it. "I'm not, Iris. I'm protecting Sophia."

After that I refused to talk to her and requested all communications take place through lawyers. Sophia had told Iris she didn't want to see her right now.

"Maybe in a while, I'll be able to talk to you again, Mama. But right now, I need to take care of myself."

I was impressed with and humbled by Sophia's maturity and courage. She and Aurora had gotten closer, and I loved watching their interactions. They were not exactly friends, neither were they mother and daughter. It was more like sisters.

But some days were harder for Sophia than others. She was healing, but she also went back to being withdrawn at times, and Dr. Ryan told me it was normal. "People have mood swings. Stop attributing everything she feels to more than it is. Maybe she had a shitty day, end of story."

So, we went back and forth between good days and bad until the bad days became far and fewer in between.

The houses sold right before Thanksgiving, and Sophia and I were technically homeless. I put our furniture and things into storage, and we moved in with my parents. Dr. Ryan agreed that it was a sound idea so that Sophia would have people who love her around her.

"Why don't you put your place on the market and just move in here?" I asked Aurora one night when we were getting ready for bed.

"You mean here at your parents' place?"

"Until we find a home for us."

She seemed to consider it. "Can't we just keep things as they are?"

That fucking hurt. She needed her condo as a safe haven, a place to escape in case things didn't work out between us.

"You don't like it here?" I asked.

"I love it," she assured me. "But...this is the Rhodes Estate."

"And?"

"This place can't be my official address."

I frowned. "Why?"

She looked embarrassed. "It's...too fairytale."

"What?"

"I feel like Cinderella," she explained forlornly, and I laughed.

"Stop it."

I lay on top of her then and kissed her mouth. "If you're Cinderella, am I your Prince Charming?"

"Right now, you're being—"

I kissed her again.

The sex had only gotten hotter even though I hadn't expected it. We were together now, and the newness of having her naked with me should be wearing off, but it didn't. My need for her only grew with my love for her.

I nuzzled her nipple and sucked it into my mouth. "I love you, Aurora," I whispered against her skin, taking in the smell of lavender, soaking in the essence of her.

"I love you too, but this house is just too much. I'll never feel comfortable here."

"It'll be for a short while," I promised her.

"But—"

I entered her then, and we both gasped, feeling that immediate connection that went beyond the physical. I kissed her softly as I moved inside her. Sometimes, we went hard, but other times, like now, we were soft and sweet, gentle, and loving. We gave each other open-mouthed kisses and aroused each other with words and touch until we couldn't stand it, and then, and only then, we let go.

I cupped her ass and began to pump into her, looking into her eyes. "I want you to live with us."

"I already am," she protested huskily.

"Officially."

She moaned when I hit her G-spot. I knew how to keep her on the edge, how to make her come—and she knew what buttons to push for me. I'd never had a partner in bed so attuned to me and my needs or one who consumed me as Aurora did.

"God, Gabriel, harder, please."

"I know, baby. I know."

She was writhing beneath me, setting off sparks inside me. The sweet loving gave way to hard fucking. I slammed into her again and again and let out a growl as I came right after she did.

I lay on top of her, shifting my weight onto my elbows. "Sell your fucking condo, Aurora, and move in with us," I ordered and bit an ear lobe.

She caressed my back. "Are you fucking me into submission, Gabriel?" she teased.

"Is it working?"
"Yeah. It's working."

CHAPTER 47

Gabriel

"Where are we going?" Aurora asked when Sophia and I asked her to go for a walk with us on Christmas Eve.

The Rhodes Estate was lit up.

Christmas was Mama's favorite holiday. We had parties, people, and enough food to feed two armies. Aurora was in awe of how we celebrated.

Aurora had moved in with us and I loved that we were all living together. I was also keen on getting started on a home for us. We hadn't set a date for a wedding, but we would once I gave her a ring and made it official.

"What kind of wedding do you want?" I asked her the previous night after we'd made love and were still catching our breath.

"Ah...I don't know. I mean, let's settle down first."

"You mean get a place of our own?"

"Yes."

I shook my head. "Stop being so cautious about us."

"I'm not," she protested and then sighed. She lifted her face from my chest and kissed my chin. "I'm sorry. I am being cautious."

"I know."

"I don't fit into your world. This house, your family...it's all so awesome. I feel like an interloper."

"You fit in just fine. I thought you'd piss Harrison off by cooking so often in his kitchen, but he worships you."

The temperamental family cook was in love with Aurora and unabashedly told me so.

"You mess up with her and I'm going to sweep her off her feet," he warned me.

"Not gonna happen," I'd assured him.

Rafe had said the same thing. He thought Aurora was "smart, good and lovely" the trifecta designed to wound any heart, even his miserable one.

But the truth was that they treated her like a sister, and I loved how they cosseted her and took her side against me. She'd never had that. My family was giving her a feeling of safety and security, wrapping her up in love and affection, so she could leave some of her insecurities and fears behind.

"Let's get married here," she suggested.

"At the estate?"

"Yes. Would Betsy be okay with that?"

"Okay?" I chuckled. "She'll be thrilled."

"Not a big wedding."

I'd had one of those; I was not into them. I didn't need a whole lot of hoopla.

"Just us and a few friends," she added.

"Done."

"Really? You don't want the big pomp and show?"

"Fuck no. I hate that. Just us and a few friends sounds just about perfect. So, when do you want to do it?"

She sighed. "Can we discuss that another day? We just started talking about it."

I laughed. She was open about how she felt, which made it easier for both of us to navigate our feelings. We still argued, and I think sometimes we did because the make-up sex was hot. But we'd gotten better at telling each other why we were saying something or behaving in a certain way.

If I came home and announced that I was in a fucking bad mood, she'd cut me slack. When she would tell me that something triggered her, I'd do the same for her. I'd never had a relationship like this before. A healthy one based on love and respect. What I had with Iris now felt even worse than it had before. There had been affection, not much respect and no love, nothing beyond obligation and duty. If I hadn't found Aurora, if she hadn't loved me, I'd have never known this bliss, this intense homecoming I felt just by being with her.

"So, where are we going?" she asked again.

Sophia held both our hands and was in between us as we walked. She was gushing with excitement. We'd planned it together; how *we'd* propose to Aurora.

She was already part of our family—the Rhodes family but we wanted a ring on her finger.

We occupied a wing of my parents' house, complete with

a living room, three bedrooms, and two bathrooms. Despite having our own space, we often found ourselves in the family room and kitchen, spending time with my parents. Rafe also started coming over more often, drawn by the lively atmosphere of the estate. Mama was thrilled, and so was Aurora. Having grown up without a family, she felt, as she put it, like she had *won the lottery*.

She and Mama had gotten closer, and Aurora was starting to help her with some of her charity initiatives.

"We're taking you to our Christmas present," Sophia informed her.

"*Our* present?" she asked.

"Yes, a present that is for you, me and Daddy."

Aurora grinned. "I can't wait."

We'd decided to take the walk before we started the Christmas Eve festivities. The Isle of Hope was draped in its usual serene beauty, the Skidaway River glinting under the afternoon sun, framed by the majestic oaks and their Spanish moss curtains.

I led us through the familiar, lush greenery of the estate, and then we veered off the beaten path.

We ended up in a clearing that offered an unobstructed view of the river, the land gently sloping towards the water, creating a natural amphitheater to the serene flow below. The air here felt fresher, filled with the promise of something new and exciting.

"Wow," Aurora said, looking around. "This is so beautiful."

"Ever thought about designing a house with a river

view?" I asked casually, gesturing to the empty space before us.

She laughed. "Which architect wouldn't? Why?"

"Well," I started, exchanging a glance with Sophia, "how about designing our house? Right here."

"Our house?" she whispered.

The words felt heavy and light at the same time, laden with meaning yet floating in the air.

Sophia smiled broadly, her heart in her eyes. "Aurora, will you marry us and help us build our dream home?"

I held out my grandmother's amethyst ring. Aurora's eyes filled with tears. "Oh my god." She put her hands on her cheeks.

"I love you. All of you. Forever," I told her.

Here, on this piece of heaven that felt suspended between the earth and water, the future seemed to unfold with limitless possibilities. The surrounding land, a blank canvas whispered of family barbecues, laughter-filled evenings, and quiet mornings watching the Skidaway flow by. The river was a constant, rhythmic presence, mirroring the steady beat of my heart, syncing with Aurora's and my daughter's.

"Yes," Aurora said, the word feeling like a key turning in a lock. "I'd love to marry you both and design our home."

She held out her hand to me, and I slipped the ring on her finger. It fit like a dream.

I stepped closer and wrapped us in a hug that felt like a promise. I held out an arm for Sophia, who joined in, making it a group embrace that sealed our new beginning.

"So, I'm thinking of a wrap-around porch to catch the sunset over the river," Aurora ventured when we broke apart, the practical part of her kicking in. The architect already looking at possibilities.

"And maybe a treehouse?" Sophia added, her eyes lighting up.

"A treehouse, huh?" Aurora mused. "That's ambitious."

"But with Aurora as the architect, I think we can make anything happen," I said, grinning as it felt like my heart might burst with happiness.

"Let me draw up some plans." Aurora put her hands on her waist, looking around.

"I want to be an architect when I grow up," Sophia declared. "Like Aurora. Then Bianca and I can both work at Savannah Lace."

She and Bianca had become friends thanks to Aurora and their Sunday sojourns to visit the great historic houses of Savannah.

"I thought you'd take over Rhodes Hotels," I said in mock despair.

"I'm sure that any brothers and sisters I have in the future will be happy to step in," she said casually.

Aurora looked at me in wonder. We hadn't really talked about children.

"Well, I am not getting any younger," Aurora declared, surprising me.

Sophia laughed. "I'd love a younger sister. I've always wanted one."

"Be careful what you wish for. You're going to be her favorite babysitter," I warned.

"I can't wait," Sophia said, her eyes sparkling with amusement. "So, how many bedrooms are we thinking in this house?"

"God, give me a breather, will you both," Aurora admonished. "What do we think about a swimming pool with a slide?"

"Oh my god, Aurora! You're my favorite stepmother," Sophia declared.

"Your only," I corrected.

The banter felt easy, natural, and full of the warmth of a family coming together. As we discussed ideas, laughed at the more outlandish suggestions, and envisioned a future on this very spot, the river bore witness to the moment we started to weave our dreams into the fabric of the Isle of Hope.

Want more Gabriel and Aurora? Read the bonus chapter: *Gabriel & Aurora Go On A Date*.

All bonus content is available on my website at www.Maya Alden.com.

Also by Maya Alden

GOLDEN KNIGHTS

The Wrong Wife

SAVANNAH'S BEST

Never The Best

Best Kept Vows

MARRIAGE BY CONTRACT

The Wrong Husband

The Wrong Bride

A MODERN VINTAGE ROMANCE

Kiss From A Rose

That's Amore

WILDFLOWER CANYON

The Wrong Ride Home

The Mountain Echoes

REGRETFULLY YOURS

Basil

Cain

About the Author

Maya Alden is a Top 5 Amazon bestselling author. She's known for her angsty contemporary romances—where charmingly infuriating heroes always find a way to redeem themselves and steal your heart.

CONTACT MAYA
www.MayaAlden.com

facebook.com/authormayaalden

instagram.com/mayaalden_romance

tiktok.com/@maya.alden.author

amazon.com/author/mayaalden

Printed in Dunstable, United Kingdom

75616002R00204